STEVE'S BARMAID

JENIFER WOOD

STEVE'S BARMAID

ABANDONED ON NIFLHEIM
BOOK THREE

JENIFER WOOD

This novel is entirely a work of fiction. The names, characters, and incidents portrayed in it are the work of the author's imagination or have been used fictitiously and are not to be construed as real. Any resemblance to actual persons, living or dead, events or localities is entirely coincidental.

Copy Editing: Alex Yuschik

Cover art: Rowan Woodcock

Cover design: Ash Raven

ISBN: 979-8-9879953-7-2 [Ebook]

ISBN: 979-8-9879953-6-5 [Paperback]

Piracy is a major issue for indie authors like me, who invest countless hours into our books. It directly impacts our ability to support ourselves and keep creating new work.

If you know someone who would enjoy this book but can't access it through legal means, please contact me at authorjeniferwood@gmail.com. If you're currently reading a pirated copy, I'd appreciate hearing from you as well. I'm committed to finding a way to get my book into readers' hands legally.

Thank you for your support and understanding.

To Kiki, whether she likes it or not.

A NOTE ABOUT CONTENT

I am a lazy reader and used to never read the content warnings. And then I realized I am also an *anxious* reader and would love a heads-up if things are about to get dark. This series is relatively light but I want to be sensitive to all readers. So, you can view this as a content warning, or you can view this as a menu.

Either way, *spoilers ahead.*

- Alien Abduction
- Mentioned parental neglect
- Religious trauma (in the past)
- Death of parents (in the past)
- Explicit sexual scenes
- Rough sex (consensual)
- Knotting
- Stretching and stuffing
- Drugging
- Kidnapping
- On page violence (minor)

If you have any specific content you are concerned about, you are welcome to reach out to me at authorjeniferwood@gmail.com.

CHAPTER ONE

BILLIE

*I*f I could cut it slinging drinks back on Earth on busy summer weekends, how hard could running a bar on an alien planet really be? It was almost time for lunch in the longhouse, but I was still inspecting the property—was this where I would find my place in the tribe? Agnarr wasn't wrong when he told me the bar was in a state of disrepair. Being one of the leaders of the tribe, he gave me permission to scope the place out on the very edge of the village, with the giant furutrés at its back, the inside covered in a thick layer of dust. One of the double doors hung off its hinges, and many of the windows had busted panes. Agnarr said it had been empty for years. The original owners had passed away, and no one had stepped in to run the business. When I inquired why it wasn't located in the center of town, with the rest of the businesses, I was informed that when it was in its prime, it was too loud for the shopkeepers who lived above their shops. I guess that was something drunk orcs had in common with drunk humans—raucous revelry at best, bar fights at worst.

I stalked around the interior, examining the state of the tables and chairs. It looked as if they were still in the same place they'd been the day the bar closed. It made me think of one of those old-timey saloons in ghost town tourist traps in the middle of the desert. Fýrifírar had no restaurants. Everyone ate communally. But they'd had a bar. I could work with a bar. Back on Earth I'd started at my restaurant as a runner and worked my way up to head bartender. I'd never really thought about opening my *own* bar, but I'd also never anticipated being abducted by aliens and dumped on a planet of orcs, either.

Yet here I was.

I hummed to myself. Could I make this work? During our previous project of redoing Piper and Agnarr's home, I'd made good friends with the Osif, the older orc in charge of all the building and woodworking in the tribe. He was a gruff old orc with a soft spot for me. He could take charge of the more complicated repairs. Cleaning the building would be no problem. Getting rid of years of grime and dust would take a lot of work, but I was up for the challenge. If I could clean puke out of the bathroom grout of my old bar, I could do this. I needed to get out of the kitchen and figure out what I would do with this new life that had been dropped in my lap. I wasn't going to waste it making giant pots of gautr. Also, if I was really honest with myself, I missed the interaction with the public. I wanted to take this new life on Niflheim by the horns and do what *I* wanted. I had been happy enough on Earth, but I was stagnating. I wasn't going anywhere. I'd never really had a time in my life where I wasn't just focused getting by day-to-day and making rent.

I poked around behind the bar, finding the usual storage. I was surprised to find a full kitchen. It needed some repairs, but had everything I would need to do food as well. Maybe I could do appetizers? No one paid for food here, so I'd have to talk with Runa, the head cook. There were stairs off the kitchen that I climbed carefully. They creaked under my feet, and I wasn't certain about the rickety railing under my hand. I reached the landing to find that the loft above the bar had been converted into a large room. A large, decrepit-looking bed was in the corner along the back wall. I was surprised. Agnarr hadn't mentioned that the owner slept above the bar. Thinking back, though, most of the shopkeepers in town lived above their shops. Could I live above a bar? *My* bar?

I turned and headed back down the stairs, deciding that was a question for another day. I carefully left the bar, using the one good door, and made my way to the longhouse, where lunch would be almost over. Leaving the kitchens to work toward a fragile dream was a bit overwhelming, considering all the changes that had happened in my life. I'd been on Niflheim for almost four of their months. I'd given up trying to figure out if time and space lined up exactly like they had on Earth. I was comfortable. The women I'd arrived with had become like sisters, and we all lived in the same row of rooms and shared a large communal bathroom. I never went to college, but some other girls said it was similar to dorming. I loved being around people, and there was always someone to talk to too late.

We were still finding our way in the tribe—figuring out how our Earth skills and interests transferred over to Niflheim. Some of the girls had it easier than others. Like Ruby. She was a nurse back home, and she'd set up shop with the tribe's healer, Emla. She found her place. The same with Liv. She'd been a veterinarian back home. The carers of the hestrs were very enthusiastic about her arrival. While I found the eight-legged horse-looking creatures a bit weird, there was no denying they were cute. Yet there were others, myself included, who didn't come with a skillset that transferred immediately. The bulk of my career had been spent learning the intricacies of restaurant and bar life. Now, I lived in a tribe that only ate communally. Cool.

It wasn't until I discussed wanting to do more than represent the humans at the tribal meetings and help out with Runa in the kitchen that Agnarr mentioned the empty bar. I almost shrieked when he explained that his dad had talked about the bar fondly when he was a kid. As the jarl of the tribe, Agnarr happily gave me permission to take over the bar.

When I peppered Agnarr with questions about the bar, he told me he had memories of his dad coming home laughing and smelling of mead. When I asked why he hadn't mentioned it before, he said it had been abandoned for so long and that he'd completely forgotten about it. To be fair, he was so sickeningly wrapped up in Piper that I was surprised he remembered anything. It was adorable and depressing. I'd never been in a serious relationship back home and I definitely hadn't met anyone on Niflheim yet.

Now, here I was, wondering if I could make the jump from bartender to bar owner. Barmaid? Barkeep? I needed something to get my mind off the whole "mate" situation that hung over my head. I was still of two minds about the Elska mate situation. Part of me was thrilled to discover that orcs —or orkin—as they called themselves, had fated mates. If my own fated mate was out there, I wouldn't have to swipe right on endless profiles and have inane conversations with men who would try to be witty and fun for approximately three messages and then ask for nudes. The other part of me was worried about ending up with a "fated" mate that ended up being a total douche canoe. Divorce didn't seem to happen here.

But none of the male orkin had caught my attention so

far. Once you got past the physical differences, like green skin and tusks, they were appealing. They were all ripped and more than a foot taller than me. The raw masculinity wasn't something you could ignore. They made human men look tiny and pathetic. I got the feeling none of them would have any trouble taking me up against a wall. I'd always wanted to date a guy that could take control physically. But I had been burned too many times to hook up with someone just because I found them attractive. So far, I'd kept them all at a distance. I didn't want to risk striking up a conversation with one of them and then have them thinking I was considering them as an option. They seemed very serious about the whole mating situation. Mate bonds couldn't form if I didn't get to know anyone. I wasn't opposed to a mate but didn't feel ready yet. Maybe once I figured out my place in the tribe.

My work helping Runa in the kitchens kept me with mainly females. While Runa's sous chef, Ottar, was very nice to look at, I noticed Joey choosing to work alongside him rather than me with increasing frequency. Besides Piper, Agnarr's mate, Joey was one of my best friends. She was a tiny Japanese woman with a filthy sense of humor, who, like me, was estranged from her family. We both felt we lacked a place where we fit in the tribe, so we joined each other in working in the kitchen.

I wasn't sure what was going on with her and Ottar, but I wasn't going to ask questions until she was willing to share. Aside from him, most of the kitchen staff was either female or at least twenty years older than me. Given how excited the tribe was for new females, I wanted this to be the time when someone finally pursued me, and I was ready to wait for that to happen. At least, I thought I was.

I sighed as I pushed open the door to the longhouse. I could wait. I'd been single for twenty-six years on Earth. What was a few more on Niflheim?

The longhouse was a riot of noise and smells, packed to the brim with everyone enjoying their meal. I hustled over to my usual table to find many of my friends still seated. I was also delighted to find Piper and Agnarr had joined us. Agnarr and Piper tended to rotate around the tables so that everyone felt they got equal time with the jarl and jarlin. Though Piper hid it well, I knew her favorite place to eat lunch was actually at home, with just Agnarr or a handful of others. She was getting used to being herself in front of the entire tribe, and I was proud of her.

I sat down, and she greeted me with a breezy smile and a plate of food. "I figured you'd get caught up looking around the bar. Did you like what you saw?" She handed me a set of cutlery and a napkin. Mothering without even realizing it.

"Ha, I did get caught up. I have some questions about it that I was hoping Agnarr could answer," I responded, taking a sip of water. Now that I realized there was a bar, I was realizing other things. Water was always the beverage served in the longhouse unless it was a celebration—like Agnarr and Piper's wedding—and then they served berry-flavored mead. Hmm... that information would come in handy. I turned to Agnarr.

"You said the bar closed when the old owners died, but you didn't tell me they lived above it." It was a statement more than a question, but I wanted more information.

"I guess I didn't think of it," he mused. "It's typical of shopkeepers to live above their shops here, so I didn't realize it was out of the norm."

"It didn't get too loud for the owners? Living above a bar?"

"Hmm, that is something you'd have to ask one of the older tribesmembers," Agnarr said. "Astrid or Runa, or even Osif would remember. I don't remember Breya and Finnr very well. They passed before my parents did, so I couldn't tell you about life living above a bar. But, I don't know, Billie —that sounds like it might be right up your alley." Agnarr grinned at me.

He did have a point. I had already garnered a reputation for being the life of the party amongst the new women. A loud, vibrant life fit me. I loved meeting new people and having conversations with strangers. It was part of a bartender's life—to dig in deep immediately.

"I do love being surrounded by a raucous crowd." I smiled shyly.

"We can tell," Piper responded. "I think this would be a good fit for you," she said, grabbing my hand.

"I also noticed that there was a full kitchen in the back of the bar," I said. "Did they serve food?"

"Já, I don't remember how that worked," answered Agnarr. "That is another conversation to have with Runa."

I tapped my fingers against my lips thoughtfully. A conversation with Runa was easily done. I saw her every morning for my kitchen work. The tiny cook was well past retirement age but didn't want to give up her domain. Ottar was willing to let her decide on her terms, quietly taking on more responsibility. I could see him taking over in the next year. I wondered what her memories were of the bar.

"So is it settled, then?" asked Joey, who'd been listening in. "Our new hang is going to be Billie's Bar?"

"Ew, gross," I groaned. "Even if I do it, I am not naming it after myself. That's terrible."

"I don't know, I think it sounds cute. You've got the whole alliteration thing going for you. Billie's Bar would be fun!" Piper gave me a teasing smile.

"No, no. We can come up with something much better."

"Come on," Joey whined. "Billie's Bar, Billie's Bar, Billie's Bar." She started chanting, with all the other women at the table joining in.

I dragged my hand down my face in defeat. There was no stopping a group of women with an idea. I rolled my eyes and smiled at the women all looking at me enthusiastically.

"You all better be ready to get your hands dirty and help make Billie's Bar happen," I said, putting my hands on my hips and giving them my best scowl.

The table erupted in cheers, and I laughed. I was a pushover. Piper hugged me and whispered into my ear, "We can find you a way out if you don't actually want to do this."

Piper was so considerate she would hate to be dragged into something like rebuilding a bar. I smiled, hugging her back. "I don't know, what do you think?" I whispered.

"I think if anyone can pull this off, you can," she said as she released me.

With the decision seemingly made, the table started to empty as people finished their meal. I had barely touched mine because of all the bar talk, so I hurried up with my lunch before heading back to the kitchens.

Billie's Bar. I could get used to that.

CHAPTER TWO

STEVE

The waves crashed on the shore steadily, soothing my frayed nerves. While our time at the seafaring tribe of the Vátrfírar hadn't gone the way I'd hoped, I could finally see the ocean. I wondered how similar it was to the sea on Earth that Mom had spent years describing to me. She'd talked about how she fell asleep listening to the waves each night in the little house she lived in before she was abducted. There was a lot Mom did not miss about planet Earth—her abusive partner and her lack of purpose came up often—but she always smiled when she talked about the beach.

At first, Dad promised to take her to see the ocean in Niflheim. But once I was born, he grew so protective of me that he didn't want us to leave Snaerfírar up in the mountains. He argued that I was too small and that it was dangerous to make the days-long journey. I argued that though I was smaller than the other orklings in our tribe, I was still sturdy enough to travel on a hestr. *Let's wait until you are a little bit older* was repeated time and time again.

All that talk of going to the beach came to an abrupt halt when Mom died before I even hit my teenage years. Losing her had shaped the rest of my adolescence, and on top of that Dad retreated into isolation. I didn't bring her up often because Dad couldn't get through a conversation about her. I still grieved her every day, but it was no longer an open wound. Yet, last summer, Dad passed as well. It had been over fifteen years since Mom died, and he'd done his best to be a happy and loving father, but I knew his soul ached for her. I was devastated that I only had enough of Mom in me to remind him of what he'd lost. Dad had been everything to me after Mom died. Now, I was essentially an orphan in a tribe where I never really felt settled. I wanted to be happy that Dad had finally found peace, but I was bitter that I'd been given to amazing parents only to have them ripped from me far too soon.

And now I stood, the only member of my immediate family left, with a whole wide world of possibility in front of me—I'd dragged my tribemates halfway across Niflheim to connect with other orkin. I tried to think of what Mom would want me to do, of what Dad would want. I wanted to see the ocean. Mom would be happy that I finally did that. I wanted to meet the other orkin on Niflheim. Maybe there would be another place where I felt I fit better. Vátrfírar was isolated up in the Fjall Mountains, rarely trading with or encountering the two other tribes we knew existed on our continent. Thanks to my mom's instilling an adventurous spirit in me, I was a wanderer. I wanted to see what else the world had to offer. I wasn't satisfied with Snaerfírar, I needed to know what else was out there.

Unfortunately, outside of the glorious ocean with its green-blue waters and foam-tipped waves, the Vátrfírar tribe was a bummer. I'd dragged my tribemates halfway across Niflheim to connect with other orkin, and the first tribe we visited turned out to be utterly lame. We talked in circles with them about how we could build relationships and communicate better, but the entire time, they had their big stupid guards watching us, suspicion evident on their faces. They didn't even trust us to eat meals with them. I rolled my eyes as I urged my hestr, Epli, forward. I should have listened to my gut and had us head to Fýrifírar first. I'd met Piper and Agnarr the winter before. Piper was losing it about the whole matebond thing. Which was fair, as humans didn't have mates. Though Mom and Dad had been mated for a long time before they had me, Mom still found it odd. Piper and Agnarr seemed much more open about interacting with other tribes. They'd willingly sought us out to figure out how to best care for Piper and their other humans. I was hopeful things would go better with Fýrifírar.

Piper and Agnarr's visit made me realize that maybe it wasn't just that I was a half-orc that made me feel like I didn't fit—maybe my tribe wasn't a good fit. From the sound of the way the Fýrifírar lived, it seemed like I would be surrounded by a much more robust community. What started as a passing idea became a fixation as we hunkered down for the snowy season. The itch to explore and meet others festered until I knew I needed to make a plan.

I was prepared for the elders to react poorly to me wanting to explore, being generally distrustful of other orkin. At first, I thought of stealing away at night. But I was at least rational enough to realize I would need the help of others if I wanted to travel, especially at the end of the cold season. I couldn't get the idea of seeing more of Niflheim and meeting others out of my head. I confided in my oldest friend, Reykr. He was at least ten árs older than I, and had stepped in as a combination of older brother and uncle when my parents passed.

He didn't love the idea of meeting other orkin, but as one of our trained guards, he hadn't gotten to use his skills in ages. He was willing to go on my mission with me, "for the adventure," as he said. I don't think he expected us to make any connections, but he was bored of Snaerfírar and hadn't met anyone to settle down with. We convinced a few other orkin to join us, now that Reykr had said he was up for the adventure. They doubted there was any merit to building relationships with the other tribes. Violence and competition were the orkin way of life, they told me. There was no point in trying to build bridges. I secretly thought Tyr and Berit were coming hoping to start fights with the other tribes. They weren't that bright.

With Reykr's influence, we got permission to go on an "exploratory mission," as the elders referred to it. I was the official representative, with the guards there to help should any trade negotiations occur. So far, zero negotiations.

Epli gave out an impatient chuff beneath me and I pulled my thoughts back together. Shit, the sun was already setting. We should have stopped for dinner ages ago. At this point, we'd be trying to make camp in the dark.

"Reykr! Why didn't you alert me it was time to stop for the evening meal?"

"I did. Twice," he snapped.

I flushed a deep green. I must have been so lost in thought that I didn't hear Reykr calling to me. Now he was annoyed. And probably hungry. "I'm sorry, I was thinking of what Fýrifírar might be like."

He grumbled. "If they are anything like Vátrfírar will you at least let me punch some of them?" .

"No. Absolutely not."

Reykr muttered under his breath, adjusting himself in his

harness. He was one of the biggest orkin of our tribe. Even with the size of our hestrs, he was uncomfortable riding all day, so I pulled Epli off of the trail, with Reykr and the rest of the Snaerfírar following. It didn't take us long before we found a small clearing where we could make camp. There were four of us so we had only brought two tents. Tyr and Berit set up one tent while Reykr and I set up another and then headed to them wordlessly. We were all exhausted.

I was anxious to get to the next tribe, but we needed to rest. This whole stupid thing was my idea and the stonewalling we received from Vátrfírar when we tried to talk trade would have made me give up entirely if I didn't have the hope of Agnarr and Piper in my mind. If we followed the plan, we still had to visit the Fýrifírar tribe before heading back up the Fjall Mountains to our boring home nestled up in the frozen peaks.

With both the tents set up, we fed and watered our hestrs before letting them rest for the evening. I volunteered to take first watch, Reykr joining me. He couldn't stop protecting me if his life depended on it. I reminded him—regularly—that I was of age, well past it. I tried not to let it get under my skin, but the whole tribe treated me like an irresponsible younger brother. I had gotten in my fair share of trouble when I was an orkling. One time, I got so tired of being cold that I tried to rebuild the fire while my parents slept. I nearly burned our house down. Then there was the time I tried to go surfing on our lake, as mom had explained to me, and nearly drowned. But all of my childhood mishaps were in the past. I wanted to prove I was a full-fledged tribe member and could contribute. And be trusted with firewood.

Reykr and I stood, alert, at the edge of the clearing. We didn't expect any trouble from other orkin, but the forest could be alive with predators. It was still early for them to come out of their winter hiding holes but a night watch was still the safest bet. We stood, watching, in companionable silence for quite a while until Reykr cleared his throat.

"As much as I enjoyed getting out of the confinement of Snaerfírar, where do you see this going? Is this just an excuse to get out of helping the tribe to prepare for the spring?" Reykr rumbled in his deep voice.

"I meant what I said when I explained to the elders that I wanted to connect with other tribes. We're so isolated up in the damn snow. I think we could all benefit from more exchange with the other tribes—and not just goods. I mean an exchange of ideas and ways of thinking," I explained.

"And this has nothing to do with being the only half-orc?"

I hesitated. I had kept my feelings of discontent to myself, not wanting my tribe to think I was ungrateful for my position and the love they'd shown me. But if I could trust anyone, it was Reykr.

"Maybe it is," I whispered into the night air. "Maybe I want to meet more orkin like me. Not just half-orkin, but orkin that are more willing to exchange technology, new ways of thinking—more progressive ideas about society. Maybe I want to see if I will feel less out of place."

"And now that you've seen Vátrfírar, do you think you'd be better suited with them?" There was no accusation in Reykr's voice, just quiet curiosity.

"Um, no. As Mom would say, they were jerks. They are just as isolated as we are—if not more. It was nice to see the ocean, though. Mom always talked about the comfort the sound of crashing waves brought her. At least I got to see that for myself. She'd like to know that I finally got out and explored." I ended on a wistful note.

I absently rubbed at the pendant around my neck. My mom had always told me it was sea glass, created by years of ocean waves. It was one of the few possessions she had with her when she was taken from her home world, a small fragment of her that I wore everywhere I went. I pulled myself out of my thoughts to realize Reykr was staring at me, eyes filled with sympathy.

"You missing your parents?" he asked.

"Mom has just been weighing on me." Since Dad passed, I have considered what Mom would want for me. "The idea that she had all these beautiful dreams about what the sea would be like here, and she never got to see it."

"Maybe," Reykr said, "You are putting all your hopes on Fýrifírar now, and I don't want to see you disappointed again."

"I know, I know." I sighed. "I just have to believe that they will be different. Agnarr and Piper were set to be the new leaders of Fýrifírar and said there were other human women. If they were willing to take in literal aliens they have to be more accepting of orkin from other tribes... Right?" I trailed off.

"Maybe." He shrugged. "Or maybe they will view us as competition and attack us in our sleep."

"Well, aren't you a delight?" I grumbled.

"I'm just saying, don't be shocked if it doesn't go according to your plan."

"Fine, fine." I waved at him. "I am approaching Fýrifírar with an open mind. It could go either way."

I'd let Reykr think I wasn't putting all my hopes on the forest orkin, even if I still was. We settled down for the night, and I fell asleep once again, dreaming of a tribe where a traveler would be welcomed. Perhaps I'd already found it.

CHAPTER THREE

BILLIE

$\mathcal{A}$s a night owl through and through, waking up with the sun was not my specialty. In fact, I loathed it, about as much as I loathed the light coming in through the split of my curtains. However, working in the kitchens meant I had to be up early to prepare breakfast for the tribe. I reluctantly shuffled out of bed and to the restroom. While Fýrifírar showered communally, we all had our own sink and toilet, for which I was eternally grateful. My hair was a chaotic mess. I was one of the only human girls that showed up with curly hair. And we weren't talking cute beach waves, either. My hair was a riot of unmanageable ringlets, used to being treated with extra attention to get it to cooperate. Now I was on an orkin planet that had never heard of conditioner. I was still working on different options with some of the other women with curly hair, but we hadn't found anything quite right.

I dressed quickly and headed to the kitchens. I showed up

just as the other cooks arrived and started on breakfast straightaway. I had become the person in charge of the gautr, a porridge that was a staple of their diet and a cross between grits and oatmeal. I wasn't a fan, but it was easy enough to make because each orc, or human, decided what kind of toppings they wanted to add. It was the sheer volume of it that we had to make that made it difficult. Even as one of the stronger girls, I couldn't lift a pot full of it. And we made four pots every morning. It hardly made my mornings cheerier.

But would working late nights in a bar be all that much better? I wasn't fulfilled working in the kitchens, I knew that. Feeding people and interacting with them while bartending was something I missed. I could come up with something better. But did I really even want a bar? I knew I wasn't fulfilled working here in the kitchens. I liked feeding people, sure. But I missed the interaction bartending provided me. I missed pouring the perfect drink or surprising someone with a new cocktail I'd come up with. I missed the stories and the secrets that were shared with me. People would tell bartenders anything and I was a rapt audience. I couldn't spend the rest of my life in the kitchen dicing potatoes—I wanted to *live* and be out amongst the rest of the tribe. I was bored as hell.

"Hey there!" said Joey from right over my shoulder. I jumped, dropping the knife and potato to the ground. "Uh sorry, didn't mean to startle you."

"Sorry, sorry, my fault. I was lost in thought." I bent to pick up the knife and potato and took them to the sink to rinse off.

Joey followed me. "These thoughts wouldn't have anything to do with *Billie's Bar*, would they?" she asked, waggling her eyebrows at me.

I rolled my eyes as I rinsed off the potato and knife. The whole idea of reopening the bar had been an idea for less than a week and now everyone was referring to it as *Billie's Bar*. At this point, even if I did come up with an awesome name for my bar, everyone would call it Billie's Bar. I hadn't even talked to Runa about it yet. Without her blessing, I didn't want to open any place that served drink— and hopefully some food.

"Maybe I was thinking about *Billie's Bar*." I said, emphasizing the name with another eye roll. "What of it?"

"So you might actually do it?" Joey squealed.

"You know, you are awfully excitable this morning."

"Hey, one of my best friends is finally taking a step toward doing something that makes her happy. That is reason enough to squeal," she said sternly.

"Is it that obvious that I don't love the kitchen?" I whispered, not wanting any of the other workers to hear. It was a valuable job, and I didn't want them to feel like I disliked their company or that I was demeaning their efforts. It just wasn't for me.

"Not to anyone who doesn't know you," she assured me. "But I see that wistful look you have on your face when you're chopping your twentieth onion for the day and know being a line cook isn't what you want."

"No, no, it isn't. And I don't think I want to take over the kitchen one day either, like someone we both know," I responded, pointing at Ottar, who had his back to us at another counter. Joey blushed to her roots. "Care to tell me what is going on there? Do I need to look at your back for marks?"

Joey covered her face in her hands, "Shhh," she hissed.

"Oh, is there something you don't want anyone to know about?" I asked raising my voice purposefully.

"Shut up, shut up," she elbowed me in the ribs.

"So you haven't imagined being his sous chef, bent over one of the counters while he—"

"Jesus Christ, Billie!" she whisper-shouted as she clapped her tiny hand over my mouth. Joey was petite, even shorter than me. Which was saying something. But she was freakishly strong. I felt as if she'd knocked some of my teeth loose.

"Alright, alright. Fine. But I want to be the first to know when the nothing becomes something."

Joey punched me squarely in the shoulder.

"Hey, you know I bruise like a peach!" I exclaimed, rubbing my arm. "I'll keep it to myself for now. But the minute—"

"The minute what?" A deep voice came from behind us.

We both turned to see Ottar standing there, quietly towering over us.

"The minute, uh, the minute..." Joey stammered, face drained of color.

"The minute Runa gets here, I want to ask her some questions about the abandoned bar," I spat out quickly, saving Joey from embarrassment.

"Hmm." Ottar looked out the window at the sun climbing above the trees. "She should be here soon. I will let her know that you wished to speak with her." He opened his mouth, then closed it as if he had been about to say something else to Joey, then thought better of it and walked off with a promptness that was unusual for him back to his workstation. Halfway there, he noticed he'd grabbed the wrong stack of trays and had to swap them out.

As soon as she was out of earshot, he hissed, "See! This is why we can't discuss my stupid crush in the kitchen. Save that gossip for our next gab fest at Piper's."

"Um, how about *thank you?* In covering your ass, I just told Ottar that I have my eye on the abandoned bar. What if Runa is offended or feels I am stepping on her territory? What if *Ottar* feels that way?"

"Runa will not feel that way. She is exhausted. Everyone

can tell she's ready to retire and spend her days at home with her mate and her grandkids. She's just waiting for Ottar to say he's ready."

I had to acknowledge that Joey's statement was true. Runa seemed frailer and frailer as the days went by. If Ottar didn't step up soon Runa was going to keel over in the middle of cooking soup one day. Joey and I went back to our tasks in silence.

I had no idea where Joey's head was, but mine was whirring about a conversation I wasn't quite ready to have with Runa. Not only was I afraid she would think I was encroaching on her job, but I was also worried she would think I wasn't grateful for all the guidance and support she had given me and the other kitchen women as we settled into our new home.

When Runa arrived, I was finally done chopping all of the potatoes and carrots for the stew. They weren't identical in size by any means, I was horrible at dicing things, but I got it done.

Gah. I slowly walked to her, twirling one of the loose curls at the nape of my neck—a nervous habit that I had never been able to rid myself of. I approached Runa and she gave me a kind, weathered smile. Even as a frail, elderly orc, she was at least five inches taller than me, requiring me to tilt my head up to look her in the eye.

"Hello, dear," she said, pulling me into a hug. Runa really did love me, which made this conversation even harder.

"Hi, Runa," I said quietly as she patted me on the head like a toddler. "Can we talk somewhere for a minute?"

"Of course, dear. Let's go to my office."

Runa had a tiny room off the side of the kitchen where

she kept track of all the food that came into and went out of the kitchen. Without her careful attention to detail, we'd probably run out of food during winter. She took off her cloak and sat down at her desk.

"What did you want to talk about, Billie?" She asked while organizing the ledgers she had heaped in front of her.

"Well, I don't know if you remember what my job was back on Earth, but I was a bartender," I said, sounding hesitant.

"I do remember. You said you loved it most of the time. but you wouldn't miss… what did you call them… lousy tipsters?" She tilted her head.

I struggled to stifle a laugh, "Lousy tippers. Most servers and bar staff depend on tips to earn a living wage where I'm from. If people don't tip, it makes it hard to pay the bills."

"Ah, right, right."

Picking up my train of thought, I continued "Well, Agnarr told me that there used to be a bar here in Fýrifírar, and I wanted to find out more about it."

To my great surprise, Runa started to look misty-eyed "Já, we did have a bar. It was a very lively and welcoming place. I worked there before it shut down. I was so sad to see it go."

"Why didn't you stay on? Run it yourself? You manage this kitchen and feed the entire tribe without breaking a sweat. You could have handled a bar!" Runa seemed completely capable of handling drunken orkin.

"This was árs ago. I was barely of age. I didn't know anything beyond *don't spill the drinks on the customers*. I wasn't ready. I would have, had I been, but I was just too young." She laughed, wiping her eyes.

"And no one wanted to take it over?" I was still confused.

"It was a turbulent time. Ulf had just died. Astrid had only been jarlin for a few árs. She was young to be stepping into the role of jarlin on her own, all while grieving her mate.

Some of the elders thought they should rule in her place as a committee until she was older. It wasn't the time to add me, a brand-new barkeep, into an already tense situation."

Runa seemed truly sad about the bar's loss, which I didn't expect. If there was a good time to discuss reopening it, it was now.

"Do you think the tribe would be ready to reopen the bar?" I asked hesitantly.

Runa looked at me shrewdly. "Do you think you have what it takes to manage a hall full of drunken orkin and humans?"

"I absolutely do. I'll definitely be hiring bouncers, depending on how seriously orkin take their drinking, but I don't anticipate that being a problem. I have cut off men twice my size."

"And you know how to make drinks?" she asked.

"I know how to mix a drink. I would have to learn how to brew liquor. Given that we have had it at our celebrations, is it safe to assume there is an orc that still remembers?"

"And who do you think that might be?" she asked me, grinning, chin resting in her palms.

"Is it you?" I squeaked in excitement. I was trying to keep it cool, but Runa seemed very pleased with this turn of events.

"Já, it's me. And, considering that it's drawing close to my time to retire from the kitchens, it is also time to pass this along. I would happily teach you."

"Really? You wouldn't feel like I was encroaching on your territory or hurting the kitchen?"

"Really. With Agnarr and Piper settled in and the tribe prospering, I think we are in a good place to reopen the bar. I don't expect you to run the kitchens; Ottar has been training for that for years, but serving appetizers or handpies at the bar? That seems incredibly reasonable."

I bit my lip—hard—to stop the tumult of questions I had. What was just a wisp of a dream was becoming very real.

"My one caution," Runa paused. "One thing I have noticed with young people is that they are always in a rush. And before you go telling me you are well above age, I am seventy-three árs. Listen to a wise old orc. If you want this to be good, *take your time*. Don't rush it just because you want it to happen. Let it marinate if you want to see your vision come to life. Think about what you really want out of this."

"Of course, of course," I responded much too quickly, causing Runa to cock a brow at me. I took a deep breath. "Yes, I want to talk to all of the orkin, specifically the elders, who would need to be involved, to make this happen."

"Well, then, it is settled. Get back to chopping. Let your mind wander and consider your path forward."

I couldn't believe Runa was on board, let alone that she wanted to help. "Can I hug you?"

We both stood, and I pulled Runa into a crushing embrace. Her body was a lot smaller than I'd imagined it would be, bonier, like if I squeezed too hard I'd break her. She had worked so long and so hard for the tribe, all those years of pre-dawn porridges and carefully prepared meals. Now it was time for us to take care of her.

CHAPTER FOUR

STEVE

I woke up to the sound of Reykr's snoring. Our tent was tiny, but that hadn't stopped him from sprawling outlimbs everywhere, leaving me pressed to the far side, with one of his hands hanging over my face. While it was nice that I was warm, I didn't really appreciate his attempt to smother me in his sleep.

"Hey." I shoved his hand off my face, and he mumbled something about breakfast. "You know, you aren't the best tent companion," I groused at him. He just rolled over and continued snoring.

I struggled out of my bedroll and slipped on my tunic and pants, pulling my boots over them. I ducked outside the tent, leaving Reykr. Tyr was already tending to the fire, heating a somewhat beaten up pot of gautr over it. *Everyone* in the tribe loved gautr. I thought it tasted like rotten fruit. I hoped that the Fýrifírar would have at least a few more breakfast offerings. I'd seen enough gautr for a lifetime.

I approached the fire with my hands outstretched, enjoying the warmth coming off of it.

"Oy," I called to Reykr, still in the tent, "If we get going we can reach Fýrifírar by the end of today."

Reykr emerged fully dressed. "What is the plan, boss?"

"Will you stop? We all know you are actually in charge here. I am just the face of the operation," I sighed.

"And as the face of the operation, what do you suggest?" Reykr continued, mocking.

I glowered at him. "We should walk our hestrs in, so we are showing we are coming peacefully and not with some battle plan. When I last saw Agnarr and Piper, Agnarr told me he was set to become the new jarl with Piper at his side, as jarlin. We should ask to speak with either Piper or Agnarr, to show respect for their joint leadership. If they ask to take our weapons, we should give them up willingly as a display of trust."

"Are you serious? You want to go into an unknown tribe on foot and let them take our weapons?" Reykr growled in disbelief. "I think we should agree on this as a group."

"Fine, let's talk it out. Tyr, Berit!" I called to them where they stood, tending to the hestrs, "We're trying to make a plan."

"Alright, what's the plan?" Tyr, the youngest, said as he dusted his hands feed off his hands.

Before I could start, Reykr interjected, "Steve wants us to walk our hestrs in and lay down our weapons as a show of coming in peace," he said derisively.

I sighed. "That isn't *exactly* what I said," I grumbled.

To my surprise, Berit spoke up, "I think that sounds fair, given how things went with Vátrfírar. I think if we approach this differently, we may have more success. Also, didn't you say that Agnarr and Piper came looking for baldrian just before the cold season?"

"Yes, and our healer Revna gave them a supply to last at least six mánuthurs with Lodin's permission."

"So don't they sort of owe us at least the opportunity to talk?" Tyr followed up.

"Já," Berit agreed, nodding, "This isn't like Vátrfírar. Agnarr and Piper know us and know we have helped them, even when we don't have the most welcoming reputation. I think your plan is reasonable."

Reykr looked around, realizing he was outnumbered, and threw up his hands. "Fine, fine. We shall arrive peacefully and give them our weapons. *But only if they ask for them.*"

"That includes the knife in your boot, too, you know. Nothing like breaking someone's trust by insisting you're unarmed and then sliding one extra knife out of a sock."

Mom had this saying I never quite understood—*if looks could kill.* I wasn't quite sure, but I believe this look that Reykr was giving me was accurate. As we reached the fork, we slowed to a stop. It wasn't long before a large male orc approached us. I placed Epli's reins in Reykr's hands and strode to meet him. I intentionally slowed my gait and placed out my hand. We grasped wrists in the traditional orkin greeting.

"Hello, I am Brandr, one of the guards of Fýrifírar" he said solemnly.

"I am Steve. We come as visitors from Snaerfírar."

Brandr's eyebrows shot up. "Steve? *The* Steve?" he questioned.

I looked from side to side, confused, as if there could possibly be another Steve standing next to me, "I guess? I am the only Steve I know from my tribe." Maybe they had a Steve in their tribe.

To my even greater surprise, Brandr pulled me into a bone-crushing embrace before letting me go to take a good look at me, "You are exactly as Agnarr described you. He and

Piper will be so thrilled you are here. Come, come, let's get you all settled. Introduce me to your fellow travelers."

After introductions, Brandr gave us the opportunity to shower and provided us with some fresh clothes, then escorted us to Agnarr's cabin. Before we even reached the double doors, they were flung open and Agnarr stepped out.

"Brandr, the other guards informed me the Snaerfírar arrived over an hour ago. Have you been interrogating them?" he asked sarcastically.

"No, I let them bathe and gave them fresh clothes. I thought they might want to freshen up before meeting the *jarl* of Fýrifírar." Brandr rolled his eyes.

However, instead of reprimanding his subordinate for giving him lip, Agnarr shook his head and punched Brandr's shoulder familiarly. The jarl motioned at the rest of us to follow him inside.

"Just so we're clear, we would have happily accepted you into our home in travelworn clothes," he called over his shoulder as he led us through the entryway.

Agnarr seemed very unpretentious and mellow, very different from the leadership I was used to. We followed him to a large dining table with platters of meat pies and other pastries. Agnarr waved to indicate that we should all sit while he passed around the food. It took quite a bit of restraint not to stuff an entire meat pie in my mouth. It was delicious. Once everyone had taken some food, Agnarr spoke.

"I must admit, after your skirmish with Magna and his followers, I am surprised you still decided to visit, given his thoughts on humans, I wasn't sure you'd still want to come."

He looked at me as if already aware I was behind the reason for the visit.

"Ah, well, we're sorry about that." I wasn't sure if he was pleased with how we dispatched of the older orkin.

"Don't be," Agnarr said seriously. "You convinced them of what we couldn't—that humans should be treated as equals. Magna and his followers are still earning their place back amongst us. Our tribe is at peace now, so I promise you won't encounter any intolerance like his here."

"Uh… sweet? I mean, thank you, that is high praise coming from you," I said, not sure how to respond to such a compliment.

"Sweet?" Agnarr asked, confused.

"It's American slang, babe," a voice came from behind me. "It means awesome."

I turned to see Piper. She gave me a big grin. "It *was* pretty sweet the way you handed their asses to them."

That phrase was new to me, but I gathered her meaning. Piper looked well. Much better than when I'd seen her at the beginning of the cold season. Her face was fuller, happier, and her wavy hair hung longer past her shoulders.

"Good to see you again, Piper. You seem well." I grinned back at her.

"I am very happy," she said, locking eyes with Agnarr in a way that was, frankly, obscene.

I looked away, blushing. At moments like that, I was painfully aware of my lack of experience with females. I'd never had anyone I wanted to look at the way Piper and Agnarr looked at each other.

"So, Lodin told us to expect you. I can't say I am surprised you chose to come before the snows melted," Agnarr said.

"That was my idea. Our guards tend to get restless during the snowy season and I was anxious to start building relationships with other tribes. Now that I had no…" I trailed off. I wasn't ready to explain my own personal reasons for coming.

"Now that you had no…?" Piper asked, picking up my sentence where I'd trailed off.

Reykr cleared his throat. "Steve has been eager to visit the other tribes of Niflheim for a fair few many árs, but our tribal leadership has always been able to come up with one reason or another as to why he should stay in the safety of Snaerfire. They are very protective of him—he's a beloved member of our tribe and one of our most valuable trackers. But Steve decided that this winter was the time. We are the lucky ones he specifically selected to join him on this endeavor. I believe your human females might have something to do with why these two came." He nodded to Tyr and Berit

"Well, we welcome the opportunity to learn from our brothers from the north, but I'd be wary of the human women. They are a force to be reckoned with," Agnarr said, taking a sip of his drink. "Is there anything, in particular, you are looking to find out?"

I could tell Agnarr knew this was more than just some peacekeeping, relationship-building endeavor. He could tell this trip was personal for me. I sighed and decided the truth was the best option.

"My mother passed long ago, and my father died recently. It seemed like the right time to step out and explore the other tribes."

Agnarr studied me, saying nothing. What was the look in his eyes—sympathy? I placed my hands in my lap, unsure of what else to say. I felt as if I had just bared my soul to the table. We sat in silence for a moment, and it was Piper who finally spoke.

"Steve, I am afraid we don't have any half-orkin here. But what Agnarr told you at the beginning of winter was true. We have twelve human women. We also have a tribe that has agreed fully and completely to the integration and acceptance of the humans. Even if you aren't certain what you are looking for, you are welcome to see if you find it here. Even if you only stay for a season."

"You'd let us stay a season?" I asked, stunned.

"There are only a handful of you, and I am sure you are willing to work to earn your keep," Agnarr said. "But why don't we see if you like it here before you make any long-term commitments?"

"I think there are some empty rooms amongst the single males, though some of you might have to take on a room-mate," Piper said.

"Oh, that shouldn't be a problem," I said. But I felt the eyes of my tribemates on me. I didn't know if *they* wanted to stay for a season. "Even if we only stay a short time, not sleeping on the ground would be great," I finished lamely.

"Well then, let's get you settled in before the evening meal. We can get your belongings taken to your rooms and we may need to pull an extra bed in from storage. Brandr, can you get their packs from the stables and I'll show them to their rooms?" Agnarr asked.

"At your service, *Jarl Agnarr.*" Brandr saluted.

"Will you give it a rest!?" Agnarr growled.

"Never."

The jarl stood and ushered us out of his home, stopping to envelope Piper in a hug. "See you at dinner, Jarlin Piper," he teased.

"You're insufferable," she said with a laugh as she waved us all out. "I look forward to introducing you all at dinner."

I was sharing a room with Reykr, but it was fine. I had my own bed and there was no guard standing outside our door as there had been in Vátrfírar. Reykr, Tyr, and Berit decided to nap until dinner, given that none of us had slept well on the road. But my mind was restless. Instead of trying to sleep I quietly slipped out of the room. Maybe I could do some exploring on my own.

CHAPTER FIVE

BILLIE

I groaned as I rose from my knees, which ached from scrubbing the baseboards. The wood was in beautiful condition, though it was hidden under layers of dust and grime. I'd pushed all the furniture into one corner so that Osif could determine what was salvageable. Then I got down to work.

The place needed to be deep cleaned from top to bottom. I washed the walls repeatedly until the water ran clear, and you could see the wood's beautiful grain underneath. I moved onto the floor, mopping until it shined. Now that the baseboards were done, it was time to tackle the windows. There were several missing panes, but I could clean the intact ones and prepare the space for the new glass. It was cold in the bar with the missing window panes, but I was sweating from all the work. I stood back and pleased to see it coming together. With each layer of dust I removed the bar felt more and more like mine.

I was on the third pass of the window, trying to get a particularly stubborn patch of grease off, when a low voice that sounded quite close said, "Wow, you are focusing pretty hard on that window."

"Jesus fucking Christ," I shrieked as I stumbled backward. In my panic, I put my foot into the bucket of soapy water and fell squarely on my ass, water splashing all over me. "What in the hell? You scared the shit out of me!" I yelled. "What do you think you are doing sneaking up on someone like that?" I was pissed as I attempted to remove my foot, which was now firmly lodged in the bucket.

"I—I had been standing watching you for quite a while. I was surprised you didn't notice me before," He stumbled over his words. "I didn't mean to startle you."

Well, you did, and now I have a goddamn bucket stuck on my foot. The least you could do is help." I stuck the trapped appendage in his direction, the seat of my pants soaked through with washwater and the rest of me feeling decidedly sorry for myself. Even my palms smarted from catching myself on the hardwood floor. This was the worst.

"Of course, of course," he said as he attempted to climb through the window.

"Dude, the doors are right next to the window."

He blushed a deep green, before walking to the doors and opening the working one. He walked to where I was sitting and stood over me, still sitting with a bucket stuck on my foot and my ass soaking wet. I didn't recognize him at all, so he definitely wasn't from our tribe.

"Okay, so, how can I help?" he asked, looking incredibly embarrassed.

"Well. You could grab the bucket and pull?" I spoke slowly as if talking to a complete idiot.

"Right, okay. Yes. I can do that," he said eagerly as he bent to examine the bucket.

It wasn't painful, but my boot was wedged in awkwardly. He took the lip of the bucket with both hands, looked at me, and said, "Steady yourself."

I planted both hands behind me where I sat, trying to anchor myself to the floor as he pulled with all his might. Instead of freeing my foot, as I'd hoped, the stupid orc underestimated his strength and lifted me completely off the floor. Then he slipped in the spilled water, causing us to fall to the ground. Whoever this stranger was, he was making a marvelous first impression.

"What the fuck was that? I said 'pull the bucket off my foot', not 'hurl me into the air!'" I cried.

"I'm sorry, I think it is more wedged than we thought. And you aren't heavy, so I guess I underestimated how easy it would be able to lift you—or throw you." He cringed.

We were now lying atop each other, limbs entangled. His muscular orc body pressed against mine, and I could feel the heat radiating from his green skin. I wanted to be irritated at this strange orc who appeared out of nowhere, disrupted my productive afternoon, and made a complete mess of the floor I'd spent hours cleaning. But as I locked eyes with him, something stilled in me. His eyes were a warm amber and apologetic, in a confused but amicable face. Even more confusing was that they looked almost human—with white sclera. How odd.

I took a deep breath. He hadn't done this on purpose. He was just a guy. It wasn't his fault I didn't notice him until he was right up on me. I took a deep breath.

I pushed myself off of him, sweeping my free leg and upper thigh over his hips. Beneath me, he tensed up, a breath catching in his throat.

Oh my god. I was grinding on a total stranger.

It was my turn to apologize, feeling incredibly embarrassed. "Sorry, I didn't mean—I mean, I was just trying to disentangle—ugh," I spluttered, avoiding eye contact.

The spilled water had turned into a small puddle, and the bucket still clung stubbornly to my foot.

The orc cleared his throat, trying to regain his composure. "Let's focus on the bucket," he said, reaching down to wrestle with it again. "I promise I'll be more careful this time." And just like that, the tension shifted from embarrassment to determination. We both tugged at the bucket, laughter bubbling up between strained breaths. Maybe this unexpected encounter wasn't so bad after all.

He finally managed to pull the bucket off, leaving us sitting on the floor facing each other. As I faced him, I could discern more details about him up close. He was an orc, but he didn't look like the other orcs from our tribe. As I had noted, his eyes matched human eyes more than orkin. He looked leaner than most of them, as well. Most orkin were stocky and built like solid walls of muscle. This orc was muscular but almost like a swimmer's body, with broad shoulders that narrowed down to a more tapered waist. I cocked my head to the side, studying him.

"Who are you?" I asked finally.

"Oh, I'm so sorry. I'm Steve." He put out his hand out to take mine.

I extended my hand, eyes wide, "Steve? *The* Steve?" I asked, grasping his large hand in some weird orkin-human hybrid handshake. Orkin gripped wrists while humans grasped hands. We ended up shaking wrists. It worked.

Steve looked at me like I was messing with him. "That is the second time today that someone has referred to me this way. What do you mean by *the* Steve?"

"Ha, I'm guessing it's you. Piper and Agnarr told us all about you. Steve, the only half-orc. And if what Magna said about you is true, you're pretty fucking badass."

Now that I knew he was Steve, it made sense. His ears were rounded and his tusks were slightly smaller. So this is what a half-orc, half-human would look like. Not bad. Not bad at all. *This is what a baby would look like if I had one. Whoa brain, where did that come from?*

Steve brought me back to my senses with a question, "Is 'badass' good? Like 'rad'?"

"Oh lord. Why do you know 'rad' but not 'badass'?" I laughed.

"The only human I knew was my mom, maybe she didn't know 'badass'?" He shrugged.

I hadn't thought about that—Steve's head must be spinning at meeting other humans. That had to be a lot to take in.

"Huh. Maybe. Well, you convinced Magna and his band of merry men that humans are not the scum of the universe so we're all pro-Steve here."

"Um... what?" Steve was looking more and more perplexed by the second. I couldn't help it. Confusing orkin with American slang was a favorite pastime of mine, and I had a brand new victim. I used Steve's shoulder for leverage to pull myself up, then put a hand out to help him. Now that we both stood, Steve was tall. Very tall. All the orcs were tall, but Steve didn't have the width of the others, making him seem even taller. That, and I was barely over five feet. Everyone was tall, even on Earth. Well, except Joey. I often wondered— probably too often— about the mechanics of Piper and Agnarr, and she was five-foot-seven.

Seeing Steve standing only cemented the surfer boy vibe. His black hair was loose, hanging to his shoulders, and it had a bit of wave to it. Nothing compared to my curls, but all the orcs I'd met so far had stick-straight, silky hair. The wave must come from his mom.

"So tell me, Steve. What's someone like you, a member of

a rival tribe, doing watching a lone human woman wash windows?"

Steve countered with his own question, "What are you doing in this broken-down building all by yourself?"

"I am working on rebuilding a bar. Not so much rebuilding as refurbishing. This one has been empty for over twenty years. I'm going to bring it back to its old glory, while adding some human touches along the way."

Steve looked around the space. Even though it was much cleaner, it still needed a lot of work. Half the chairs and tables we sat at needed to be replaced because they were too beaten up. I knew nothing about woodworking, and the bar top itself was rough and uneven. I wanted to talk to Osif about sanding it down and refinishing it. I still had at least a month of work ahead of me, or more than that if I kept up my work in the kitchens and continued to refuse help from my friends. I knew I'd only be able to go so long before they forced me into helping their help—and I was grateful. I'd explained to him what I was doing in the bar, but he had yet to explain to me what he was doing in our tribe.

I took our conversation back to my original question. "Alright, Mr. Steve, your turn. I explained what I'm doing in an empty bar. Your turn to explain why you are at our tribe."

Steve shifted from one foot to the other, as if weighing how much to tell me. I already knew he was accepting of humans, based on his treatment of Piper and Magna alone, but that didn't tell me why he had traveled all the way from the snowy mountains to us. He continued to stay silent.

"Are you just really into humans?" I asked, raising a suggestive brow.

"No—no." He put up his hands. "Well, I mean, yes. But not like that. Well, maybe like that? I don't actually know. I just—"

I cut into his spluttering. "Oka-a-ay, buddy, we're gonna need to take a seat."

I steered Steve to one of the tables and chairs awkwardly arranged in the corner of the bar. Steve flopped down and dragged a hand over his face. It was only in the sunlight streaming through the half-grimy window that a sprinkling of five o'clock shadow glittered on his face. For some reason, this made him even more attractive.

I loved a man with stubble.

CHAPTER SIX

BILLIE

*A*ll I had asked him was what he was doing in our tribe, and he clammed up and got weird. We had been having a good conversation, maybe even leaning toward flirting, and now he looked uncomfortable. Something about why he was here had made him feel uncomfortable. I was puzzled about this while the silence grew.

Unsure of what to do next, I went with what I knew—humor. "Okay, you don't want to tell me why you're here. Are you a spy?" I raised my brows at him in question.

"No—no. Definitely not." He looked horrified.

"Definitely something a spy would say." I tried to say it with a straight face, but I broke and started laughing. "Okay, if you aren't a spy, why can't you tell me why you're here?"

"It's just a whole bunch of personal baggage that no one needs to hear," he mumbled, not looking me in the eye.

Ahh, okay. Bartender mode activated. I was used to many a patron unloading their trauma on me. People I didn't even know would pour their hearts out to me. I was a therapist paid in tips.

Steve needed someone to listen to and had stumbled across the perfect person. "Well, I am here and willing to listen. This is a judgment-free zone. Trust me, in my line of work I have heard some crazy shit. Hit me with it."

"Half of that was slang, wasn't it?" he asked, giving me a grin.

"Sure was. You'll get used to it. Now I can tell you need to talk, and I am here to listen." I nestled my chin in the heels of my palms as if I had all the time in the world to wait for him to open up.

I was fascinated by this half-orc. It must have been really interesting to grow up with a human mother and an orkin father—and be the only one of his kind. I wanted to know more about him. And it didn't hurt that he wasn't bad to look at, either.

"Okay, okay," he began reluctantly. "I'm the only half-orc in my tribe. Both my parents have passed away, and I never truly fit in. Discovering humans had arrived here and escaping my parents' expectations motivated me. My mom, who missed Earth, taught me about it—Halloween, pop-tarts, music, and electricity. She loved my dad and me, but the realization she could never return home weighed on her." He continued, and I nodded in encouragement. "After her death, I felt even more adrift. My protective father kept me from exploring. I'd ask to go to the beach to honor her memory, but he would tell me it wasn't safe. Only when he passed did I consider the idea of leaving to see what else was out there."

"You're carrying guilt," I said.

His brows furrowed. "How did you know?"

"Well, your parents' passing freed you, yet you feel guilty for wanting more than your tribe offers," I explained.

Steve's jaw dropped. "Are you a mind reader?" he asked.

"Yep. Mind reading." I managed to say it with a straight face.

"Really?" Steve asked, eyes wide, putting the boyish look back on his face.

"Yep. All humans can do it. So you better be careful with what you think about around all these human women," I said, leaning back in the bar chair and raising my brows.

Steve blushed green and looked down, directly at my wet boobs. Immediately realizing he had made things worse, he looked up at me, horrified, and even more green.

"I wasn't—I'm not thinking—well, now I am!" he cried.

I couldn't help but bust up laughing, "No, no. No one on Earth can fucking mindread. Sorry, I will stop teasing you for a bit, but only because you just bared your soul to a complete stranger. And then accidentally checked out my tits."

Steve breathed a sigh of relief as I let him off the hook, but he was very focused now, keeping his eyes on my face. "Okay, so if you aren't a mind reader, how did you manage to figure me out in one conversation?"

"I was a bartender back on Earth. I served alcohol to people. It doesn't teach you mind reading, but it does teach you how to read people. They'll confess their deepest secrets over a drink." I toyed with the empty, long-forgotten bar glass that was on the table between us, thinking about my old patrons. I wondered what it would be like to serve orkin.

"And people just open up to you because they are drinking?" He seemed confused.

"I just listen. It's that simple. Most people—or orkin—just need someone to listen to them. It sounds like you need to decide what *you* want. I am working on the same thing." I finished, feeling as if he'd just shared so much of himself I could give him a bit of understanding of me.

"You aren't happy with Fýrifírar?" he asked, brows raised.

"I'm not unhappy. I just need time to settle. This very bizarre abduction has given me time to figure out what I want, but it's still been really different from what I'm used to. So, you and I are kind of in the same place," I said truthfully.

The cogs in my mind were whirring. This orc was new to our tribe, looking for a purpose. I was on the same trajectory and could use the help getting the bar back in operating order. Maybe having him stay would be good. I found that working with my hands let my mind wander and figure things out.

I made up my mind. "Would you want to stay here for a while? All of the girls are still figuring out their new lives. You can figure it out with us," I offered. Also, I would love help with the bar. Maybe this unexpected and surprisingly wet—"I couldn't myself "—meeting could benefit both of us.

"That would be… really, really great. I don't know how my tribemates would feel about staying." His face went from hopeful to downcast as if his friends would ruin his chance to finally figure himself out.

"Then fuck 'em," I said, leaning back in my chair.

Maybe Steve was just as lost as I felt, needing time and space away from home to figure out what he really wanted and who he really was.

I assessed him, wondering if he ever got the chance to just be. "If they're your friends, they will know you are going through something, and this is what you need. If they aren't, then why do you care what they think?"

"You make it sound much easier than it is," he said ruefully.

"I've been burned too many times to let myself get hung up on what other people expect of me. I still get nervous about it, but at the end of the day, I need to do what is best for me. It's hard, especially if you feel like you might need to take a different path from your friends or family members. Hell, I nearly had a meltdown telling the head cook I wanted to open a bar instead of chopping potatoes for her. But I did it."

"You'd let me help?" Steve asked.

"Well, if it were completely up to me, I'd put you to work now. But we need to check in with Agnarr. This is above my pay grade. You'd have to go to the boss for that kind of permission."

"Will you just say normal words?" he huffed.

"Mmm… no." I smiled brightly. "But I will take you up on your offer to help if Piper and Agnarr are okay with you staying." Still twirling the glass in my hand, I realized Steve's showing up might have solved many of my concerns in one fell swoop. I had an eager and willing orc to help me with my bar.

"Do you think they would be?"

"Well, they just took in twelve human refugees. I don't think they'd turn down an orc willing to do manual labor." I laughed. "We can talk to them about it at dinner tonight. I'll even stand next to you so you don't get nervous. Speaking of which," I said, looking out the window, "the sun is starting to set. We should get dry clothes before heading to dinner."

We both stood, and he looked at me thoughtfully, "You're the first human I have had a real conversation with outside of my mom."

"And? Do we live up to the expectation you built in your head?"

He pursed his lips as if thinking it over.

"Hey! I just gave you some solid life advice!" I cried.

He laughed. A hearty booming laugh that made me feel warm down to my toes.

"Yes, you live up to expectations. I think maybe I have made my first human friend?" He asked hesitantly.

"Yes." I nodded, finding the concern in his voice adorable. "You have made your first human friend. Now go get some fresh clothes for dinner."

Steve headed out of the bar, brow furrowed. How would working with him on this project go? I'd flirted with some of the orkin from the tribe but hadn't built a solid foundation with any of them outside of Agnarr and Osif. Agnarr was *very much* taken, and Osif was at least thirty years older than me. I loved working with him. He reminded me of my grandpa.

Steve's vulnerability struck a chord within me. He was one of the most open orkin I'd met here. Like me, he was adrift. Where I was struggling to fit into a new world, he straddled two cultures, trying to find where he belonged. But something about those hazel eyes, warm with laughter, fascinated me. After everything he must have gone through, always being different, the only half-orc in so many tribes, he still smiled and still wanted connection and understanding.

Was making friends with a male orc a good idea? I was a flirt by nature, and this often led to men thinking I was up for anything, and in the past—I was. Casual hookups were fun and easy until someone (usually me) expected more, and things got complicated. I shook my head. Steve was too innocent to be a casual thing. Or anything for that matter. Based on his dad's protective nature, I doubted he had much experience with females. But I could be a friend, a confidant. I'd been around the block too many times to think of him otherwise. What was I getting myself into? This might be a bad idea.

CHAPTER SEVEN

STEVE

A human friend. I made a human friend on my first day Fýrifírar.

The Fýrifírar orkin could not be more different than the Vátrfírar. Agnarr and Piper welcomed us with open arms and already offered to let us stay the season. And now with Billie's Bar, I would have a chance to contribute during my stay.

I didn't have any questions. My mind was made up. I was staying. I found Billie fascinating—no mesmerizing. And the idea of seeing if I might fit into a different tribe was too difficult to say no to. I chewed on my lip, thinking about what my tribemates would say. Reykr would stay whether or not he wanted to because he wouldn't leave me. Tyr and Berit could make it back together if they wanted to leave. Considering I was still suspicious of their reasons for coming, it might be better if they didn't stay. I had a feeling they only joined to get a look at the human females. If they left, at least they could report back to the tribe that the other tribes or wild animals didn't kill us.

I headed to my room and let my mind wander back to Billie. She was unlike anyone I ever met. She was so candid and open it made it easy for me to talk to her. I'd told her more about my fears and hopes than I'd ever told anyone, and I just met her. There was zero judgment in her questions, just curiosity. I wanted to know more about her. For the longest time, I thought it would be getting out and seeing what was beyond my village. But what about after that? I didn't have any answers. Billie made me think beyond just gaining my freedom.

And then there was Billie herself. I had now met exactly three human women: my mom, Piper, and Billie. Billie didn't look like any of the other women. For one, she was even shorter than all of them. Her curly brown hair was a wild mane that gave off the impression of someone who wasn't to be tamed. Though she was tiny, she had a curvy figure. In the brief moment I inadvertently glanced at her chest, I wondered what it would be like to cup each of her breasts in my hands. Her tapered waist flared out to generous thighs, and I found myself thinking about what her backside would look like, pondering if her skin was as soft as it looked.

I shook my head, trying to get a hold of my thoughts. I had never considered anyone romantically—male or female. I felt almost guilty for thinking about her like that. I had been stuffed into the role of baby brother for so long, that sex, of any variety was off the table. Many orkin had stepped in to help raise me after my mom's death. Obviously I'd never been interested in any of them; that would have been weird. Instead, I had a bunch of loving uncles, aunts, and older mentor figures, not unlike siblings. There wasn't room for romance in any of those relationships. And there weren't many females in my tribe that came of age at the same time as me. Billie was the first female I'd met who hadn't patted me on the head like a child.

I opened the door to mine and Reykr's shared room to find him already dressed. He looked at me quizzically.

"Why are you all wet?" he asked.

"It's a long story involving a bucket," I said surly. "I don't want to get into it. Do we have anything I can change into?" My encounter with Billie was wild, strange, and wonderful, and I wanted to keep to myself a little longer.

"Odin brought us some fresh clothes—they are closer to our sizes this time. He's a sweet orkling, but once you get him talking, he doesn't stop. His mom, Torah, oversees laundry," he explained, indicating a pile of fresh clothes on my bed.

I quickly changed. "Alright, let's get going," I said, grabbing my cloak.

There was a crowd at the doors to the longhouse. It wasn't until I looked to the head of the crowd that I noticed Brandr holding the doors open for everyone to stream inside. He gave us a friendly nod and then tilted his head toward a table at the front of the longhouse, where Piper and Agnarr were already seated. Tyr and Berit were already seated with them. And directly to the left of Piper, I was surprised to see Billie—deep in conversation with Piper. I blanched instantly. *Was she already asking Piper if we could all stay? Was she telling Piper I accidentally got her stuck in a bucket? That I thought humans could mindread?*

I followed Reykr to the table, where Reykr sat across from Piper, leaving me to sit across from Billie. Billie and Piper halted their conversation.

"Steve!" Piper exclaimed. "Billie was just telling me about how you ran into her at the bar."

I looked to Billie and she gave me an almost imperceptible shake of her head. Ah, okay, she hadn't told Piper everything about the meeting yet. I returned my attention to Piper.

"Yes, while my tribemates took the afternoon to nap, I decided to explore a little. I hope that's alright?"

"Of course, of course. We trust you." She waved me off as if my concerns were unnecessary. "Billie was saying you might want to stay the season?"

At this question, Tyr, Berit, and Reykr's eyes all swiveled to me at once. I cleared my throat and shifted uncomfortably. Billie probably didn't realize I hadn't discussed the idea of staying with them. I hadn't because it wasn't a discussion I wanted to have, but my mind was made up and I wasn't going to let them unmake it for me— as it had been so many times in the past. The silence stretched on, with more eyes on me, Agnarr's now included.

I cleared my throat again. "I did tell Billie I might like to stay the season, if you'll have me. I could help Billie get the bar up and running and do other work around the tribe to earn my keep. I hadn't gotten a chance to discuss this with the rest of my tribemates, but I plan to stay."

Rekyr looked unphased, sipping his drink as if he'd expected this all along. Berit and Tyr immediately put their heads together in whispered conversation. Billie, Piper, and Agnarr all looked thrilled.

"Well, I think we are all eager to get *Billie's Bar* open," Piper said with a laugh, emphasizing the name, as Billie cringed. "I think it would be lovely if you stayed to help, Steve. She hasn't been as accepting of help from others, so she must see some promise in you."

I blushed, unsure of how to take the compliment. But I was pleased to be welcomed.

Reykr crossed his arms over his chest and gave me a shrewd look. "You know I'll stay if you stay. I might even be able to help out with the bar if Billie will have me." He glanced at Billie.

Billie assessed him, taking in his giant frame."I think we might find some use for you," she replied flippantly. "What of the rest of your compatriots?"

Tyr and Berit paused their whispering, both their forks held aloft when they realized we were waiting for a response. They nodded to each other before nodding to us.

"We'll stay," Tyr said. "We can also help with the bar or do other work around the tribe. It is better than sitting around Snaerfírar waiting for the snow to thaw."

Agnarr's brows rose. "Should I be worried that the four of you seem so eager to stay away from home for more than a season?"

I had the same questions in my head about Tyr and Berit. I couldn't help but wonder if the much larger female representation in Fyrfire made up their minds. I decided to keep my concerns to myself for the time being.

"No, no," I assured him. "Lodin knows we are trying to build relationships. He will likely assume we have either been eaten by skogkatts or made headway with one of the tribes."

"Well, then consider it official. You are welcome to stay with our tribe for the season and make yourselves useful however you see fit."

"Thank you, Jarl Agnarr," Reykr rumbled next to me.

Agnarr waved his hand dismissively. "Please, just Agnarr. Now, let's eat. I am sure your fare on the road left much to be desired."

We all helped ourselves to the piles of different dishes on the table, and I enthusiastically attacked my food. I was still hungry from trying to eat on the road. I tried a bit of everything and found their cooking to be just as good, if not better, than the cooks of Snaerfírar. They had three different types of meat pies that I had to stop myself from shuffling into my mouth. As I got my fill and slowed down, I looked up and saw Billie looking at me thoughtfully. I cocked my head to the side with a silent question. Why didn't she tell Piper about the bucket and our conversation? Billie just winked at me. She whispered something in Piper's ear that made her smile, and she stood up.

"I'm heading to bed, all," Billie said. "After working all morning in the kitchen and then all afternoon in the bar, I am exhausted."

I'd already cleared my plate and made my mind up quickly. "Let me walk you back to your room?" I asked.

She looked at me with brows raised before giving Piper a quick look. Piper shrugged. Whatever language they were speaking, I wasn't privy to it.

"Sure," she said casually, "that would be nice."

I stood and followed her out of the longhouse. Once I caught up with her I had to slow my pace because her legs were much shorter than mine. Walking next to each other, our height difference was even more apparent. Her head barely reached the middle of my chest. It also made it very easy for me to see down the top of her tunic. I couldn't help but notice her breasts were significantly larger than any of the other females I'd seen. They looked so… soft. I quickly averted my eyes when I realized this was the second time I'd ogled her in one day.

"So you're staying," she said. It wasn't a question.

"I am. Are you okay with that? I know we discussed it as a possibility, but I made it official with Agnarr without further conversation. I just volunteered to be your assistant until you finished the bar. That's a lot of time with me, isn't it?" It came out as a question laced with uncertainty.

"I am happy to have your help. And you need someone to help you work through all of this." She paused. "But you shouldn't rely only on me. You should talk to Agnarr and

Brandr, too, and be more honest with Reykr. He'll want to know how much you're struggling with figuring out your place without your parents if he's a real friend. I am always willing to listen, but I don't want to be your sole source of advice."

"You're right. I think having new perspectives might help me figure out what I am looking for…"

We must've reached Billie's door, because she stopped walking. I just stood there, not sure what to do next. We stared into each other's eyes for a beat.

"You don't have a lot of experience with females, do you?" she asked, tilting her head to the side.

"No. No, I don't." I stuffed my hands in my pants pockets. "I wasn't interested in any of the orkin from my tribe. None of them were born around the same time as me."

"So you've never been interested in… anyone?" she looked surprised.

"Nope. Well, unless my hand counts," I said before I stopped to think better of it.

"Steve!" she gasped, clutching her chest.

I was mortified but realized she was laughing. I'd made Billie laugh again. I couldn't help it, but I started laughing too. We both kept laughing until she paused to wipe the tears from her eyes.

"Well, Steve, at the very least, I can teach you a little more about females." She said, cocking a brow.

"I—I—that sounds good," I stammered.

She turned and opened her door. "Goodnight, Steve."

"Goodnight, Billie."

CHAPTER EIGHT

BILLIE

The next morning, I was up with the sun, heading to the bar. I was very surprised to find Joey there. "What brings you here?" I asked suspiciously.

"You're going to trust the orkin from Snaerfírar to help you with the bar, but not me? No way." She crossed her arms in front of her chest.

"Is Runa okay with you missing kitchen duty?" Runa had been fine with me leaving to work on the bar, but more people taking off would have a big impact on food prep times. Was I stealing Runa's staff? Ugh, I didn't want that at all.

"Agnarr and Piper are fine with it, and that's enough for me," she said.

"So we both have permission to work on the bar full time?" I asked, surprised.

"Yep. I talked to Piper about it last night. They think the bar will be great for the tribe, and working with the Snaerfírar will be excellent for tribal politics. You know, finally getting the tribes to talk to each other about trade, alliances, disaster relief, blah, blah, blah. Piper and Agnarr go nuts for that stuff. They see this as a huge step forward for the tribe. They have no hesitation."

"Wow. Well, okay then. Thank you." I pulled her into a hug. "I appreciate your willingness to help my dreams come true."

"Bitch, as if I would do any less," she whispered in my ear before releasing me. "When do you think the Snaerfírar will show up?"

"I don't know," I said, chewing my lip. "I didn't realize that he might want to do it full-time if he only plans to stay the season."

"Don't you mean them? There are four of them."

"Right, right." I blushed. I had clearly only been considering Steve.

"Speaking of *him*—what is going on there?" Joey waved her hand between us.

"With Steve?" I asked, confused.

"Duh, with Steve. Don't act like an idiot. He walked you home last night. Did he push you up against a wall?"

I blushed even further. How had Joey sussed out the tiny ember of a flame that was starting between Steve and me? It was so small that I wasn't even sure it was real. I was attracted to him, and I was pretty sure he was attracted to me, but that was it. I wasn't telling her anything.

"Nothing is going on with Steve. He needs a friend. And the dude has zero experience with women. I doubt he's ever seen boobs. He couldn't handle me."

"I dunno. I know your boobs are the size of dinner plates, but his hands looked pretty big from where I was sitting."

"Joey!" I hissed.

She shrugged. "I'm just saying. It looked like he was into

you. And it could be pretty fun to date someone like Steve who had no expectations—he could learn a thing or two."

I squinted at her, unwilling to admit that there was merit to the idea as we gathered the supplies for the days work.

"What about you and Ottar, hmm?" I asked, changing the subject.

"Alas, I was mistaken. I caught him making out with Bo in the pantry yesterday." She gave a dramatic sigh.

"Oh, well, Bo is cute. Ottar's got solid taste."

"I know, right?!" she stomped her foot and huffed. "Ugh, if I didn't have a stupid crush on Ottar, I'd be happy for them. At least they're getting some. And you could be getting some, too." She raised her brows at me.

"You've seen me with Steve like once. There's nothing there."

"Hello? Did we not just talk about him walking you home? And… I heard you laughing outside your room on my way to mine." She sounded sheepish.

Okay, if *anything* were going to happen with Steve, I would have to keep it on complete lockdown. Joey was too nosy for her own good.

"Honest to God, woman. He's been here one day, and you are already spying on us?"

"I just happened to walk by at the right time," she said, feigning innocence.

"Yeah, yeah." I rolled my eyes. "Listen, maybe there is something about him. He's so open and honest. Vulnerable with me from the first minute. He doesn't have the tough macho facade. But I know I'll end up screwing it up, so I don't even want to bother."

"What do you mean by screwing it up?" she asked.

"I fall for a guy, and I want to sleep with him. We fuck, it's great, then I start sharing my feelings and he freaks out and leaves."

The look of sympathy Joey gave me was enough to show me she understood. I didn't want to be just a warm body. What I knew of Steve so far would have had me jumping into his bed in the past. He was kind and thoughtful. He listened to me when I was sharing about myself. And he was hot as hell. But his inexperience and my mess of past 'relationships' might make for disaster. For now, I was going to be his friend. If something developed... later, it would develop later.

"Okay, so you aren't ruling Steve out as an option?" Joey asked, pulling me out of my thoughts.

"No. I am not ruling Steve out. He feels like an innocent little bean and I don't want to wreck him completely."

"He's a grown-ass man—er, orc. He can decide if he wants to be wrecked by you."

"Ha, ha. I will keep that in mind," I said as I started to stalk the bar, looking for places that needed work. "You're happy to help with this? It's a lot of physical labor."

"Oooh, of course!" Joey said.

"You know, there are four new orkin here. And that big one—Reykr? He was giving off definite daddy vibes." I raised my brows at her.

"Oh lord, I did notice him. He's huge!"

"Something you'd be into?" I asked suggestively.

"I mean, I'd love to, but I don't even know how that would work mechanically. I am barely five feet tall!"

"Piper doesn't seem to have any complaints. Maybe you can ask her if she had to work up to it?" At this, we descended into a fit of giggles.

We looked around the bar a bit more and decided it was time to ask the Snaerfírar to join us. There was a lot of heavy lifting—we needed to empty the bar completely. We headed to their rooms and knocked on one of the doors. No one answered for a moment, so we knocked again.

After what felt like an eternity, but was only a few minutes, the door opened. Steve stood in the doorway shirtless and barefoot, wearing nothing but pants that weren't fully laced up. Oh boy. I opened my mouth and closed it, not trusting myself to speak. I knew most orkin were muscular, but Jesus Christ. He was lean, with broad muscled shoulders, impressive pecs, and just the hint of a six-pack above the cut of his hip muscles that pointed directly toward a black happy trail. He was hunching a bit as if that would hide his naked chest or his bright green cheeks. I blinked and blinked again. *Holy fuck, how was I going to be friends first with Steve?* I could feel myself growing damp just at the sight of him shirtless.

"Hi!" Joey finally said.

"Hi," Steve responded, a little too brightly, as if he was trying to make up for being half-naked and barely awake.

Sensing I'd lost the ability to be coherent, Joey continued.

"The tribe has relieved Billie and me of our duties in the kitchen so we can work on the bar full time. We were hoping you all would be willing to join us?" Joey said brightly.

"Yeah, yes, of course!" Steve responded, dragging his fingers through his hair. He turned to look behind him, where Reykr was still asleep in bed.

My mouth finally decided to work, "Why don't you get some breakfast and meet us at the bar in about an hour?" I suggested.

"That sounds great," he said, but remained standing in the doorway.

I gave him an awkward smile. "I guess will see you in a bit?"

"Sure."

"Alright. Bye then!" I said it little too loudly as I pulled Joey away from the door and down toward the path.

We walked briskly for a few moments in silence before Joey asked, "So how long are you going to wait to fuck him?"

"Gahhh! This is what I'm talking about!" I waved my arms in the air. "I am terrible at friends first, fuck later. You saw him."

"Um, I think I saw *you* seeing him," she said. "You need a better poker face."

"Do you think he noticed how awkward I was?" I asked, concerned.

"No, he was just as awkward. But I think you are right about him being clueless about women. He was too busy being embarrassed that he was still asleep to notice that you were drooling."

"Oh fuck you, I was not drooling." I shoved Joey off the path.

"May as well have been," she teased, rejoining me.

"You're going to make keeping things friendly and professional impossible, aren't you?" I huffed, starting to walk faster than her.

"Maybe." She kept up with me easily, still enjoying pushing my buttons.

"You know, you're lucky I like you. Otherwise, I'd banish you back to the kitchens to pine over Ottar while he feels up Bo in the walk-in."

Joey was mock-offended. "Well, that would be just plain mean."

"Fine, fine. But seriously. Let me navigate Steve?" I asked plaintively. "Who knows, under all those muscles and vulnerability, he might be the same type of dude to completely ghost me."

"Alright, I will be on my best behavior, scout's honor," she said, linking her arm to mine.

We continued to the bar in silence. The image of Steve, shirtless and rumpled from sleep, was burned into my brain. Without warning, the image of me licking down his happy trail popped into my mind.

Fuck. Friends. We were going to be friends. I was determined to see what this could be before I started anything physical with him. If I really did want to find a *mate* here in my new life, jumping into bed with Steve wouldn't end well, considering his inexperience and my past.

STEVE

Shit. Well, that could have gone better. I wasn't doing a good job proving my worth here if, on my first morning, Billie and Joey found me still asleep. I didn't want them to think we were lazy.

I shook Reykr awake and nearly got a face full of his fist as he woke up swinging. Reykr did not like waking up early.

"We need to go. Billie and Joey just stopped by on the way to the bar, and work starts this morning." I pulled my tunic on over my head.

"Already? The sun is barely up." He grimaced, stretching his arms over his head.

"Do you want to make a bad impression in Fýrifírar?"

"No, but I also don't want to be awake right now," he complained.

"Are you sure about staying here for the season?" I asked. "I won't be hurt if you decide to head back. We just agreed to a solid few months of hard labor."

"You know I don't like being stuck up at Snaerfírar. When I became a guard member, I thought I would see more action than the wayward bjorn that wandered into our territory. Plus, I'm not leaving you here alone."

"You know, at some point, you will have to give up trying to protect me."

Reykr had been my rock for the last ten árs, but I didn't want him to stay just because of me. I felt at ease in Fýrifírar and didn't need his protection.

"Já, I know," He said. "But it isn't now. Not while we're in an unfamiliar tribe and you are surrounded by the unknown." His tone was clipped.

With that, the conversation was done. I wasn't mad about Reykr staying, but I wanted him to stay because he wanted to, not because of any sense of obligation to me.

I attempted to change the conversation. "They told us to stop by the kitchens and get something to eat before heading to the bar. We can grab Berit and Tyr on the way."

It wasn't long before we stood in front of the dilapidated bar. The inside might be sparkling clean thanks to Billie's efforts, but a lot more work needed to be done on the exterior and the interior before the bar could be up and running. From the looks of it, the roof needed to be repaired—if not replaced. Several window panes were missing, and most of the furniture wasn't salvageable.

I wandered through the property, looking for Billie and Joey. The roof made the most sense to start with. Any repair that would make a mess would need to be cleaned before we worked on the inside. I didn't have a ton of woodworking experience. All of us were taught the basics as orklings, but only the carpenters knew the finer details.

I walked back out of the bar to find my tribemates had been joined by Billie, Joey, and an older orc I hadn't met yet.

They were deep in conversation. Billie's eyes lit up when she saw me.

"Morning! Glad to see you put some clothes on," she teased.

I blushed. There was something about the way Billie spoke to me that made me feel warm and weird all at once. I tried to brush it off.

"Will you introduce me to..." I trailed off, gesturing vaguely at the orc that had joined us.

"I'm Osif, the head carpenter of Fýrifírar. I am helping Billie here with the bar. Now that we have more hands this should go much more quickly." He rubbed his hands together eagerly. "So how much do you know about repairing a roof?"

"Uhh.. Not much," I said honestly.

"That's okay," Billie said. "I don't know anything about roofs and Osif promised me we would be able to manage it."

I honestly wasn't super pleased with how close Billie seemed to be with Osif, but I reminded myself that he was at least thirty àrs her senior and likely had a mate.

"Well, it looks as if I am going to take the lead, and that is no problem," Osif said. "We need new materials for the roof and new panes for the windows. We are also going to need new furniture, but that is something I would rather take on by myself. So why don't the Snaerfírar come with me to get lumber while the women clear out the attic space?"

"Um, I can lift lumber!" Joey interjected. "I'll head with you to get lumber. Steve and Billie can start on the attic."

"Já, I can work on the attic with Billie, if you'd rather go get lumber," I said, trying to be as accommodating as possible. Maybe Joey just had a passion for lifting heavy objects

A look I didn't quite understand passed between Billie and Joey, but neither said a word. Joey headed off with the rest of my tribesmates and Osif, leaving me alone with Billie.

I studied her uncertainly. Was she annoyed at being left alone with me? Her cheeks were tinged pink.

"I guess we should head up to the attic?" She glanced at me.

"Alright, we can grab the cleaning supplies on the way up."

We entered the bar and climbed up the stairs. They groaned and creaked underneath our weight. "These will need to be replaced, too," I commented.

"Yeah, or reinforced. Along with the railing. There is a lot of work to be done." She sighed.

"Hey, that's one of the reasons we agreed to stay. We want to help," I reassured her.

"I know. I want to ensure you know what you're getting yourself into," she said, looking around at all the repairs that needed to be done. The whole building looked as if it was sagging under the weight of dirt and grime.

"Já. None of us are master carpenters, but we've all come together to build new homes at Snaerfírar. We will be able to get it up and running. I can't wait to see you behind the bar pouring drinks."

Finally, we arrived in the attic. This wasn't a storage attic, as I expected, but the home of the previous bar owners. There was a large bed in the corner, a small kitchen, a dining table and chairs, and a door to what I assumed was a washroom. Even the fireplace was continued up into this space.

"Oh, this isn't an attic," I said in awe. "This is actually super cozy. And well-outfitted, despite the age."

"Yeah, I noticed when I first inspected it. It doesn't look like it has been touched since they passed. All of this furniture will likely have to go. That bed doesn't look salvageable. Not that I am particularly interested in sleeping in a dead person's bed." Billie made a face.

"How do you think we will fit everything down the stairs?

They are pretty narrow," I said, walking around and looking at the furniture. "The chairs would likely fit, but the dining table and the bed would have to be taken apart."

Billie looked around at the furniture, hands on her hips, lips pursed.

"Well, we only really need to take the salvageable stuff down the stairs, so it doesn't get more damaged. What if we got rid of the rest of the stuff a much quicker way?" She gave me a mischievous look.

"Okay, and what would be a much quicker way?" I asked, wondering where this was leading.

"What if we just threw it out the window?" She gestured to the large window at the front of the attic.

"You can't be serious." I moved in front of one of the chairs as though it were at risk of imminent defenestration. "Th-that just isn't done."

Billie was unlike anyone I'd ever met. She was seriously suggesting throwing old furniture out a window. Who would think of that? I couldn't tell if I was terrified of her or enraptured by her.

"Why not? It's not like it will matter if it gets broken. This old stuff will probably end up being used for firewood."

"And what do you think Osif would say to this plan?"

"I happen to think he would say it was brilliant," she said, puffing out her chest and smiling.

"Well then, you're the boss." I bowed.

"Oooh, does that mean I can boss you around?" She teased, tossing her curly hair to one side.

"I am at your service." I smiled suggestively and then blushed at my forwardness. *What has come over me?*

"Oh, don't tell me that. I might abuse my powers."

"Why don't we start by emptying this attic? Then you can think of other ways to use me," I said.

"Oh, I can think of many ways to use you," she replied tartly.

I could feel the heat radiating off my face. I needed to change the subject, having realized how forward I was being. "Should I run downstairs to get an axe to chop up some of the larger items?"

She laughed at my clear discomfort. "That sounds like an excellent place to start."

When I returned with two axes, I was greeted by a vision of Billie levering all of her petite body against the window sill in a doomed but desperate effort to pry it open.

I placed the axes against the wall and rushed to help her. The window was probably stiff from having been shut for árs. Billie was pulling at it with all her might, but it refused to budge.

"Why don't you let me try?" I asked, startling her.

She let out a breath of exhaustion. "Yeah, I've given it all I've got, and it won't move."

I stepped forward and examined the window. It looked designed to open upwards, with a large lip along the bottom and a small latch. The window was still locked.

"Did you consider unlatching it before trying to yank it open?" I pointed at the latch.

Billie put her face in her hands, mumbling something.

"What was that? I couldn't quite hear you," I teased.

"No, I didn't see the damn latch," she muttered.

"Would you like to be the one to unlatch it, or shall I?"

"Oh, just get on with it and open the stupid window," she said, rolling her eyes.

I was discovering I liked embarrassed Billie. Embarrassed Billie was adorable—flustered and pink-cheeked. Was I... flirting? We took turns embarrassing each other. I put the thought out of my mind as I easily flipped the latch and opened the window. It was large enough to fit most of the furniture, but the dining table and the bed would have to be cut up.

"Alright, boss, what is salvageable, and what is being tossed out the window?" I asked. I was hesitant about the plan, but Billie was in charge.

Billie looked around at the furniture carefully, running her fingers across the dining table.

"You know what," she said suddenly, "I want it all gone. I want to start from scratch. I've never gotten to pick out my own furniture—it has always been hand-me-downs. With all the help I am being offered and the tribe's clear investment in reopening the bar, I think I should get new stuff, right? This stuff looks like it is at least fifty years old," she said, wincing. "Not like I'm ungrateful, but—"

"I don't see why not." I kicked a chair leg, and it bowed. "We have Osif willing to teach us and plenty of eager novice woodworkers. A new set it is!"

With that, I swiftly picked up a dining room chair and easily chucked it out the window. Then we heard it crash to the ground outside the bar.

"Steve!" Billie gasped.

"What? You said all new things?"

"Yes! But you can't just throw a chair out a window without checking if—you know—there is someone on the ground below? What if you just knocked out Joey or Reykr?"

I blanched. Reykr would be fine if someone hit him with a chair, but Joey was tiny, even smaller than Billie. I rushed to the window and peered out. No one outside and nothing on the front lawn other than a very broken chair.

"We're safe," I said, breathing a sigh of relief.

"Okay, next time you throw something, at least check first?" She laughed.

"Yes, boss."

Billie grinned at me as she picked up another chair,

looked out the window, then dropped it with a resounding crash.

"I think this is going to be kind of fun," she said, picking up another chair.

We spent the rest of the morning clearing out the attic, starting with the pieces that easily fit through the window. We chatted as we emptied the space. Billie was easy to talk to and was as curious about my life as I was about hers.

Hearing about her family made me feel more at ease speaking about my own truthfully.

"I was the youngest of three," Billie said. "But none of us were close. Our childhood wasn't the best. My parents were very religious and didn't really care about us as long as we did what we were told. I wasn't allowed to date. I wore a purity ring, and my virginity was my entire value. Whatever my dad said was law, whether or not he understood the consequences of it. The three of us scattered as soon as we hit eighteen," she explained.

There was a flatness to her voice, as if she was trying to hide a pain that wasn't fully healed. "Where did your sisters go?" I asked.

"They both fled as soon as they could. They distanced themselves from the family as much as possible. Because I was the youngest, it was harder for me to just *run* when I definitely should have," her breathing hitched.

"Eventually, even though I couldn't imagine leaving my parents, I had to. I needed a life of my own. I found a job and a roommate and moved out. I stayed local, but I was no longer under the thumb of my parents. I was free to figure out my future. I ended up working at a restaurant and was happy there, but I didn't have any long-term goals. That's what I am doing now that I am here. Making long-term goals. Billie, the bar owner." She grinned at me.

I reflected on her upbringing. Orkin were communal by

nature. We ate together, often lived with our parents until we took mates, and rarely left our tribe of origin. All of this had always felt irksome, but I brushed it off. Now, it made me wonder if the human part of me wanted to make my own way—forge my own path. Whatever guilt Billie had felt about leaving her parents behind, she had clearly moved past it.

"How did your parents react to all of you leaving?" I asked.

"They were surprised, honestly. I think they thought that because they didn't hit us and they fed us, they were exemplary parents. But the reality is a lot more goes into parenting. They never really *saw* any of us. I think people of their generation had kids because that was the norm, not realizing how badly you can fuck up a kid. Now it is becoming more common to choose not to have kids."

"Are you angry at your parents?" I asked.

"No. Just sad. Sad for them because they don't understand why we don't have a relationship. Sad for me because if I ever do decide to have children, I don't have a model of what a parent should look like. I'll probably do the opposite of whatever my parents did. I wouldn't want my kids to meet my parents. I wouldn't want to expose them to their archaic way of thinking. Honestly, having parents that follow a religion that is thousands of years out of date sucks balls," she said, looking downcast.

"Hey, I don't think you need to have had great parents to be a great parent. Just recognizing what your parents lacked in raising you sets you up to be a much better mother someday," I responded, trying to comfort her. "I think of some of the things my parents did and how I would do them differently. I wouldn't have stayed holed up in the mountains, even if we did have an orkling. I would travel, show them different places on Niflheim, and go on adventures together. I know that is what Mom wanted deep down, but she was too scared to expose me to the unknown. And I don't think Dad ever wanted to leave."

"You'd want to take an orkling on adventures?" Billie asked, grinning.

"Yeah, maybe?" I shrugged, but was smiling. "I'd want them to see the ocean and meet the other tribes. Maybe we could explore the forest. Snaerfírar has hunter cabins that are nestled around the Fjall Mountains. We could explore and stay in the cabins." I thought wistfully about what it might be like to have a mate and an orkling that I got to raise with the freedoms I never had. I had never considered orklings before. It seemed out of the realm of possibility before Billie. But here she was, encouraging me to create a future I wanted.

"You have put a lot of thought into the life you want," she said, looking at me with what seemed to be admiration. What could I have said to make her admire me?

"Well, I had a lot of time stuck up in the mountains thinking," I said ruefully.

"Do you see yourself doing this traveling and adventuring with a certain someone?" she probed.

I felt myself blush. "There was no one in my tribe that I wanted as a mate. After a while, I stopped considering any of them. I knew if I was going to take a mate, I would have to find someone outside of Snaerfírar."

"So, is that what this mission is? A hunt for a mate?" she asked outright.

"It's been so long since I considered anyone. It hadn't really crossed my mind." I'd come to Fýrifírar looking for connection—and understanding. Not a mate.

"So focused on figuring out your future that you didn't picture a partner?"

I could tell she'd traveled this same path. "I guess, yeah."

"Well, maybe it is time to consider if you want one. Especially if you see orklings in your future."

"Do you want one?" I asked. "I mean, do you want a partner?"

Immediately, I wanted to hide under a large piece of furniture. How could I even ask that? But Billie didn't seem to mind.

She sighed, "That's… complicated. I always thought I did, but my relationships with men have been one dumpster fire after another."

"Dumpster fire?" I asked.

"Mmm… Shit show? Disaster. One disaster after another."

Well, now I had learned two more human terms: shit show and dumpster fire. I filed them away for later use.

"Why were these relationships *dumpster fires?*" I asked, making her laugh.

"Well, I have a bad habit of jumping into things physically and then getting my heart all caught up in what the guy only saw me as a hook-up."

"Hook-up?" I asked.

"You know, casual sex, no strings attached."

I nodded like I understood, though I definitely didn't. I couldn't imagine being casually intimate with someone. Maybe it was my lack of experience, but the idea of sharing a bed with someone and then treating them like it wasn't a big deal made me feel ill. Billie must have seen the look on my face.

"Not something you'd be interested in?" She leaned forward.

She already knew that I lacked experience, so there wasn't much harm in sharing more. Plus, Billie didn't seem like she would judge anyone.

"Maybe it is because I haven't been in a romantic relationship, but I can't imagine doing intimate things with them and then pretending as if it hadn't happened. What is the point?"

"You don't ever want to have sex just to have sex?" she asked.

I just sat there blinking. I had no idea what the right answer to that was or if there was a right answer.

"Uhhh…"

"Okay, so maybe you and I are more alike than I thought." She chewed her lip thoughtfully. "We are just coming at it from opposite ends of the spectrum. Whenever I sleep with a guy, I find myself wanting more. I don't want to hook up with him and then continue about my life as if it didn't happen. I want to see if there is the possibility of a relationship, of a future. What it sounds like is that is what you want as well; you don't have the same kind of baggage I bring to the table."

Billie was using the term baggage in a way I was unfamiliar with, but I didn't see any of her past experiences as an issue—if anything, they'd helped her grow. "You say it like it's a negative thing," I ventured. "I think you've spent a lot of time figuring out what you want. In doing that, you've decided what you definitely don't want. That seems like time well spent."

"It does seem like time well spent. And it has given me plenty of opportunities to learn what I like and hone my skills," she said, licking her lips.

It took me a second to follow her meaning, "Billie! You can't say things like that to an inexperienced orc like me!" I put my hands in my face in mock embarrassment, trying to hide my laughter.

"Maybe that's my goal," she laughed, grabbing a small end table and chucking it out the window.

CHAPTER TEN

BILLIE

Steve and I were still gleefully eulogizing chairs before pushing them to their inevitable death out the upper window when the rest of our group returned. I'd had a delightful morning getting to know Steve. It was dangerously fun to shamelessly flirt with him and see if I could make him blush. I also learned a lot more about his upbringing and his tribe. He had been unhappy for a long time. I hoped that however things landed here at Fýrifírar he found the future he was looking for.

"Oy, you up there!" Joey's voice floated in through the open window. "What the fuck have you done to the front lawn?"

I poked my head out the window to see Joey and Steve's buddies had returned, along with Osif and some other orkin I recognized from Osif's workshop. They were all carrying building materials.

"Hello! We cleared out most of the attic!" I called down to them.

"That's fairly obvious," Joey called back up while gesturing at the yard full of broken furniture. It looked like a table and chair leg graveyard, with deep divots in the ground where pieces had landed.

"It was the most efficient way," I replied airily. "We've cleared out most of the attic!"

"No way!" Joey called back. "I'd never have guessed! Can you just come down here?"

"Fine, fine. We're going to need some help with the larger pieces anyway."

I headed to the staircase to find Steve had been staring at me as I leaned out the window.

"You know, if you like what you see, all you have to do is ask," I teased. Steve snorted, blushed, and then smiled in that endearing, embarrassed way he did.

I headed down the stairs and didn't hear Steve move to join me on the rickety stairs. Perhaps I'd given him something to think about. I enjoyed flirting with Steve, and he seemed to enjoy my company. I was going to have to be careful with the flirting, though. I wasn't sure where this could go yet. I rolled this over in my head as I walked out from behind the bar to the small crowd that had gathered on the front lawn. I approached Osif, as he would be in charge of the operation.

"We have managed to empty most of the living quarters, but we need help with the bed and the dining table," I told him. "They wouldn't fit out the window."

"You chose quite a unique way of emptying the attic." Osif nudged a splintered drawer with one foot. "This is impressively destroyed."

"It seemed effective," I said, unrepentant in what I still thought was an excellent plan.

"Well, excluding the dents you've made in your front lawn, it was effective." One of his workers was circling a chair that seemed to have exploded on impact.

"What have you done with Steve? You didn't chuck him out a window, too, did you?" Joey piped up.

"No, he's still upstairs. I was actually surprised he didn't come down to join me when you all arrived. Maybe he's starting to chop up the bed." I shrugged.

Joey gave me a quizzical look but said nothing.

"Alright, well, we should get all the pieces out and start on the roof if we want to get it reframed today." Osif turned to his men and the Snaerfírar. "Head up and help Steve with the last of the furniture." Then he turned to me. "Since you chose such an *enthusiastic* method of emptying the living space, we will need a pair of hestrs and a cart to carry off all this furniture. We can chop it up to serve as communal firewood. Why don't you—" he pointed at Joey and me "—head over to Alvis and get us a cart?"

Joey linked her arm in mine as we walked.

"Where's your head?" she asked, as if she could tell I was already a million miles away.

"I don't know. Everywhere. Can I run a bar? Is flirting with Steve dangerous? Do I want to sleep above a bar? Do I want *something* with Steve, or do I just want to fuck someone?" I sighed.

"Well, I can answer some of those for you quite easily," Joey said.

"Oh really? You know me *that* well?" I mocked.

"Yes, yes, I do. First. Yes, you want to run a bar. You hate being stuck in the back of the house and not interacting with everyone. Remember when you chatted up so many of the cooks that breakfast was half an hour late? You have so much personality it's practically spilling out of you. And yes, you want something with Steve. You also want to fuck him, but I am pretty sure you want *something* more. The question is if you can keep your pants on long enough to establish a foundation."

"Hey! Rude!" I elbowed her in the side as we walked.

"The only one I don't know the answer to is if you want to sleep above a bar. Depends on how loud you are when you have sex. You strike me as a screamer."

"Joey!" I gasped, in mock horror. She did have a point. I was more worried about the noise of the bar, not the noise *I* would make. That was a new consideration.

"Is anything I said a lie?" she asked innocently.

I rolled it around in my head. Nope. She was pretty dead on.

"I don't know how to be friends first," I whined, giving up any attempt at saving face about my feelings for Steve.

"Well. You be friends first by sharing about yourself—open up. And by learning more about him. You never stop talking, so I can't see how you'd have difficulty establishing a friendship."

"Um, I'm a good listener too, thank you very much," I huffed.

"Maybe work on things together where your hands are busy so you don't accidentally grope him?" she suggested.

"Oh my God. You are the absolute worst."

"Am I? Or am I practical?" she said knowingly, tapping her temple before we both busted out in a fit of giggles. We laughed until tears were leaking out of our eyes.

I leaned against her and said, "I don't know what I'd do without you"

"Probably fuck Steve."

She was probably right.

I sighed dramatically. "Okay, I shall be friends first. It doesn't seem that hard. Just talking to him while we emptied the attic was nice. It was good to find out more about him."

"You're welcome," Joey said, flipping her hair.

"I knew you engineered that!"

"Um, duh. What kind of wing woman do you think I am?" She looked offended.

We started laughing again but were getting close to the hestr stalls and had to pull it together.

"Straight face, soldier, we have some hestrs to obtain," I said as we strode toward the stables.

STEVE

I watched as Billie and Joey walked away from the bar arm in arm, and wondered where they were headed. As much as I had wanted to follow Billie down the stairs to greet everyone, I had to sit down on the sagging bed and think of shoveling hestr shit in order to get my raging boner to subside. I couldn't help but admire the curve of Billie's backside when she leaned out the window to talk to Joey, and my cock stood up at attention almost immediately.

I took some deep breaths as I sat on the bed. I couldn't deny that I was drawn to Billie. She was so easy to talk to. I felt as if I had spent my whole life keeping secrets, and they just started pouring out of me the minute I met her. And it wasn't just because she was human. Joey and Piper were nice and fun to talk to, but they didn't make me feel like I felt about Billie. Also, Piper was mated to Agnarr so thinking of her in that way never entered my mind. Joey was funny and good-natured, but I didn't feel like there was something *there* like I did with Billie. She felt like a kindred spirit in trying to figure out what she wanted out of life, not just what she was handed. It didn't hurt that I was also clearly physically attracted to her.

I put my head in my hands and tried to piece together all of my fragmented thoughts. I had taken this trip in hopes of better understanding who I was and what my future held, but so far, the only person I had opened up to about it was Billie. She had extensive experience with sexual partners. I had zero. Surely she'd want someone more like Reykr, who'd fucked his fair share of the females back home. At least he'd know what he was doing and not be a fumbling virgin stuck in an attic trying to hide his erection.

I exhaled and sat up, dusting off my pants. The bed was pretty ancient and wouldn't be a great loss, that was for sure. Who knows how many generations of dust bunnies had called that thing home? Billie asked me if I would like to stay and help build the bar and find my place. We had time.

I moved toward the landing to head down but was surprised by Reykr on the stairs.

"Lost in thought again?" he asked.

"Er…" I wasn't about to tell Reykr that I'd been sitting in an empty room waiting for my cock to behave. I tried to stop the blush creeping up my cheeks.

"Would a certain mouthy female have something to do with it?"

"Hey! Don't call her mouthy," I snapped. "That's rude. She's talkative."

"Oh, oh, I see. I've hit the nail on the head there. Someone has developed a crush on little Billie."

"I just like talking to her, okay?" I huffed.

"Okay, then I shall ensure you have plenty of time to talk to her. For now, should we call the rest of the bunch and get this bed and table sorted so we can start on the new roof?"

"Yes." I waved a hand at him. "Call them all up. If we cut the rest of this into pieces, we should be able to get it out in no time."

By the time Billie and Joey returned with a cart pulled by two hestrs, we had emptied the rest of the attic and made good progress removing the old roof. It would be a several-week project, but it would go quickly with so many of us working on it. We piled all the old furniture into the cart, and Billie and Joey headed to Osif's workshop, promising to stop by the kitchens to get us food.

Soon, it was well past midday and work on the roof was hot but progressing nicely. Shingles flew onto the ground to join the dents in the lawn, and just as my stomach was beginning to rumble, Billie and Joey were back with baskets of food and a few blankets for us to sit on.

"I thought we'd have a picnic," Billie explained as she spread the blankets on the grass.

I gathered that a picnic involved eating food outside on the ground. While I would rather have a chair, I was grateful to be eating outside. There was no doubt I smelled from all the manual labor I'd been doing all morning. An outdoor picnic with Billie sounded much better than sitting in close quarters with a bunch of strangers in the longhouse. Though, given the opportunity to shower, I wouldn't mind being in close quarters with Billie again.

CHAPTER ELEVEN

BILLIE

The next several weeks went by in a blur. We worked from sun up to sun down. While I knew I was taking on a big project, as I saw the sheer physical labor involved in redoing the roof, fixing the windows, and adding stabilizing beams to the ceiling, I realized I wouldn't have been able to do this without orkin help. Joey and I pulled our weight, and I was continually astonished by her physical capacity, given her tiny size. Watching her lift tables on her own was impressive. She was a force to be reckoned with. By the end of the first three weeks, we had all what I had started to think of as "the big stuff" done. The roof and exterior were finished, and finally—the doors and windows were fixed. The bar was completely clean inside and out. It was time for the interior work.

Over the last several weeks, I was with Steve constantly, but generally in large groups. We all got to know each other as we worked and chatted. Steve was funny in a quiet, unexpected way. Sometimes, his jokes would almost slip under the radar, and I would chuckle to myself. He was curious about anything and everything. He didn't stop at questions about the humans or Earth. One day, he asked me to explain a telephone. Given his dated understanding of Earth, it took much longer to explain than I expected, but I didn't mind. He wanted to know everything. He made me think of someone who had been told "don't ask questions" his entire life and was now making up for it with an unending quest for more information. It was both endearing and overwhelming. I didn't know all the answers to his questions, but he always appreciated whatever I could tell him.

One morning, while we were working together on installing window panes, Steve asked me to explain a cassette player.

"My mom said it was a way to play music but never really could get me to understand beyond that," he said.

The wheels turned in my head. I didn't even remember the last time I had seen a cassette tape, considering how technology had advanced since his mom had been abducted. Her knowledge of Earth stopped in 1991, so Steve's knowledge of Earth also ended there.

"Well, it is a little box with two speakers, and noise comes out of them. You put another tiny box inside of it and press play, and it plays the songs that have been recorded onto the tape. We no longer use them, so I am unsure if I am explaining it well."

"You mean you don't listen to music anymore?" He was confused.

"No, we still do! It's just that the technology has changed a lot since then. Now everything is cloud-based."

"Music comes from the clouds on earth?" Steve looked shocked.

I did my very best to keep a poker face and not laugh out loud, having to breathe through my nose several times.

"No. Not actual clouds," I said trying to keep my voice even. "Everything is virtual now, you don't need to physically own a cassette to play music."

"But how does the cloud know what music you want it to play if you don't have the tape?"

"I really don't even know how it works, honestly. I know we've advanced far beyond cassettes." I shrugged.

It was these little interactions with him that pulled me to him. He wanted to know and experience so much and had spent so much time wanting to know so much and having no one to ask.

I was also getting to know the other Snaerfírar, and they were solid, if somewhat quiet orkin. I was usually the one that got everyone to laugh, a role I also played at home. I loved the group that we had all working toward my dream. Longing for more alone time with Steve, I concocted errands that would only involve the two of us. Whenever we worked, my eyes strayed toward him, and I hoped it wasn't my imagination that I felt his eyes on me, too.

It was a few more days of solid work after the roof was finished when we ran into a problem—we hadn't picked out any interior furnishings. Osif wanted me to have the final say on all the bar decor and tasked me with meeting with the appropriate merchants. I was ready to ask Joey to spend the morning shopping with me when, to my pleasant surprise, Steve volunteered. I gave Joey a furtive look, and she just gave me a barely perceptible smile back.

I had a list of all the things that I wanted to look at and it would take all morning, if not all day. Here I was, finally presented with some time alone with Steve and I was nervous. I had developed a major crush on him, but nothing was going to happen if we were never alone.

"Ready for a day of shopping?" asked Steve.

"I mean. I can *shop*. Are you sure you can keep up with me?" I teased.

"I shall even carry parcels," he said with a straight face.

I laughed. "Alright, let's be off."

It was a bit of a walk to the town center as the bar was right on the edge of the village. Suddenly all of my thoughts shriveled up, and I couldn't think of a single thing to talk to Steve about. We walked in companionable silence for awhile until, much to my appreciation, Steve spoke.

"So, now that you are seeing the bar come together, what are you thinking?" he asked.

"What do you mean?"

"Is this still what you want? Is this still your dream?"

"Oh…" I hadn't given it much thought in the last several days.

"Not so sure anymore?" he asked.

"No. I think—" I struggled with conveying my jumbled thoughts "—I think, I am more sure."

"How so?"

"I want something that's mine, something I can see grow and then feel accomplished afterward. Building this with my own hands has made me incredibly proud." I turned to him. "What have you been thinking while we worked?"

"I like it here," he said simply.

"Oh?"

"I have felt more free to be myself around you, around the other Fýrifírar. I always felt like I asked too many questions —'too many whys'—as my dad would say. I have learned more about humans, other orkin, and myself in the last several days than I have in my entire life. You've been a big part of that, Billie. You are endlessly patient with my questions and my need to know anything and everything. You haven't noticed, but you are the one who keeps answering my questions when the others have long since stopped." He blushed a shade of olive green as he looked down into my eyes.

I held his gaze, feeling like it was the moment to ask if he wanted something more from me. He'd just told me how much he loved spending time with me. If that wasn't a clear signal, I didn't know what it was.

"I have noticed that you have slipped into our community seamlessly. I love talking to you, too. I love your questions and your curious mind. I love that you don't look at me like a zoo animal because I am human. I love that you are so determined to decide what you want out of life. I find it incredibly... attractive." I fidgeted with my cuticles, not making eye contact.

I was almost certain we were on the same page, but it was still hard to be the first one to say it out loud.

Steve looked surprised. "You're attracted to my mind?"

"Well, I am attracted to a whole lot of you, but your mind is what got me started," I said, feeling my face get hotter.

"I am attracted to your mind... and all the rest of you, too," he mumbled the last part.

"I'm sorry, what was that?" I tipped my head closer and held a hand up to my ear, as if to hear him better.

"I am... drawn to all of you, Billie." He sounded more confident but was still blushing.

Oh, shit, we were really having this conversation. My heart felt like it would come out of my throat, and my hands were clammy, but I was doing it. I hadn't been imagining those stolen glances. I wanted to be smart about this. I wanted to do this right. With all our endless conversations, I had never explained dating, human or otherwise.

"Well, do you want to do something about this mutual attraction?" I asked, my stomach feeling like it was full of snakes.

Steve's jaw hung open at the knowledge that we had similar feelings. It took him a minute.

"Uhhh… what do humans usually do?" he asked.

"Well, we would go on dates. Do things together, just the two of us. See if our attraction grows?"

"I would love to spend more time with just you," Steve said earnestly. "What kind of things could we do?"

Jesus Christ, why am I so nervous? Keep it cool, Billie. Okay, you both expressed interest in something. Just suggest something, anything. Come on, brain!

"We could go on a walk?" I suggested.

What the fuck? A walk? Who am I, an 80-year-old bird watcher?

Steve furrowed his brows in confusion. "Aren't we currently going on a walk?"

"Technically, yes, but when you go on a walk as a date, you usually go someplace scenic and maybe pack snacks or a picnic?"

"Oh, I would like to do that with you," he said, still blushing. "Uh… do we just like… do that now?"

I laughed. "We're supposed to be picking out things for the bar, remember?"

While I loved his excitement, I knew there were other things we needed to consider. I didn't know how the tribes would feel, his or mine, if we started dating. And given my bad luck with relationships, I wanted to keep this just between the two of us for the time being. Not only did I not want tribal politics involved, but I also didn't want to be peppered for details as the first woman, outside of Piper, who had pursued something with an orc. I didn't want the opinions of all the girls.

"So, not now. But when?" Steve's lips were twitching like he was trying to stop himself from grinning.

"We could do that tonight, if you'd like?" I offered. "I have wanted to check out the glowing mushrooms on the forest's edge, but it is only worth going at night."

"I've never seen them up close either. That sounds like a fantastic *date*." He emphasized the last word, causing my stomach to feel even more squirmy.

Now we had a date planned, and I had to spend the entire day with him calmly picking out furnishings and pretending like I wasn't thinking about everything from what to wear to whether orkin expected shaved vulvas.

I had to reel myself in. For one, I was determined to take this slow. If I had learned anything in the several weeks last week of working with Steve, if I was going to date him, I was going to date him for real. He was not the type of guy that would want to do casual. He had never been in a relationship before. I wanted to set the right tone. That meant no fucking on the first date, especially considering his lack of experience. I mentally removed shaving from my to-do list.

We wandered through shops, where I picked out beer steins and glassware. I chose gas lamps and candles for the tabletops. I wanted everything to feel warm and cozy, so I chose jewel-toned fabrics and tableware. Steve and I continued to chat as I made my decisions, and I purposefully offered him the ugliest option available just to see if he'd tell me he hated it. I showed him some particularly horrendous patterns for curtain fabric.

He cringed and said, "I think you can do better."

"Ha! You passed the test!"

With a baffled look, he said, "What test?"

"These are terrible. I wanted to see if you'd agree with me just to be nice."

He looked relieved. "I considered it, but you've always been honest with me, so I decided to go with honesty, even if it hurt your feelings."

I almost melted into a puddle. I would never get over the

lack of facade Steve had with me. True honesty, no guessing games. I was dangerously close to handing my heart over then and there. Maybe it was my terrible past experiences making the bar for a good guy staggeringly low, or maybe Steve was just that amazing. Maybe both?

We finished up shopping. I had opted to have everything delivered to the bar once it was ready, so as it reached late afternoon, Steve and I stopped just at the edge of the center of town. Everything was electric around us as neither of us moved to head to our respective rooms. I finally broke the silence.

"Why don't we get cleaned up, and I'll grab dinner? We can meet at the edge of town just before sunset?" I asked.

He hesitated. I panicked.

"Do you not want to go anymore?" I was prepared for him to have completely changed his mind after spending the day with me. "If not, that's totally okay—"

Instead, he cut me off. "No! It's not that. I promise." Sweat beaded at his temples. "I just don't really know what to wear to a date, and I've been using the tribe's extra clothes because we're staying longer than we planned. They don't fit a half-orc very well. Some of them are baggy, and some of the pants are too long."

This orc was going to kill me dead with his vulnerability.

"Oh." I breathed out shakily. So this was just a clothing emergency, not an I've-decided-you're-a-little-too-much-after-all emergency. That was fine. I could solve that. "Wear something you feel comfortable in. These mushrooms are a bit of a walk. Also, clean clothes are a great start," I added with a grin.

I'd seen Steve in all states of cleanliness as we'd restored the bar. I wouldn't have cared if he showed up in his work clothes.

"Okay, I can do clean."

Just as he was about to walk away, I thought of something.

"Steve?"

"Yeah?"

"Can we keep tonight just between us?" Steve cocked his head to the side, brow furrowed. "All the girls will want to know every detail about everything, and I'd like to see what we can be without their input, if that's okay."

"I'll tell Reykr I am tired and going to bed early. I also don't need Reykr, and the guys peppering me for details about my *date*." He smirked.

"Oh good, I'm glad we agree." I hesitated for half a second before I stood up on my tip toes and brushed a small kiss on his cheek.

"See you in an hour!" Then I turrned and left before he could respond. When I snuck a look over my shoulder, he was still standing there, hand pressed to his cheek, lost in thought.

CHAPTER TWELVE

BILLIE

The next hour flew by in a whirlwind. I got ready as quickly as I could. On the way out, I looked at myself in my mirror and deemed my appearance suitable for an orkin date before rushing to the kitchens. I wanted to pack up food before anyone got there for the last meal and peppered me with questions. Anything that looked portable I grabbed and shoved into a basket, then dashed out to meet Steve. As I walked, I realized I still had a solid few minutes until sunset, so I slowed my pace and took a couple deep breaths. I didn't want to show up harried and panicked.

Yes, I was nervous. I'd spent the last several week getting to know Steve and consciously trying to keep my flirting in check. I didn't want to be the hit-it-and-quit-it girl anymore. I considered the other relationships I'd had—if it was even worth calling them that. They were long-term, no-strings hookups, always on the down-low. The guys I slept with always wanted me to be their secret sidepiece. They were there for my tits and ass, but I wasn't for taking home to mom.

Starting things with an actual date was a huge step. And the more I learned about Steve, the more I wanted to learn. His childhood hadn't been unhappy, but even though he didn't say it in the group, I could tell he resented that he was still treated like the kid brother. No one was ready to let Steve become a man. Or… orc? Steve loved to talk and I was ready to listen. We would very likely have a lovely time. Why was I so in my head about this date? Was I making the same mistake by keeping this—whatever we were—secret with Steve?

TWO YEARS EARLIER…

My phone buzzed in my back pocket. I knew who it was before I even pulled it out.

> Eric: Wanna get out of here?

I didn't have to give up my prime real estate on the balcony, red solo cup in hand, to know Eric would be watching me from across the lawn. Subtlety was not his strong suit. *Do I want to leave with Eric?* I sighed. Everyone was at the point of being sloppy drunk, and I was still sober. I wasn't having any fun, so I might as well have a little bit of fun with Eric.

> Billie: Sure.

> Eric: Okay, I am going to head to my car, but wait a few minutes?

I rolled my eyes. He didn't want anyone to know we were hooking up. We all hung out in the same friend group and he said it would "make things weird." I knew what it meant. It's what all the guys meant. They wanted me for my body, for my curves, but they didn't want anyone to know that they wanted me. Billie, here with a great rack and ready for a good time. I watched Eric leave and headed over to Dre.

"Hey, I'm gonna head out," I said to my best friend of fifteen years.

"You sure?" She looked up at me from her boyfriend Nathan's lap. I knew an engagement ring was coming soon.

"Yeah, even though I'm twenty-four, Mom still gets pissed when I come home late. Rants about being on the road with drunk drivers."

"Okay, well, text me when you get home."

"Will do," I said, knowing I wouldn't.

I headed out to the front to find Eric leaning against my beat-up Honda Element. She was old and hand-me-down, but I loved her. And the seats in the back folded completely flat. I unlocked it and hopped into the driver's seat while Eric got into the passenger side.

"Where to?" I asked, knowing the answer.

"Oak Tree?"

"Yeah," I said and turned the car on, heading for the bowling alley.

We lived in such a small bedroom community that there weren't really any "bad" parts of town, but the bowling alley was a dive, and no one paid attention to cars parked there overnight. I pulled into the back of the lot and we both folded down the backseats without speaking. After a quick and fairly unsatisfying fuck in the backseat of my car, I dropped Eric off at his car. As I went to drive away, he called to me.

"Hey, where are you going to tell Dre you went?" he asked, stuffing his hands in his pockets.

I rolled my eyes. He was asking me if I was still okay with keeping it a secret. He didn't want Dre to know he was treating me as a side chick because she'd kick his ass on my behalf. As Eric studied me in concern, all the faces of the prior dudes who'd treated me like this popped up in my head. Suddenly, I felt gross.

"You know what. Fuck you. I'm done being just an easy lay for you. No. I won't tell Dre. But only because I am embarrassed that I let you treat me like less than a person for this long. You can use your own damn hand from now on."

With that, I sped off home, leaving Eric with his jaw hanging open like a dumbass fish.

I pulled myself back to the present. I hadn't thought about Eric in years. He was the last man I let use for my body. Was I setting myself up for the same treatment by wanting to keep Steve a secret?

No. Steve wasn't like that. He already told me he was drawn to me. He wanted me for all of me.

I hoped.

STEVE

Billie had brushed her lips across my cheek. I didn't even know what to call what she did. Did orkin do that? I pressed my hand to where her lips had been. They had been warm and soft. I wondered how the rest of her would feel. I quickly shook myself out of it and hurried off to get ready for our *date*. I wanted to shower and change my clothes, maybe even polish my boots. They'd taken a beating during our work.

I showed up to our agreed meeting place early and flustered. I was wearing my nicest clean clothes. I shuffled nervously with my hands clasped in front of me, unsure of what to do as I waited. What if she didn't show up? She'd wanted to keep this secret, which seemed logical, but what if she was embarrassed of me?

I felt the crushing weight of inexperience. I knew nothing of how to "woo" a female. My knowledge of sex and relationships all came from talk in the sauna with Reykr and the other guys. I didn't even know if she would expect something entirely different as a human. I shook myself. This was Billie. The woman who had spent the last several weeks making all of us laugh as we worked ourselves to the bone to see her dream come true. I was thinking about the way her face lit up as she got a laugh out of me when I saw her approaching, carrying a basket and a rolled-up blanket.

"Hi." She waved as she approached.

"Hi."

We just stood there smiling at each other like two idiots for a moment. I bit my lip. Somehow, calling this *dating* had made it feel very real.

"Do you know the way?" I asked finally.

"Yes. It isn't far." She tentatively linked her arm in mine so she could lead the way. At least she had some idea of what she was doing.

We headed out of the village on a path that took us into the Niflfýri, or Forest of Mists as the humans called it. The sun was still a sliver in the sky, but the shadows were lengthening, and everything was tinged with the blue of twilight.

We walked silently and I tried to take in everything I could about Billie. This is the closest I'd ever been to her. Her hair was damp and smelled wonderful. It took significant willpower not to bend down and bury my face in her curls. They were amazing. She always had her hair pulled back when we were working, but by the end of the day ringlets were slipping out around her forehead and at the nape of her neck. I had thought more than once about dragging my tongue along her neck to taste her. I was even more enamored with all of her curls on wild display.

I wanted to say something, anything, to get the conversation going. For the first time, I found myself out of questions. She seemed happy walking arm-in-arm, but I realized she was still carrying the basket and the blanket.

"Here, let me take the supplies," I said, reaching across her and accidentally brushing my arm against her chest.

She looked startled but not displeased as I took the items off her. She didn't comment on my accidental invasion of her space but blushed as she handed me the basket and blanket.

"Thank you," she said. "Where did you tell the guys you were going tonight?"

"I didn't run into any of them. I figured I would let them think I was exhausted from my day with you."

"And how did I exhaust you?" she asked, arching a brow suggestively.

"I just meant—I mean…" I stammered.

"I'm just teasing you." She brushed her now free hand down my arm and looked up at me.

I felt like my skin was on fire. "We're gonna be okay," she said. "This is supposed to be fun. We already know we like spending time together. This is just taking it to the next level, right?"

I wasn't sure if she was reassuring herself or me—or both of us. I let out a slow breath.

"I really like talking to you," I said. "I don't see how talking to you more would be anything but enjoyable." I pulled her closer to me as she stumbled over one of the cobblestones.

"I like talking to you, too."

We walked in comfortable silence for a bit before Billie spoke again.

"Have you ever seen the glowing mushrooms before?" she asked.

"Not at night. I have seen them during the day, but they look like ordinary mushrooms then."

"I've never seen them at all. I haven't strayed from the village since we were dumped here. I didn't feel safe."

"Any reason?" I asked.

"Well, once you realize that being abducted by aliens is an actual viable option, you aren't keen on putting yourself in a position to be re-abducted. I felt safe within the confines of the village." Her face was scrunched as if she was admitting something embarrassing.

I'd never thought about having a fear of being abducted *again*. That would be terrible.

"But, now?" I asked.

"I trust you to keep me safe if any alien baddies show up," she said, batting her eyelashes adorably at me.

I puffed out my chest. "It would be an honor to protect you from alien baddies."

Billie just laughed and continued to pull me toward our destination. We reached the part of the path where the cobblestones turned into packed dirt, signifying the beginning of the forest and the end of Fýrifírar territory. It wasn't long before the mushrooms started to pop up like jewels along the path. It was almost dark, so the glowing mushrooms provided most of the light.

Billie approached them, squatting down to look more closely.

"These are like something you'd find in a 1970s blacklight poster," she said as she stroked a finger across the head of one of the mushrooms.

I squatted down next to her. "I'll have to take your word for it because I don't know what half of that means."

The mushrooms really did look magical, glowing all colors the rainbow and bathing the path in a soft light. I set down the basket and the blanket and walked to inspect another, larger patch of mushrooms. They were all over the planet, but seeing them up close was very different. As I investigated, Billie busied herself by laying out the blanket and basket for us. Wanting to get at least to sit with her before night truly fell, I left the mushrooms and joined her.

"What did you pack for us?" I asked, sitting down across from her.

"A little bit of everything, but mainly gautr, because I know it's your favorite," she said, giving me a smile.

Oh no. Was I going to have to pretend to enjoy gautr? Why would she think I liked it? I must have done a terrible job hiding my horror because she started laughing.

"What's so funny?" I asked.

"I think you and I might be the only ones in Fýrifírar that hate gautr. I noticed you always skip it at breakfast because I do, too!" She laughed.

Relieved, I started to laugh with her. I loved the way we laughed so easily together. Billie had an excellent sense of humor.

"It tastes like rotten fruit to me," I said. "I don't get it!"

"Rotten fruit is being generous. It smells like feet and has the texture of already chewed food." She made a gagging face and kept laughing.

What she'd actually brought were two of my favorite

things: the meat pies the kitchen made and the sweet pastries they sometimes had at breakfast.

"How did you know these were my favorite?" I asked, grabbing a meat pie.

"You haven't been the only one paying attention," she said, taking a meat pie for herself.

"Is it that obvious that I've been watching you?" I asked. I didn't realize I'd been so obvious, but considering it landed me here on a picnic with Billie, I had no regrets.

"Only because I've been watching you right back." She bit her lip, looking up, blushing. One of her curls had fallen into her face as she'd arranged the food. I reached out a hand to tuck it behind her ear, and to my surprise, she leaned into the touch, leaving my palm cradling her cheek.

"Are you super hungry, or could we put off eating for a bit?" she asked, tracing a finger across my knee.

I swallowed. I knew nothing about physical intimacy, but I was ready for whatever Billie wanted.

"I can wait on food, but you'll have to lead the way."

"Oh, I can do that," She moved the basket of food that was between us and scooted closer to me until we were knee to knee, both sitting cross-legged.

She reached out and stroked a finger along my jaw.

"Do you know what kissing is?" she asked. "Piper said Agnarr didn't."

"I have seen Agnarr press his lips to Piper's the way you did to my cheek this afternoon," I said, growing hot all over at the feeling of her finger on my jaw.

"Would you like to try it? Are you okay with me being your first kiss?" She traced her finger down my neck, causing me to shiver.

Her voice was breathy in a way I hadn't heard before. Did this mean she was aroused?

"I—I am okay with that," I stuttered.

My heart was practically beating out of my chest. Not only did Billie want to kiss me, she was asking me if I was okay with it. I was definitely okay. I was so okay that I felt my pulse under every inch of my skin. She got up on her knees so we were at eye level and leaned in close.

"We're going to take it slow," she said, stroking her hand down my arm. "Tell me if I do anything you don't like or that makes you feel uncomfortable."

At this point, my skin was on fire with the sensation of her touch and the anticipation of whatever she was going to do—I didn't care what it was. She placed her hands on both my shoulders and made eye contact one last time before leaning in. She brushed her lips against mine gently, almost hesitantly. They were soft. So soft. I wasn't sure what to do with my mouth, so I remained still. She pressed her lips against mine again, this time more firmly, before slipping her tongue out and dragging it across my bottom lip. Suddenly, I needed more. Billie's lips on mine made me feel like it was just the two of us, learning each other, cherishing each other.

CHAPTER THIRTEEN

BILLIE

I moved my hands away from Steve's shoulders, threading my fingers through his soft waves as I leaned into him. I'd thought maybe the tusks would feel weird, but they were just part of him. As I dragged my tongue across his lower lip, he seemed to realize there was more to kissing than just pressing your lips together. At first, he started to lick my lips and then my cheeks. I giggled.

"No, no, keep it to lips for now. We can lick other places later." I grinned.

I pressed my lips against his again, gently pulling at his lower lip with my teeth. He opened for me, and I slowly started to explore his mouth with my tongue. He let out a low groan as our tongues started to stroke each other. I tightened my grip on his hair and attempted to shift closer to him but was blocked by how he was seated. He was getting the hang of this, and I wanted more. His textured tongue was unexpected but felt incredible against mine.

I pulled back to look at him. His hooded eyes told me everything I needed to know. He was enjoying this as much as I was.

"Can we—" I faltered. "I want to be closer to you."

Without a word, he picked me up as if I weighed nothing and placed me in his lap, my legs slung over his hips while he sat cross-legged.

"Is this okay?" he asked, voice husky.

"I'm not crushing you?" I asked, skeptical. He was taking my whole weight on his thighs.

"You barely weigh a thing," he said, sliding his hands up and down my sides from where he had lifted me. "Can we try that again?"

"Oh, do you like kissing?" I asked with a smirk.

He didn't respond, instead pulling me towards him. Our lips met again, and this time, he was much less hesitant. He explored my mouth with his rough tongue, leaving no inch of me undevoured. My mouth was his for the taking, and I could feel heat beginning to pool in my core as he attempted to devour me. I broke away from him and caught a definite look of disappointment before I started kissing down his neck.

"You kiss other places?" he asked, sounding astonished. "You said no licking yet!"

"You can kiss anywhere," I whispered into his ear before gently biting the lobe.

I felt him gasp, "Does this feel good?"

"This is… incredible," he said breathlessly. "Can I kiss you more places, too?"

"Of course." I continued to kiss up and down his neck.

To my surprise, he planted several small kisses across my cheeks and the bridge of my nose.

"I love these little spots," he said, touching my cheeks where the freckles would be. "What are they?"

"They are freckles." I laughed. "I'm quite fond of them myself, but I've never had someone want to kiss them."

"I want to kiss you more," he said, dragging his lips down my neck like I had kissed his. He stopped as he reached my collarbone and licked up the column of my neck, stopping with a gentle nip of my ear, the way I had. He pulled back.

"You taste incredible," he murmured, voice filled with need.

I pulled myself closer to him as I kissed down his neck again. As I continued, I felt a telltale bulge start to swell beneath my ass. Oh, he really liked kissing. The question of whether his cock would be more orkin or more human flitted across my mind. Whichever, it was large. I ground my hips down, letting him know I liked the feeling of his cock pressing into me. His hands slid lower down my back and he paused.

"Is this still okay?" he asked.

"Please" was all I said before taking him by the mouth again.

I hadn't had a solid makeout session in a long time. Most guys were too focused on the end goal to realize that foreplay was just as important. Steve's fingers dug into my ass, massaging me through my pants. We continued kissing as I ground into his lap, sucking on his lower lip. I felt like a horny teenager and couldn't keep my hands off him. I ran them up and down his muscled back as I learned the inside of his mouth. I needed more. But was this too much for a first date with an inexperienced guy like Steve? I had no problems hopping into bed on the first date in the past.

But that wasn't what I wanted with Steve.

I pulled back and studied him. "Do you want to stop? I know all of this is new."

"I would love to keep going if you are comfortable." He

shifted so I could feel his erection lining up with the juncture of my thighs.

Without another word, I yanked my tunic over my head and tossed it aside. I leaned back with my arms supporting me so Steve could get a good look. He devoured my chest with his eyes before snapping them back up to my face. If I ever had any doubts that my tits would have the same effect on an orc as they did on a man, those were gone.

"Do you like what you see?" I teased.

"I, er, they're amazing," he said, hands twitching at his sides as if they were going to reach out and grab me involuntarily. "But why are they tied up?"

"When you have tits this big, you have to wear something to carry them," I said as his eyes dipped back down to my chest. "Otherwise, they're a pain."

I was a size triple-D, if not more, back home, but it turns out bras don't exist in Niflheim, and I was abducted in my pajamas. The tailor in town very awkwardly but kindly made some of us bigger girls bandeau-style bras that... mostly worked.

"I could carry them for you," Steve said earnestly.

"Just walk around behind me all day, arms wrapped around me, holding my boobs up?" I laughed.

"That actually sounds great." He said, eying my still-covered chest unabashedly.

I loved that we could talk and joke while being incredibly turned on. I leaned forward and undid the bandeau's tie, tossing it aside with my shirt. "Why don't we just see if you like the feel of them for now?"

Steve's eyes were as wide saucers as he saw my exposed breasts. I wouldn't be surprised if drool started slipping from his mouth.

"I can touch you?" he gasped.

"I wish you would." My voice dipped low.

Instead of grabbing a handful, as I expected, he traced the slope of my breast to the tip of my hardened nipple with a single gentle finger. I felt a shiver run down my spine.

"Are you cold?" he asked.

"No, you're keeping me plenty warm."

He cupped my breast, feeling the weight of it, before flicking his thumb across my nipple. I arched into his touch.

"So you like it when I touch your nipples?" he asked, gently rolling the pointed tip between his thumb and forefinger.

"Mmm," was all I could get out as he added his other hand. It felt like an electric zing straight from my nipple down to my core.

"Can I kiss you here?" he asked, kneading my flesh. All I could manage was a jerky nod.

Steve licked his lips before kissing his way from my collarbone down to the valley of my breasts. He dragged his tongue from my sternum to one of my nipples before closing his lips around it and sucking. Oh, Steve was a fast learner, and it was going to kill me. The feeling of his hot lips and textured tongue toying with my nipple had pleasure radiating out of me. I wanted more of him.

I slipped a hand between us and rubbed his hardened length through his pants with the heel of my balm. Steve's body tensed, and he let out a low moan. I felt my insides clench as I wondered if he would fit. I shook myself. It was too soon for that. We said we were going to take this slow. No sex tonight. I couldn't do that to Steve. He had no experience. But that didn't mean I couldn't show him other things.

He groaned against my chest as I continued to stroke him up and down through his pants.

"May I?" I asked.

"Mmmph," was the only response I got as he switched his attention from one nipple to the other.

I brought my other hand between us and loosened his pants before dipping my hand inside. I gripped his cock, sliding my hand up and down. I felt Steve tense underneath me as I explored. This was definitely an orc cock, based on Piper's description. I felt a textured pattern along the length. I needed to see more.

"Can you help me out here?" I whined, trying to pull at the laces of his pants.

"You want to see my cock?" Steve's eyes were hooded with want, but he chewed his lip.

"I'd like to do much more than see it." I stroked his length up and down again, this time more firmly.

He groaned and leaned his forehead against mine, taking a shuddering breath. He pulled me up to my knees momentarily while he pulled his pants down to mid-thigh, freeing his trapped cock, seating me back in his lap. I gasped as I looked down at it.

It was magnificent. Swollen and darker green than the rest of Steve's skin, and larger than any human dick I'd ever seen. There were faint ridges and swirls up and down the length of it with a bulbous protrusion at the base, which Piper had explained to me was a 'knot.' The tip of his cock was even darker green, poking out of his foreskin, and leaking quite a bit of shimmery fluid from the slit. I ran my thumb through it before bringing it to my mouth. Steve watched in astonishment as I sucked his cum off my thumb.

"You want to taste me?" Steve blinked, watching me. As I savored his sweet muskiness on my tongue, I knew exactly how our first date would end. Not only did I love cum, but I loved a good blow job. Now that I knew orc cum was much milder in flavor than human cum, I was even more excited.

"I would very much like to taste you, but I think we'll need to reposition. I can't do what I want while sitting in your lap." I scooted myself off of him. Without a word, I pulled his pants down as much as I could with his legs still crossed. "Come on, work with me here," I said.

Steve uncrossed his legs and shifted his pants further down to his thick thighs. I knelt next to him and continued to survey. I could now see his balls, covered in silky black hair, below his knot. Again, like his cock, his balls were much larger than a human's. I fondled each one of them softly, earning me enough muffled groan from Steve. I dragged my fingers across his dripping tip again, using his precum to slick my hand up and down him. He was so large and swollen I couldn't wrap my fingers all the way around his cock. It was hot to the touch, just like the rest of him. Drool pooled in my mouth as I imagined wrapping my lips around his cockhead.

"I'm guessing you're unfamiliar with the idea of a blow job?" I asked as I continued to pump him. Steve was clearly having trouble concentrating because he didn't even respond, just continued to stare down at my hand working him.

"Steve?" I paused.

Our eyes met and I took the opportunity to give him a deep kiss, tangling my tongue with his. He definitely liked kissing.

"Do you like when I use my tongue when we kiss?"

Silent and wide-eyed, he nodded.

"I can do that to your cock now, if you want."

"Is that what you want?" he asked, looking amazed "Is that something humans do?"

Oh, this sweet baby virgin. I was about to rock his world and I was dripping wet just thinking about it.

"Yes, it is something humans do," I responded, giving him another stroke.

He let out a strangled moan. I kissed him again, tangling my fingers through the hair at the nape of his neck. He immediately slid his tongue out this time and began an enthusiastic exploration of my mouth. He was sloppy, but a quick learner, and I moaned into our kiss before pulling away.

"Lean back," I instructed.

Steve leaned back, resting on his elbows, giving me better access to the goods. I wrapped my hand around the base of his cock and bent forward over him.

I was going to rock his world. I fucking loved giving head.

CHAPTER FOURTEEN

STEVE

I barely understood how it happened, but Billie knelt in front of me, completely topless, with my swollen cock in her hand, as she stroked it slowly up and down. Her soft hand wrapped around me was already making my vision hazy. I didn't know pleasure like this existed. I was going to explode at any minute, and then Billie asked if she could kiss and lick my cock.

I breathed deeply through my nose and nodded. The idea of her soft lips wrapped around me sounded too amazing to turn down. My eyes were half-open, in some dream state, like none of this could be real, but every touch anchored me to this moment. Billie scooted forward to give her better access to me. Her full breasts were on display and unlike anything I'd ever seen or imagined. They were larger than my hands, with dusky pink nipples that puckered when I touched and licked them. She really seemed to like it when I sucked on them, and it made my cock leak even more copious amounts of precum. Sadly, her breasts were now out of reach as she knelt over my lap, but I was too curious about what was going to happen next to stop her.

She grasped me firmly around my knot and then took my whole cock head into her soft, warm mouth. I jolted involuntarily at the overwhelming sensation. Stars danced in front of my eyes as her tongue slid down my length. She just continued, taking as much of my cock as she could, all while still pumping the base of me with her hand. Her tongue dragged along the underside of my length as she took me deeper. Then I felt her suction her lips around me and suck up and down with her mouth at the same pace she pumped me with her hand. The onslaught of sensation was almost too much for me. Not only was I experiencing pleasure I didn't even know was possible, but it was being provided by Billie. Billie, who I'd watched and admired for weeks. I bit down on my hand to prevent myself from letting out a strangled cry.

"Billie," I moaned, "that feels incredible. But I don't want to choke you, and I'm going to go off any second."

Billie popped her mouth off my cock and looked up at me through her lashes.

"What if I want to feel your cum shoot down my throat and taste all of you?" She asked, never stopping the slow, steady rhythm of her hand.

"You—you want to swallow my cum?" I could barely get the words out because, first, I was completely shocked that was something she'd want to do, and second, she hadn't taken her hand off of my cock. My brain was shortcircuiting.

"Absolutely," she said. "Just let me know when you're close. You can also set the pace, you know. Just use my hair to move me up and down so I can learn how fast you like it."

I was at a loss for words. I just stared at her, slack-jawed, like an idiot. She gave me a wicked grin and leaned back down. The sensation of her hardened nipples resting across my hairy thighs was almost more than I could bear.

This time, instead of taking my cock into her mouth, she dragged her tongue from my knot to my tip, before licking up the pre-cum that continued to flow from my slit. I throbbed at her attention, my balls tightening, ready for release. After she had sufficiently licked every part of me, she took my cock back into her mouth and wrapped her fist around my knot again. She slid and sucked me up and down, but a little too fast, and I tentatively grabbed her hair.

"Slower, deeper," I barely choked out.

Billie adjusted, taking her time as she wrapped her lips around me, dragging her tongue along the underside of my cock in a way that made me feel as if all my nerve endings were lighting up. She took me as deep as she could, and I felt myself brush up against the back of her throat as she tried to swallow me whole.

"Billie, I'm gonna—" I began to say, but it was too late.

My cock swelled and pulse as I exploded. Stars swam in front of my eyes as I came harder than I ever had. Billie was undeterred as she pumped and sucked me through my orgasm as if wanting to wring every lost drop out of me. When she finally sat up, she had an adorable dribble of cum leaking out the side of her mouth. I wiped it up with my thumb and she pulled my thumb into her mouth, sucking off every last drop. Something about her sucking it was incredibly erotic.

"You like my cum?" I asked, bewildered.

No one had ever tasted my cum before. I didn't even know that was a thing.

"I loved it. I loved seeing you lose control because of what I was doing to you. How was that?"

"*How was that?* Are you serious? I will have this evening

etched into my memory for the rest of my life as one the best experiences I have ever had!" I cried.

"Well, that's really only the beginning, but I think it is a good start," she said, climbing back into my lap. She wrapped her legs around my waist and placed her head between my collarbone and jaw, breathing deeply. She sighed.

"How is it that you smell so good?" she asked.

"Uhh.. Soap?" How could she be attracted to my smell? I knew mates were drawn to each other's smell, especially during intimacy, but I immediately dismissed it. We only had one-quarter orc between us. And she was human. She wouldn't be able to smell me in that way.

"No, I know what our soap smells like. It is something completely you. It's intoxicating." She took another sniff of my neck before licking the lobe of my ear.

I buried my face in her hair and realized she also had a distinct smell that was her own—not the smell of the soap, though. She smelled sweet, like a fragrance I didn't have a name for. I inhaled again as she lazily stroked her hands up and down my back. After a moment, I realized I hadn't done anything for her. She'd just made me orgasm harder than I ever had and now was sitting in my lap, stroking me lazily, not asking for anything in return.

"Uhh, Billie?"

"Hmm?"

"What about you?"

She pulled back, confused. "What about me?"

"Well, shouldn't I..." I trailed off, having no idea what I should be offering, so I just gestured vaguely toward her lap like a moron.

"I would love that, but it is a little more involved for me, so I think we can save that for a second date—that is, if you want to go on another date?" She chewed on her lower lip, as if my answer would be anything but yes.

"Are you kidding me? I don't want this date to end." I pulled her into an embrace.

I wanted to hold her so close to me that I absorbed her. I dragged my fingers slowly up and down her spine, inhaling her scent. My cock perked up again. I felt her chuckle.

"Ready to go again already?" She smirked.

"Is that not normal?" I asked, surprised. "Orkin can come many times in a row."

"Hmmm, Piper neglected to tell me about that part," she said as she pulled out of our embrace, smiling. "That will come in handy if we continue down this road."

"*If?*" I asked, my voice taking a very inopportune time to crack.

What did she mean by 'if'? This was the most amazing date I'd ever been on, even considering I'd never been on a date. Maybe Billie didn't have as good of a time as I did. She seemed to enjoy kissing and liked me playing with her breasts, but maybe she'd had better. She'd hinted at having a lot of relationships in the past. I would understand if she didn't want an inexperienced orc she'd have to teach every step of the way. I scrunched up my face, trying not to think about how much it would hurt if she just wanted to be friends after this.

"Hey, hey," she said softly. "Where'd you go?"

"Well you said *if* we go on another date. Do you not want to?" I dragged my fingers through my hair and averted my eyes, afraid of her answer.

Billie looked nervous. "Steve, I very much want to go on another date with you, but I need this to be different from the relationships I have had in the past. I mean, based on you being… you, I am not particularly concerned, but I have some unlearning to do. Most guys I've gone out with I have wanted a second, third, fourth date, and they've ditched me once we've fucked. So I get scared to get my heart involved."

"So these men just wanted sex, not a relationship?" I asked, unable to keep the disgust out of my voice.

"Pretty much." She shrugged.

"And you wanted a relationship?"

"Not always, but a lot of the time. I would hope for something more, but I would just get ghosted."

I cocked my head to the side. "Ghosted?"

"The people I was seeing would just disappear. I'd never hear from them again," she said, stroking a strand of hair behind my ear, "I guess it would be hard for you to ghost me, but I could wake up and find out that you all decided to head back to your tribe in secret." She smiled sadly.

I didn't know how to explain to Billie that she would have the opposite problem with me. After one date, I was already worried about falling too fast. I would never *ghost* her. I never wanted to let her out of my sight. I entertained a brief fantasy of kicking Reykr out of our shared room, just so Billie and I could fall asleep in each other's arms. Reykr could share with the other two, instead.

But based on what Billie had explained to me, I didn't think asking to move in with someone on a first date was normal, so I would have to assure her without overwhelming her.

"I definitely want to go on another date. And another. And another." I couldn't help it. It just slipped out.

Billie laughed and pulled me in for a kiss. She tasted of my cum, and somehow, this made me even harder.

"I have no hesitation. I will go on as many dates as you want. But we should stop here for the night. I want to be able to sneak back into my room before anyone notices I am not in the showers."

She climbed off my lap and began putting her breast contraption and tunic back on, and I was sad the moment she covered up her glorious chest. I never wanted her to wear a tunic again.

"We need to get back," she said. "You're still okay with keeping it quiet so we don't have the entire tribe watching us?" she fidgeted with her tunic.

I dragged my fingers through my hair. "Yeah, I don't want any of the guys asking me about this yet." I wasn't sure I was ready to tell anyone, even Reykr.

"You go and head back to your room. I'll wait a few minutes before I head to mine." I sighed at the thought of her leaving. "When can we go on a date again?" I needed to know before I let her leave.

"Are you free tomorrow night?" she teased, knowing I was free every night.

"Yes, of course."

"I'll think of something fun," she said before giving me one last kiss and heading back toward the village.

I didn't know what she had in mind, but I hoped it would set me on fire like tonight had. I felt more radiant than the mushrooms, glowing brighter than the moon. I couldn't wait to get even closer to her.

And if that involved even fewer clothes, well, I'd be thrilled.

CHAPTER FIFTEEN

BILLIE

I was practically buzzing as I headed back to my room. The sun was fully set and I could slink in, unnoticed. Laying back on my bed, I replayed the events of the *date* in my head. Though it was technically a date, we didn't even get through our dinner before we started groping each other. It felt good to kiss Steve. Really good. While the last few weeks of getting to know him had been agonizing at times, when all I wanted to do was jump his bones, it would be worth the wait. At least, that's what I was telling myself.

I laid down on my bed and thought of Steve's lips on my neck and chest. I knew going further on our first date wasn't a good idea. We both wanted this to be more than a casual hook-up, but now I was wound up like a top. I loved a good blow job, and giving Steve his first one was terrific. Even his cum tasted good. I couldn't get the image of his astonished face when I wrapped my lips around his cock out of my mind. I smirked at the knowledge that I would forever be his first, in hopefully many things. His lack of experience made everything feel like a new and surprising adventure. The knowledge that I would get to be there for all of these new experiences caused me to feel warm down to my toes. I couldn't wait to show him everything we could do to make each other feel good.

As Steve's every touch, lick, and kiss whirred around in my brain. I propped myself up on my pillows, and I slid my hand down the waist of my pants, yanking my bra under my tunic and giving myself access to my nipples. I dragged my fingers through my folds and was unsurprised to find myself swollen and soaking. It had taken all of my willpower not to strip off my pants and ride Steve's cock while we were in the woods. I stroked my slit up and down, wetting my fingers before I brought them to circle my clit. I massaged my tits and pinched my hardened nipples. Steve had gotten me so heated I was going to come hard and fast. I switched to circling my clit with my thumb so I could dip two fingers inside, pumping in and out.

I whined in frustration that my fingers were no comparison to a cock, let alone a giant orc cock with extra bells and whistles. I continued to pump my fingers while adding more pressure to my clit. I tugged and pinched my stiff nipple, thinking of Steve's teeth dragging across it and licking me with his rough tongue. I bet his tongue would feel incredible on my clit. The texture of it made me light up in ways I'd never though possible—I wondered what oral would be like with him. And with that thought, I combusted. I clamped down on my sad, pathetic fingers, wishing for more. My toes curled as an orgasm ripped through my body, causing me to twitch and moan. I panted, realizing I had been holding my breath. If I could come like that, just thinking of Steve... I was a goner.

I snuggled into my bed and was pleased to find I still

smelled like him. I drifted back off, trying to come up with other *date* ideas.

The next morning, I was at the bar early, trying to be chill and not think about Steve. We had made significant progress and were getting down to the finer details. Osif and I had gone through paint samples and sconces until I was so bored I couldn't see straight. I wasn't an interior designer and was completely over all the decision-making. I had finally roped Piper in for some of the aesthetic choices so she could help me cut down my options. Today, we were sanding down the interior walls of the bar and relacquering them. I understood almost none of the process, but Osif assured me it would be straightforward. I was surprised but pleased to see Steve walking toward the bar alone.

"Where's your band of merry men?" I called.

"My what?" he asked, looking confused.

I laughed. I would never tire of confusing orcs with slang.

"Where is the rest of the gang?" I asked.

"Oh, at breakfast. I said I wasn't hungry. I hoped maybe I'd get a moment alone with you if I showed up early. " He was blushing deep green.

"Oh really?" I sauntered up to him and wrapped my arms around his neck. "What did you hope to do with that moment alone with me?"

He wrapped his arms around me, eyes hooded with lust.

"I dunno, I was a big fan of that *kissing* that you taught me," he said, brushing his lips along my neck.

I broke out in goosebumps at the gentle caress, and pressed myself against his warm body. Wrapping my fingers in his hair, I pulled him away from my neck and to my mouth. He crushed his mouth into mine, devouring me eagerly, stroking his tongue inside and tangling it with mine. I curled my fingers into his hair, pulling him even tighter to me, wanting to press every part of my body against his. His arms tightened around my waist, and I felt him growing hard between us.

I kissed his neck, and he buried his nose in my hair.

"You didn't shower. You smell of us." His voice came out low and tortured.

"Is that bad?" I asked, confused, pausing my kisses down his neck.

"It is just going to distract me," he murmured.

"Mmm," I hummed as I continued kissing his neck. "Well, you will just have to think about what is in store for tonight."

"Oh? Have you come up with any other *date* ideas?" He chuckled.

"Emla has been fiddling around with mead recipes, and I thought maybe we could go berry picking to do a berry mead. She said only one type grows this time of year, and the bushes are wild just a bit south of the village." I pulled away. "How does that sound?"

"I think it sounds like we should probably go earlier rather than later—you can't berry pick in the dark." He gave me a wag of his brows, causing me to laugh. He clearly wanted to explore more now that we'd started down that path.

"And it wouldn't have anything to do with your impatience to be alone again?" I smirked.

"Not one bit," he said before pulling me in for another deep kiss.

I loved that Steve was no longer shy about touching me. I stroked along the inside of his mouth with my tongue, earning a deep groan from him. I was growing flushed and could feel myself starting to dampen my underwear. I pulled away.

"We need to stop before anyone else shows up," I breathed.

He let me go and stepped back. I clapped my hand over

my mouth to stifle an eruption of giggles at the sight of the enormous erection tenting his pants.

"Um… can you do something about that?" I asked, waving vaguely at his dick.

"Hey, this is your fault!" He ran a hand down his face in embarrassment as he tried to adjust himself to make it less noticeable.

It did nothing. If anything, it made his erection more noticeable.

"Sorry, not sorry." I laughed, trying to feel bad for his predicament but failing. "Think about old people or something. Old orcs! Think about old wrinkly orcs!"

Steve gave a weak chuckle, a hand still covering his face. He took a couple of deep breaths and looked down to see nothing had changed.

"I'm going to stroll around the bar and inspect the exterior walls, ensuring all the lacquer has dried well," he grumbled.

As he walked away, I could hear him mumbling, "Old orkin, old wrinkly orkin."

I was still chuckling when Joey strolled up, right as Steve slipped around the backside of the bar.

"What are you so happy about? And why weren't you at breakfast?" She squinted suspiciously.

"Oh, I am just—er—really excited that it is starting to get warmer?" I fumbled.

"And breakfast?" she asked, brow cocked.

"I went early. I wanted to see what the bar looked like as the sun rose."

What the fuck am I talking about? I wanted to see the bar at sunrise? I would need to get better at lying to Joey real fast.

"Suuuure…" was all she said before heading into the bar.

I grimaced as I watched her walk away. I didn't want to keep things from Joey, but I didn't want our budding relationship to be the talk of the tribe. She didn't seem mad, just as if she didn't believe me in the least. She would be the first person to know—when it was time.

All of my helpers started showing up, including Steve's gang. Reykr came up to me immediately.

"Steve wasn't at breakfast and was gone when I woke up this morning," he said brusquely. "Do you know where he is?"

"I haven't seen him. Maybe he went to the showers early?" I suggested.

This was a much better lie than watching the sunrise over the bar. *Bonehead, Billie.*

Reykr cocked his head to the side, squinting as if he was deciding whether or not he trusted my lie. Then, to my great embarrassment, he leaned in and smelled me. Not too close, but enough to make it weird. His eyes went wide, but he said nothing.

"Um, are you *smelling* me? Because maybe that is normal for orkin, but that is definitely not normal for humans." I raised my brows, disturbed.

"Sorry, I just thought—you know what, never mind." Without further ado, he walked away from me to join the group.

I worried. What if he could smell Steve on me? I knew that orkin had a better sense of smell than humans did, but I didn't really think anything of it until just now. Fuck. A shower would be necessary after our berry-picking date tonight.

Osif arrived, and we began working on the interior walls. Steve joined us just a few minutes after we had all started, and no one seemed to notice. He gave me a heated look as he walked in and then looked crestfallen when he saw he couldn't work beside me. I had Tyr to my left and Berit to my right. Steve would have to pick a different spot to work. I sighed but knew it was probably for the best not to spend the entire morning with him

We all focused on sanding down the walls for several hours. Tyr, Berit, and I made small talk, but it was all surface-level. I hadn't gotten to know them like I had gotten to know Steve or even Reykr. I had grouped them in my head as "dumb jock types" which probably wasn't fair, but they didn't seem to have much to add to the conversation whenever we spoke, and they always traveled in a pack.

I focused on sanding down the exposed wood. Trying to get some conversation rolling while doing the tedious work, I started with the best question I could think of.

"So what did y'all have for breakfast?" I cringed inwardly at how inane the question was.

"Gautr," they responded in unison.

"Is it the same as the gautr you have at home?" I asked, hoping I could learn more about them and the Snaerfire.

"Not quite," said Tyr. "I don't think we have the same dried fruit up in the mountains as you have down here, but it is close enough. Your cooks are excellent."

"Is how we eat different from how you eat at Snaerfírar? Do you all eat together?"

I'd never specifically asked Steve if they all ate communally because I assumed it was a standard orkin practice.

"Já, though our longhouse is smaller than yours," Berit answered. "But it has fireplaces at both ends because of the cold."

"Do you miss it?" I asked. They'd now been at Fýrifírar for more than a month, and while I knew Steve was more than happy to be here, I often wondered if the others were only staying because of him.

"Já, but I don't miss the cold." Tyr said, "The warmer season is already starting here. It will be cold for at least another several weeks in Snaerfírar."

He moved closer to me as he spoke and I could almost feel him taking a whiff of my hair. I tensed as I waited for him to say anything. He just raised his brows at me and said nothing.

"Okay, that is the second time one of you has smelled me today," I said, calling out the creepy behavior. "It is considered weird at best and outright rude at worst to smell someone during casual conversation."

Berit looked alarmed and placed his hands up in the air as if to say, *I come in peace.*

"Sorry, we do have a keen sense of smell, and you smell different today," he explained, still looking concerned that I might slap him.

"Good different or bad different?" I asked.

"Um…" He was purposely not meeting my gaze.

Did I smell *bad*? I knew I hadn't showered last night after our date, but I had showered right before. There was no way I smelled like stale sweat or a locker room.

"Well…" I prompted Berit as he just stared at me like an idiot.

"Not bad," he clarified. "Definitely not bad. Just different." Tyr nodded along with him.

"Well, could you refrain from smelling me in the future?" I asked. "It gives off major creeper vibes."

"Major what?" Berit looked confused.

Ah, here was where their lack of knowledge of slang was sometimes annoying. "It just makes you seem like you don't have good intentions, and it feels like you're invading my personal space," I explained.

I was used to weird patrons who got way too close to me or, worse, touched me when they were trying to order. This gave me immediate flashbacks to a regular who liked grabbing my arm whenever he wanted another beer. I was not a fan. The two of them stared at me like idiots with their mouths open. They clearly needed time to process my boundaries.

"Why don't we just get back to work?" I asked.

I was fine not getting to know them more if they were going to be weird. I wasn't interested in friendship with two male orkin who would likely leave at the season's end.

I could ignore them and focus on my work. We had the entire interior of the building to sand down. I could focus on work. Osif had claimed the actual bar top for himself. I saw him crouched over it, sanding meticulously, completely absorbed in his task. Steve, Joey, and Reykr were together, and I was surprised to see them working in complete silence. Usually, you had to stuff something in Joey's mouth to get her to stop talking. I briefly considered joining them to break the silence but decided to let it be. Maybe they were just absorbed in their work. I shrugged and returned to the patch of the wall I was working on. Perhaps Joey was harboring something for daddy-vibes Reykr.

By lunchtime, my arm was numb from sanding, and I was starving, having not actually had breakfast. Luckily, one of Osif's carpenters had grabbed lunch for all of us, and we sat out on the grass outside, enjoying the warm weather while we ate. I was still with Tyr, and Berit, and I sighed when Steve sat down with Reykr, Joey, and Osif. More uncomfortable small talk. At least they hadn't tried to smell me again since this morning.

"What kind of alcohol will you carry in the bar?" Berit asked.

I was surprised but pleased at his further attempt to make conversation.

"Emla said mead is what is most common here and what she knows how to make. So, I'll start with that before I expand. I am going to look at different flavorings, though. This afternoon, I'm going to try the berry patch Emla suggested. It's just a bit outside of the tribe." I took a sip of water

"Ooh, could we join you?" Tyr asked eagerly.

Fuckity fuck sticks. Dating someone in the same group of "friends" where we saw each other every day was already proving to be a challenge, and we'd only had one date. Thinking on my feet, I threw out another lie. "Ah, actually, I am going with Joey. She and I need some girl time. We haven't gotten to hang out with the two of us in a while because we've been so busy with the bar." I tried to keep the hesitation out of my voice.

I groaned inwardly. I guessed I was telling Joey today.

Tyr and Berit accepted my explanation and went back to their lunch. Breathing a sigh of relief, my eyes strayed over to Steve to find him staring at me with barely concealed hunger on his face. I felt myself flush and gave him a look that I hoped conveyed, *stop being so obvious*. I went back to my food. I tried not to think about how difficult this was and instead focused on my berry-picking date. I wondered if we'd pick any berries.

CHAPTER SIXTEEN

STEVE

The entire morning was torture. By the time I had gotten my cock to obey orders, everyone had started working on the walls. Billie was sharing a wall with Tyr and Berit. I was surprised to find myself curling my hands into fists. Tyr was talking to Billie, making me want to punch him in his stupid face. I shook myself. Is this what jealousy felt like? I didn't want any of my tribemates talking to her. Or even standing near her.

I grumbled but joined Reykr and Joey on the opposite wall and got to work. Reykr was usually quiet, but Joey was also working silently and was not her usual talkative self. The entire morning, I had a weird, tense feeling. I wondered if I should try to make conversation, but decided to get down to the work at hand and not try to force anything.

It was hard to keep my mind off of Billie as I sanded down the walls, but I couldn't risk having to run to *adjust* myself. I thought about our home tribe and wondered if anyone missed us. This tribe seemed much more tightly-knit than mine, with everyone being friendly with everyone else. It was refreshing after coming from someplace more reserved. I wondered what it might be like to stay with them permanently. Reykr and the others wouldn't want to remain here, but over the past few weeks, I found myself caring less and less about what they decided and wanted to decide for myself. Maybe Billie was having that impact on me. In our conversations, as we worked, it sounded like she had learned the hard way to do things that made her happy and not worry about what others thought. I felt like maybe I was getting there.

I was relieved when Osif called for a lunch break. The weird, silent tension between Reykr and Joey was uncomfortable, and I was tired of working alongside them. I was going to join Billie for lunch but was once again blocked by my own tribemates. I humphed as I sat down with Reykr and Joey, stuffing a meat pie into my mouth. At least the food here was good.

"Do you think we'll finish today?" Joey asked eventually after we'd sat in awkward silence for several moments.

Reykr let out a laugh that caused him to choke on his meat pie, requiring me to give him several hearty pats on the back.

"So, I'll take that as a no?" Joey sassed.

I was very surprised to see Reykr blush. "No, no, I'm sorry. I think this sanding business will be several more tedious days."

"Ah, yeah, I was afraid of that." Joey's shoulders slumped.

We had been working on the bar for a long time. The finish line was in sight, but everyone was getting tired. And now I needed to figure out why I wouldn't be joining them and continuing this afternoon. Billie and I hadn't discussed what ruse we would use to skip out on afternoon work.

I finished my lunch and stood. I was still formulating a plot in my head as I brushed the crumbs off my hands. Billie stood at the same time as me, but instead of looking at me, she called Joey.

"I told Emla I would have some berries for her to sample by tomorrow. Do you want to come with me? Let's have some girl time."

I tried to hide my confusion. I looked at Billie, and she gave me a quick look that told me she was lying.

"Sure, sounds better than more sanding." Joey stood, brushing off her lap.

"Steve, do you want to walk part of the way with us?" Billie asked me. "Agnarr has asked to be updated on the bar, and I figured you'd like to see him." She was clearly trying to stress the unspoken meaning of her words.

Everything clicked together in my head, and I tried to sound casual when I realized what was happening. I joined Billie and Joey as we headed down the path toward the longhouse. We walked in tense silence until we rounded the bend and were out of sight and earshot of the bar. Joey stopped, crossing her arms over her chest.

"Alright, it's time to fess up. I know you don't want to go berry picking with me," she said, giving her best friend a knowing look.

Billie looked embarrassed but held her chin aloft.

"Steve and I went on a date last night, and—"

Immediately, Joey was jumping up and down and squealing. "I knew it! I knew there was no way you went to bed early!" She pumped her fist toward the sky with success. "So am I your cover?" she asked, practically dancing with excitement.

"Yes, if you wouldn't mind," Billie said, trying to keep her voice low. "I would appreciate it if you told everyone that you and I went berry picking this afternoon."

"Sure, sure. Anything for you, babe. What are you actually doing?"

"We're going berry picking," Billie said.

Joey put her hands on her hips and pouted. "That's a lame-ass date, Billie."

"Well fuck, we're on another planet with no electricity. What are we supposed to do? Go to the movies?" Billie rolled her eyes.

"I dunno, you could take him to the caves that Piper told us about," Joey suggested.

"Joey," Billie had a note of warning in her voice. "The caves aren't really an appropriate place for a first *or* second date, are they?"

I couldn't read what was going on between the two women, but they seemed to come to an unspoken understanding.

"Ah, yes. That makes sense. Well then, I guess enjoy your berry picking? Where should I go so people think I'm with you?" She smirked at Billie with such mirth that I could tell she was enjoying tormenting her friend about this.

"Go take a nap or a nice long shower," Billie said, dismissively waving her hand.

"Fine, that will work. I guess I'll go enjoy my unexpected afternoon of freedom," Joey said, giving me a knowing look.

I raised my hands in defense. "I don't even know what's going on right now."

Joey gave us one last knowing look before heading to the cabins.

Once she was out of sight, I turned to Billie. "So I guess we are telling Joey?"

"There's no one else I trust to cover for us," Billie said. "And she can be a blabbermouth, but she knows this is important to me."

"She knows *what* is important to you?" I asked, wanting to hear her say it out loud.

Billie blushed but lifted her chin. "You and me. I want you and me to be something. Isn't that what we agreed to?"

"Já, it is. And it is what I want to do," I said, pulling her close.

She let me wrap my arms around her for only a moment before she pulled away.

"Not on the main path," she hissed. "Then everyone will know. Wait for later."

Thinking about the rest of the afternoon, another worry cropped up. "What if someone asks Agnarr where I am? What will he say?"

Billie rolled her eyes. "He'd probably say, 'eh, I dunno, maybe he went for a walk.' Agnarr is super mellow. We should be fine unless Reykr gets it in his head that he should do some investigating."

As much as Reykr was invested in knowing where I was, I knew he wouldn't abandon the project to look for me.

"Meet behind the kitchen in fifteen minutes?" I asked.

"Yep." Billie grinned.

Then, as if she was thinking about what we were actually going to do while berry picking, I was hit with her delectable scent. I was still trying to figure out why sometimes she smelled stronger than others. It felt like something I should know. I shook off the thought and quickly kissed Billie on the head before walking toward my room. At the very least, I could change before our date. I straightened up, then glanced down at myself and snorted. Sawdust and food crumbs probably wouldn't add to the allure.

BILLIE

I didn't have time to shower, so I hoped whatever smell the orkin had noticed wasn't a bad one. I couldn't smell anything, but Steve had said I smelled like *us*. If I was honest, that made my heart go a little gooey inside. I watched him walk away before I realized I was supposed to be headed to the kitchens. I grabbed some baskets for berry picking and food for dinner. I was heading out when Emla called to me.

"Billie!" She waved me down. "I want to give you something to take with you on your afternoon with Joey." In her hand, she had an earthenware jug with a cork stopper. "This is the first batch of mead I have so far. It's the standard honeyed mead. Why don't you and Joey try it while you pick berries? You can tell me what you think."

I took the jug from her hand. Did I want to have a drink with Steve? Maybe.

"Thank you. We will try it and report back. And thanks for supporting the new bar."

She patted my arm and waved me off. I exited the back of the kitchen to find Steve leaning against one of the walls, his hands in his pockets. He looked—the only world that came to mind was edible. He gave me a soft smile as I approached him.

"Hi." I breathed, standing as close to him as possible.

"Hi back." He smiled and tucked a curl behind my ear.

My hair was still in a bun from working all morning, but as usual, the ringlets around my face and at the nape of my neck came free.

"Want to go berry-picking?" I asked, holding up the baskets for berries and the basket of food I had packed.

I was already anticipating very little berry picking, but I wasn't sure what we'd get up to. I wanted Steve to set the pace at something he was comfortable with.

He grabbed the heavier basket from me and looped my arm in his. "Lead the way."

We headed down the meandering path toward the berry bushes that Emla had told me about. On the way, Steve peppered me with questions about tugboats, his latest obsession of Earth nautical inventions. Laughing, I explained them, and the conversation turned to the morning's work.

"I hated that I couldn't talk to you all morning," Steve said. "I got stuck with Reykr and Joey. I don't know what is happening with Joey, but she wasn't her usual talkative self, so we worked silently."

"Hmmm…" was all I responded.

"That 'hmmm' sounds like you know something." Steve raised his brows at me.

"I think Joey might have a little crush on Reykr. What's the story there? Why hasn't he settled down? He's at least ten years older than you." I often wondered about the stoic, barrel-chested orc graying at the temples, but it never felt the right time to ask. Steve took a moment to answer.

"I think because he stepped in and helped raise me when my mom died, he never thought about looking for someone. My dad became a shell without her. Reykr did everything a parent should do, but he was only in his late teens. By the time I was of age, most of the orkin in our tribe that were of his age had settled down. Maybe he likes the quiet."

While it was an unfortunate situation, it wasn't Steve's fault. Yet another burden that wasn't his to carry.

"You can't blame yourself for Reykr still being single," I said gently, touching his arm. "He made that choice, and while it was a sacrifice, it was a sacrifice he made willingly."

I could tell Steve was considering my words, but he said nothing.

"Hey, who knows? Maybe something is blossoming between him and Joey," I continued. "Maybe Reykr needed to escape Snaerfírar as much as you did."

Steve paused. "You think Joey and Reykr could work? She's so small and loud. I mean that in a good way—I don't know that someone like Reykr could manage that amount of energy."

I laughed. He wasn't wrong. "I think you underestimate Joey's determination. If she's got her eye on him, Joey is nothing but determined."

We continued discussing Reykr and Joey's viability as we reached the berry bushes. Once again, I laid out a large blanket, and we set our baskets down. The bushes were in a small clearing, each plant as tall as I was. On closer inspection, they were close to some berries back on Earth, but not exactly the same. They reminded me of blueberries crossed with a grape, deep indigo but oval in shape.

Steve inspected them next to me. He pulled off a berry and popped it into his mouth.

"Any good?" I asked. Normally, I wouldn't eat random berries from an unknown bush, but Emla assured me these were edible and would not poison me.

"It's sweet but tangy, and the berries kind of pop when you bite down on them," Steve said, picking another one.

He held out the berry to me between his thumb and forefinger. I think he expected me to take it using my hand, but instead, I wrapped my mouth around his two fingers, pulling the berry into my mouth with my tongue. Steve's face went from surprised to heated as I sucked on his fingers. I slid my mouth off of him and bit down on the berry. It had the texture of a blueberry but was much more flavorful. I briefly wondered how it would taste with a honeyed mead but was distracted by the look Steve was giving me.

"Do you want to wait on the berries and do something else?" I asked, my voice dipping low.

"Well, we've sampled them and know they are good, so we deserve a break," Steve said, voice dipping low.

"I think that sounds like an excellent idea," I said, wrapping my arms around his neck.

CHAPTER SEVENTEEN

STEVE

I was alone in an isolated berry patch in the middle of the afternoon with Billie nuzzling my neck. I was the luckiest orc on the planet. After everything that had happened between us the night before, I was eager to explore more of Billie. As much as the sight of her sucking my cock had been my complete undoing, I knew there were many more options we hadn't tried. I wondered if she'd let me put my mouth on her the way she put hers on me. *Is that something humans do?* I wondered.

We both looked around, taking in the surroundings while pressed against each other.

"What are you thinking about?" Billie asked.

"Oh, I was just thinking of what we might try today." I had no idea what was on the table.

"Oh, I thought we were here to pick berries." She smirked before continuing to kiss down my neck.

"For some reason, I don't quite believe you." I slid my

hand into the curls at the nape of her neck, angling her face up toward mine. I tilted my head down, and we met with a hungry kiss. I pried her lips open, then devoured her with my tongue. She was an intoxicating mixture of her usual sweetness and the berries we'd sampled. I ran my tongue along the inside of her mouth and tiny teeth, wanting to savor every part of her. She responded in kind, tangling her tongue up in mine. She pressed herself against me as if trying to meld with me completely. I wrapped one hand tighter around her waist and dug my fingers deeper into her hair. I wanted to consume her and was growing harder by the second. Just as I started to feel self-conscious about it, Billie wormed her hand in between us and started stroking up and down my cock through the fabric of my pants.

She pulled away from my lips and continued kissing down my neck, stopping to lick along my collarbone. "Well, the options are pretty endless," she said between kisses.

It was hard to think with her rubbing my cock and kissing me. The sensations were overwhelming. If she kept at it, our options would be very limited.

"Can I, er, can I touch you the way you touched me?" I asked as she continued to distract me.

"Mmm, of course, reciprocation is always welcome," She paused her kisses to check in on me. Her eyes were hooded with want, and she still hadn't stopped dragging the heel of her hand up and down my cock. "But only if I get to see this bad boy again later."

"Uh—deal." I was so turned on by Billie's clear infatuation with my cock that I was going to come at any moment.

"Okay, you can touch me anywhere you want. Follow your intuition. I will try to keep my directions to a mini-mum." Amusement twinkling in her eyes

I wasn't sure what she meant but was eager to find out. Her willingness to try *anything* with me was almost more than I could handle. I pulled her in for another kiss, but instead of wrapping my hand around her waist, I slid it up the front of her tunic. My hand came in contact with skin rather than her bra. I found her breasts bare, nipples hardened. I gasped in surprise.

"No breast holder today?" I asked, rolling a nipple between my forefinger and thumb.

"I thought I'd come prepared. I took it off on the way to the kitchens." She smirked.

I groaned as I continued to explore each breast, paying extra attention to her nipples now that I knew she liked them being touched. We continued to kiss, but I wanted more. I wanted to touch her everywhere.

"Can you take this off?" I waved at her tunic.

"How about a piece of clothing for a piece of clothing? I want to be pressed up against your warm chest," she dragged her finger down my torso.

I couldn't get my tunic off fast enough, throwing it aside. She removed hers as well, her glorious breasts and tight, puckered nipples on full display. I massaged her tits, flicking my thumbs over the hardened tips, earning me a low moan from her. Bending down, I pulled one of them into my mouth, sucking on it, then flicking my tongue back and forth across the stiff peak. Billie tangled her hands in my hair, pulling me closer. I wasn't sure who was enjoying this more, her or me. The moans coming out of her were making my cock throb so hard it hurt. I switched nipples, dragging my teeth along the other, then licking away the sting.

Billie's fragrance was heady and overpowering, and I wanted to do more. I just wasn't sure what *more* looked like. I pulled away from her chest. Her eyes were heavy-lidded, and her cheeks and chest were bright pink.

"What else—" I didn't need to finish my sentence.

Billie grabbed my hand and pushed it down the front of

her pants, then pulled me in for another kiss. I had heard enough conversation from the other guards and seen enough naked orkin to know what fucking was—I'd actually witnessed it on more than a few occasions in the sauna—but I wanted to find out about everything that led up to it. Billie shoving my hands into the front of her pants was definitely a cue. I explored her stomach and hips with my fingers before sliding my hand lower to the crux of her thighs. I traced my fingers over her mound and through the silky hair covering it. Taking my hand lower, I reached her damp folds. This had to be where I was meant to be. She was hot to the touch and wet. I dragged my fingers up and down, exploring her before spreading her lips apart with my two fingers. I slid along a small bead of flesh at the top of her lower lips. She gasped into my mouth as I glanced along the nub before suddenly gripping my hand. Fuck was I doing something wrong?

Billie looked at me, concerned. "This is kind of a big step. I should have double-checked but got caught up in how good you felt—are you okay with this?"

I dropped my jaw, shocked. "I am very okay with this. Feeling you this way is incredible. I thought you stopped me because I had done something wrong."

"Oh no, definitely not. That spot you just glanced your fingers along was my clit. It is very sensitive. Think like my nipples but to the extreme."

I slipped my fingers across her clit again, trying different strokes to see what worked. Billie panted as I circled its edges, slipping her hands into my hair and pulling it tightly into her fingers. The reactions she gave me were driving my need higher and higher. I felt as if I might combust at any moment.

"Can we sit or lay down, maybe? I want better access to this divine cunt of yours," I asked, not letting up on her clit.

Billie looked at me in surprise. "Who taught you the word cunt?"

"The other guards mainly. And Reykr. We're a community that bathes together. I knew what a cunt was before I knew what it was for."

"Ah, and you'd like better access to my *divine* cunt?" She teased.

"Yes, please." Unable to keep the eagerness out of my voice.

I wanted to put my mouth on her the way she had on me. Billie released me, smiling, as she pulled off first her boots, then her pants, leaving her completely nude in front of me.

"Lay down and spread your legs," I said, surprised at the command in my voice.

"Oh really? Giving orders now?" Billie arched a brow at me.

"Oh shit, was that too demanding? I mean, will you please lie down? You got to see all of me yesterday. I want to see all of you." I spit the words out very quickly.

"I happen to like it when you're bossy," she said. "Tell me what you want, Steve. Maybe one day you can be in control." Billie wrapped her arms around me and gave me a deep kiss while brushing her hardened nipples across my chest. She then laid down on the blanket, leaning up on her elbows and with her knees spread wide. "Tell me what you want from me. Is this what you had in mind?" she asked.

I tried to keep my mouth from hanging open as she lay, spread out before me, completely bare.

"Yes, yes, it is," I choked out.

I dropped to the ground, positioning myself between her knees. Ahh, there was that scent again. It seemed to radiate out of her core. I pulled each of her thighs a bit wider so I could fit my shoulders between them.

She had silky curls covering her mound that were the same color as the hair on her head. Her lips were swollen and glistening pink. With the way her legs were bent, I could just barely see her clit and the slit where I assumed my cock would go, based on all my conversations with the other guards. That, and the fact that my cock started to dribble excessively just at the sight of her lower lips. At this angle, it didn't look big enough to accommodate my cock, but that was a worry for later. I admired her cunt for so long she started to shift.

"Er, do you not like what you see?" She looked uncomfortable.

Fuck. That was the last thing I wanted to make her feel—it was the exact opposite. I loved what I saw, every inch of her soft skin. I wanted to devour her. Her scent was driving me insane.

"No, I love it," I responded, voice husky. "Can I kiss and lick you the way you did to me?"

Billie simply nodded.

"You may have to give me some direction." I hesitated.

"I am sure you will be able to follow my responses, but I can help," she said, smiling down at me.

Finally, Billie was bared to me fully, her perfect soft stomach and flared hips all pointing me toward her wet core. Already wedged between her thighs, I licked her slit from bottom to top. I was rewarded with a delightful little squeal from Billie, but I wanted to take my time learning her. I licked up each side, devouring the musky, sweet taste that was all Billie. Once I had given thorough attention to each fold, I used my fingers to spread her wide. Ah, there was the tiny bead of flesh that had made her go wild before. I slid my tongue around it, not wanting to touch it directly and over-stimulate her.

I tried circling it with the tip of my tongue, stopping

every few seconds to drag it across gently across the entirety of her clit.

"There!" Billie cried as I flicked my tongue across her sensitive button again.

I continued flicking back and forth across the bead of flesh. Billie writhed underneath me before clamping her thighs around my shoulders and digging her fingers into my hair. I didn't let up because seeing her come undone made it hard for me to keep myself under control. Seeing how much she enjoyed this was enough to make me go off.

"More," Billie panted as I continued. "Put your fingers inside."

I wasn't even sure what that meant, but I tried to follow direction. I used one hand to spread her folds so I could continue to lick at her clit, but I brought my other hand to her slit and dipped it inside. She was warm and oh-so-wet. I explored her channel with my fingers, never letting up with my tongue. The noise that escaped Billie was more like a breathy scream than a moan. I saw her eyes scrunched up and her mouth in a perfect "o." She dug her fingers even tighter into my hair, so I continued to pump in and out of her with two fingers while licking her clit with my tongue. Suddenly, Billie's whole body locked up. I felt her channel clamp down on my fingers, and a gush of fluid covered the lower half of my face. I licked up every last drop of it, delighting in her taste. Billie didn't know it yet, but this was enough to make her my everything.

CHAPTER EIGHTEEN

BILLIE

I came so hard my vision was spinning. Steve's textured tongue and unbridled enthusiasm took me from zero to one hundred in no time. I was panting as I recovered. My legs flopped open, and I was unable to stay up anymore. I was still on my elbows, and I peered down at Steve.

"Was that okay?" he asked, concerned.

I took a deep breath. "That was more than okay. That was amazing. I think I might need some water before we continue."

Steve opened the basket of food and pulled out a flask of water. He handed it to me, and I took a deep swig. He also took a drink before setting it aside.

"Continue?" he asked, sounding almost embarrassed.

I looked to see the front of Steve's pants wet. He'd come just from making me come. Oh, that was fucking hot. I wanted to lick him clean.

"Pants off, Steve," I directed.

"But I've already—"

"Yes, and I want to lick you clean," I responded. "We aren't wasting a drop of your delicious cum." Not only did I love blow jobs, but the fact that orkin cum tasted better than human cum? Oh lord, help Steve.

Steve looked surprised but fumbled with the laces at the top of his pants. He seemed nervous. I got up on my knees and scooted over to him to help. I kissed him as I undid his pants, finding my taste on his lips surprisingly erotic. He kissed me back tenderly, pushing my lips apart with his tongue. We slowly moved from a tender kiss to devouring each other greedily as I pulled the laces of his pants apart and shoved them down. They'd been loosened before, but this was the first time I saw everything fully displayed. His cock, balls, and thighs were covered in cum.

"Lie back and take these all the way off," I instructed.

He did, and finally, we were both totally naked. In a berry patch. Just outside of the village. And I could not bring myself to care.

He lay back propped up on his elbows to watch what I was going to do. I knelt next to him and admired his soft cock. I wondered if I could get it hard again with my tongue.

I licked down his happy trail before tonguing him every-where. His cum was sweet, and I was already addicted. I traced my tongue down each thigh, savoring the twitches and groans it was earning me. His balls were far too large for me to fit in my mouth, so I explored each of them with my tongue. I was pleasantly surprised to see his cock already starting to swell. I licked it clean, from root to tip, watching it grow with every pass of my mouth. The braided ridges became more pronounced, and the knot at the base bulged out as I continued to savor his cum. I knew most guys needed a bit of time between orgasms, but this seemed surprisingly quick.

By the time I had licked up every last drop, Steve's cock was hard and bobbing in front of me, the tip poking out of his foreskin and starting to leak. I marveled at the swirled, ridged patterns that ran along it and wrapped around his fist-sized knot. My core clenched at the idea of trying to take him.

But I hesitated. I could give him another blow job, but I really, *really* wanted to fuck him. We were supposed to be taking this slow, yet here we were with both of us very clearly ready for more. I wanted anything to climb on his lap and see if I could take his ginormous orkin cock. And I wanted to see his face in wonder when he realized that as great as blow jobs were, sex was even better. I gave him one last lick from root to tip before sitting up.

"Do you want to stop?" I asked, trying to keep my tone neutral. I didn't want to pressure him anything.

"Do you want to stop?" He asked, clearly in pain at the mere idea of stopping here.

"No," I said, not letting him finish his question. God, I was eager.

"Neither do I," he said, looking up and down my naked body. He reached out and brushed a thumb over one of my peaked nipples, causing a shudder to ripple down my spine.

"Well, usually, if this were another guy, I would have a conversation about STIs and protection, but orkin don't seem to have any STIs, and I am drinking the birth control tea you have here. So that's covered."

"What?" he said quietly, still toying with my nipple.

He hadn't heard a word I said.

"Steve." I snapped my fingers in front of his face.

He looked up, shocked. "Sorry. Your breasts are just so… mesmerizing," he said, stroking my peaked nipple.

"How would you feel if they were bouncing up and down in front of you while I rode your cock?" I asked.

"Is that an option?" His voice went up an octave.

"Yes, that is very much an option." I bit my lower lip, thinking of everything Steve would find completely overwhelming. I relished in being the one to show him all the options

I swung one leg over his waist so I was straddling him, his cocked trapped between us. I felt a twinge of nerves. He was *large,* larger than anyone I'd ever been with. And I still didn't really know what to make of the knot. Piper didn't seem to have complaints about it. Or about Agnarr's size, so. I slid my wet folds up and down his cock without taking him in. He felt good. Really good. I adjusted my movements so I could watch his reactions. Between the enthusiastic oral he'd performed and the fact that I was already wet and ready to go again, it didn't take long for me to feel like I was on a Slip 'N Slide—a braided textured Slip 'N Slide.

Steve groaned and puffed out a breath. "Is this—are we having sex?"

It took all my might not to laugh. "No, Steve, I was just making sure I was wet enough to take you. You are quite large."

"But that felt so good," he said, surprised.

"Well, yes, that does feel good. But I promise sex will feel better." I leaned in and kissed him deeply. "Imagine thrusting your cock in and out of me, rubbing all your amazing ridges into me. I am dripping just thinking about it. And you're forgetting my only experience thus far has been with human cocks. They don't come this large, and they don't come with the extra bells and whistles." I gasped as I felt his ridges run up and down me.

Steve's jaw hung open in shock, brows raised. He looked

like I had just simultaneously given him all of Santa's Christmas presents. For a second, I worried he might pass out.

Finally, he asked, "Bells and whistles?" faintly.

"Some of this may be new for you, but a lot of it is new for me, too. Human cocks don't have ridges or swirls or a… knot? That's what it is called, right?" I asked.

"Yes, it is called a knot. It will lock us together, trapping my cum inside, making it more likely for …" he trailed off.

"More likely for me to get pregnant. I get it, but as I explained while you were staring at my tits, I am on birth control. So you can fill me with every ounce of cum that you want, and I still won't get pregnant." Even though I had no desire to get pregnant, the idea of him stuffing me full of his cum made me giddy with pleasure. I wanted all of it. Gallons of cum. In the past, I'd had partners with condoms or partners that came on my stomach or back—but this was going to be my first time having someone come inside me.

The look Steve gave me was almost feral. I lifted myself up on my knees and grabbed his cock between us. It was sticky and so warm. I slid the head of his cock up and down my slit, enjoying the surprised look on his face.

"Are you ready?" I breathed, notching his large head at my entrance.

Silent, vigorous nodding. *Was I ready?*

I slowly started to sink down on him. I gasped as his cock breached me. There was far more pressure than I expected, and he was already stretching me. I placed my hands on his shoulders and continued to press down further, determined to swallow him up. I took a deep, shuddering breath as I felt him slide further in. He looked down at where we were joined and then up at me in shock. I stroked his face and kissed him.

"Is this good?" I asked.

"I—you're so tight and wet, and you've only barely taken part of me. I can't imagine it getting any better. What if I don't fit?" He looked panicked.

I could feel his taut muscles beneath me, trying to hold back from thrusting up.

"We will fit, I promise. Women's bodies are miraculous things." And just as I stopped thinking about the stretch and pinch, I slid down further. "Kiss me, pinch my nipples. It will help me loosen."

Steve didn't need further encouragement. He dove down and sucked onto one of my nipples like a starving man. He laved and sucked at one until he came off with a pop and switched over to the other. I fisted my fingers in his hair to pull him closer to me while he aggressively sucked each one of my breasts. I could feel ribbons of pleasure shooting out from where he had my nipple gently clamped in between his teeth. I groaned and felt myself slip further down his cock.

Steve looked down between us to see I had taken more than half of him. He felt like nothing I'd ever experienced before. My body couldn't decide if it was too much or not enough. I slowly rose and sank back down to see how it would feel. I let out a gasp. I was right about those ridges. They felt incredible dragging along my tight channel. I rose and slid back down again, this time earning a groan from Steve. I locked eyes with him as he dragged his hands all over my back and sides, stopping to pluck at my nipples, pulling me closer and closer as if he wanted to become one with me.

"Is this okay?" I asked. This was his first time, after all, I wanted to make sure he was comfortable.

"I think life-altering would be more accurate," he groaned, stroking his warm fingers up and down my spine before pulling me in for a kiss. He sucked on each of my lips before slipping his tongue inside. This was a hungry, greedy kiss.

I stopped thinking about him fitting inside me and the mechanics of everything for just a moment and kissed him just as greedily. I tangled my tongue with his before lightly biting his lower lip. He wrapped his arms around me tighter as if trying to consume me. He delved his tongue into my mouth, and I whimpered at the onslaught of sensation. For someone who had only been kissing for two days, Steve was amazing at it. I lost myself in his kiss, and then I felt myself sink further and further, until our thighs finally met. I was completely seated on his lap and had taken almost his entire cock, still sitting just above his knot. But I was determined. I had never felt stuffed so full in my life. I felt every ridge, braid, and vein that spread across his cock. I let out a whimper.

"Is it too much?" Steve asked, stroking my cheek. I could tell by his tense thighs that he wanted to thrust upwards but was waiting for my response.

I breathed through my nose. "Not too much, just let me control the pace for a bit?"

"Of course," he said eagerly.

I pulled myself up on my knees, him sliding almost entirely out of me before I sank back down. Oh, that felt incredible. I repeated the motion again, keeping my eyes on Steve. His gaze went from astonished to dreamy with lust as I set the pace: slow but measured, sliding him almost all the way out, then sinking back down on him. As I grew wetter and was able to accommodate him more easily, I picked the pace up, rising up and then slamming back down on him. I was hot and slick. Steve's hands and lips were everywhere as I raised and lowered myself. It was as if he couldn't get enough of me. He settled on digging his fingers deeply into my hips and panting into my ear as he kissed and nibbled my lobe. Sweat formed at my temples, and my thighs burned, but he felt so good that I didn't care. I ratcheted up my pace, causing a squelching slurping noise every time he slid in and out of me. Pleasure pooled in my core as he filled me again and again.

"Billie," he panted.

"Hmm?" was all I could manage.

"Let me take over?"

It was as if he could tell I was out of practice and needed to swap.

"Yes, please. Where do you want me?"

"On your back, spread your legs," he ground out.

I cocked a brow at him, surprised at his tone.

"I mean, only if you are okay with it," he added meekly.

Oooh boy, I could not wait to meet unrestrained Steve.

"I am more than okay with it. I happen to love it." I kissed him and moved off his lap before spreading out on the blanket.

Steve crawled over me, sliding in between my legs. He grabbed his glistening cock and slid it up and down my slit, grinning.

"Oh, did you like it when I did that?" I asked

"Mmm," was all he responded before he notched himself at my channel and thrust into me with teeth-chattering force. He placed his elbows on either side of my head before licking up the side of my sweaty neck. "I loved it."

Steve then buried his face in my neck and started to thrust, slow and even. He felt different at this angle. Good different. I felt as if I might be ready to take his knot. I wrapped my legs around his hips and met him, thrust for thrust until he was pistoning in and out of me, and I let my legs fall open, admiring him as he thrust into me. And then there it was, a small feeling of pressure and then a retreat. I locked my legs around him, encouraging him to thrust further. He steadily thrust in and out of me, delving deeper with each thrust. And then I felt it—a pop. He'd knotted me and slid all the way in. Steve let out a garbled cry, and I felt my eyes beginning to well up—not because it hurt, but because it felt so good.

"Hey, hey, is this too much?" Steve looked concerned, knot buried deep inside me.

I sighed in the exquisite pleasure the knot was providing, "This is amazing."

He kissed me gently and then continued to thrust, slowing his pace, now with his knot popping in and out each time. I felt as if he was reaching the very end of me every time he thrust. I wrapped my arms around his neck and my legs around his waist. Everything was lighting me on fire. The feel of my sweaty boobs sticking to his chest, the smell of him musky and citrusy, and all Steve. The feel of his ass clenching underneath my legs. With every thrust of his hips, I felt myself coiling up when, suddenly, he changed the pace. He was no longer pistoning into me, but rutting into me with such force that I could feel his balls slap against my ass. I whimpered under him, threatening to combust from the sensations. His breathing quickened on the nape of my neck as we were both were panting from the pleasure and exertion of it all.

"Oh, fuck, Steve," I panted.

"Billie. You feel so damn good. You're so tight. I have no idea how this is working."

He hammered in and out of me, each time his knot dragging along my sensitive flesh, causing stars to burst before my eyes. My toes curled, and I arched my back into him, meeting him with every thrust as we moved together.

"Steve, I'm gonna—" but I couldn't even finish the thought. He gave two more powerful thrusts, and I felt him spurt hot cum all along my walls. I hung on, panting as I felt myself clamp down on him, emptying himself into me. I tossed my head back, letting out a ragged groan as he pressed into me one last time before collapsing. My arms and legs went limp at the sheer force of my orgasm, and I lay there, breathing heavily, with Steve atop me.

CHAPTER NINETEEN

STEVE

I barely shifted my weight in time to stop myself from crushing Billie with my much larger frame. We lay there in silence for a moment, both sticky with sweat and panting. My heart was pounding against Billie's. We were still joined at the waist, with my knot wedged inside her tight seath. I attempted a small movement so I would be able to look Billie in the eye. She moaned at the movement of my cock, still trapped inside her, and I felt her clamp down on me, causing a tingle of sensation down my spine. I managed to shift to one side so I could prop myself up on my elbow and take her all in.

Her face was flushed pink, and sweat made her little ringlets even more pronounced around her hairline. Her beautiful chest was still heaving, her eyes still dark. I skimmed my fingers up and down her side, enjoying the feeling of her soft skin. I wasn't sure what I was supposed to do *after*, so I wanted to let Billie lead the way. I had never had a mating of any kind, but that definitely wasn't something casual for me. I hoped it wasn't for her, either.

"How was that?" she asked.

How was that? I had no idea what the appropriate response was. *Life-altering? Mind-blowing? An out-of-body experience? Beyond anything I'd ever dreamed of?*

"Do you want the truth?" I asked.

At this, a look of concern flashed across her face. Oh, that's not what I wanted.

"I didn't want to overwhelm you," I explained hastily. "It was amazing. Lifechanging. I have never come so hard in my life. Watching you come while clenched around my cock will be seared into my brain forever."

Billie looked relieved. "Oh—you scared me."

Then, it was my turn to get nervous. I had never fucked anyone before. What if it wasn't any good for her? The way she clung to me, digging her tiny fingers into my back and wrapping her legs around me to pull me closer, all pointed toward her enjoyment, but how was I to know?

"Was that—was that—was I okay?" I asked hesitantly. "I know that I am not as…experienced at this."

Billie stroked a finger down my jawline. "That was incredible. I have never had a guy make me come twice. I can't believe you're new at this. I can't believe I am saying it, but that might be the best sex I've ever had."

I blushed. "Well, you made me come twice. It seemed only fair."

Billie laughed. "That is not at all how things usually occur, but I could get used to it."

This reminded me that Billie had been with others, several others. I didn't like the ugly feeling that grew in the pit of my stomach when I thought of Billie atop someone else, crying out someone else's name. I didn't want to admit my jealous thoughts. She had a right to a past just as much as I did, but I owed her honesty.

"Sorry. Just mentioning how things had been different for you in the past made me picture you with others. I—I didn't like it," I finished lamely.

"Ah, that's reasonable," she said, nuzzling my neck. "I wouldn't like to picture you with anyone else, either. I know we have pretty different past experiences, but I promise there is only you now."

"So, does that mean you want to be my chosen mate?" I asked.

I had wondered how this might work. There seemed so little orc between the two of us that it felt unlikely that any Elska bond would happen. But, we could be chosen mates. Billie looked surprised.

"Chosen mates are like spouses, right?" she asked, eyes wide. "It's a pretty permanent decision?"

Oh no, I'd asked too soon. I was scaring her off already. She'd had more casual partners than I'd had. Maybe she wasn't ready to make this permanent?

I cleared my throat. "Yes, mates are usually taken for life." I was a bundle of nerves as I watched her take in the information.

"When I got to this planet, I was excited about the idea of an Elska mate—someone destined for me who I didn't have to look for. But I don't think we have enough orkin in us to be fated." I was so tired of looking for my person on Earth that I started to think there wasn't anyone for me. "Here, fated mates solved that problem. But we aren't fated, are we?"

"No, I don't know if we have enough orkin blood between us to form an Elska bond," I said truthfully.

"But you could probably bond with another orc, couldn't

you? What if there is someone else in my tribe that you are destined for?"

I shook my head vigorously. "I would deny the bond. There was no one else for me, Elska or not. Now that I know you—now that I've been with you. You are all that I want."

Billie considered what I'd said momentarily, still tracing her fingers up and down my side. I assumed she was trying to reassure me, for which I was grateful.

"You'd be willing to deny an Elska bond for me?" she questioned after a time.

"Yes," I responded, undeterred. "You are my everything."

"Could we do a hybrid human-orc relationship to start?" she asked after a time. I could tell she was hesitant to dive into full-blown mates.

I didn't love the sound of that, but I was willing to listen.

"Tell me more," I said.

"Well, we'd continue to date, and then, if things went well, we'd decide whether or not to make this permanent when the season is over. If we decide to make this permanent, one of us is going to have to move, except I don't know that either of us is ready to make that decision yet."

I hadn't thought about that. Forever meant one of us saying goodbye to our tribe forever. And yet I didn't even need a moment to process. My mind was made up. I was staying. I'd already considered staying before Billie and I talked about a relationship. I fit in much better with the Fýrifírar than the Snaerfírar, and my only hesitation had been whether they'd allow me to stay. Surely, if I was going to take Billie as a mate, they would let me. Then, really, my only issue would be a difficult conversation with Reykr.

Billie wasn't ready for forever today. We could continue to "date" until the end of the season, and then I would tell her I'd decided to stay.

"Okay, so we continue to date." I paused. "Can we continue to do this?" I gestured at our still-connected bodies.

Billie, smiling as always, said, "Yes, we can continue to do this. I am going to insist upon it."

I sighed with relief. Then, I asked the last question on my mind. "Do you still want to keep it a secret?"

I honestly didn't know what answer I wanted. I was undecided.

"I think so." Billie's brows furrowed in uncertainty. "I like having something that's just ours for now. Without everyone watching, it gives us more time to decide on the future."

She had a point there. I didn't want the whole tribe watching this unfold. If Reykr knew I was interested in one of the humans, he would automatically worry about whether or not I'd come back home. And I also liked that it was just between us—well, and Joey.

"You may have to remind Joey to keep it a secret," I said.

Billie rolled her eyes. "Oh, trust me, I am well aware. Um… now that we've had our serious 'what is this relation-ship' conversation, do you think you could tell me how long we're stuck like this?" She waved at our joined hips.

"Oh! I have no idea. I've never knotted someone before." I blushed with embarrassment. Billie was really seeing my lack of experience.

She looked slightly surprised, then shrugged. "I guess that makes sense."

Billie pulled me in for another kiss. I didn't think we would ever be able to part if she kept kissing me, but I decided to keep that to myself.

BILLIE

I was in the showers, thoroughly washing so that no one would smell Steve on me in the morning, when Joey busted in.

"Well?" she demanded.

"Well, what?" I said, just to annoy her.

"Well, what happened with Steve?! You just slipped back in from berry picking, didn't come to dinner, and now you're showering alone." She crossed her arms and frowned at me, clearly disgruntled.

I laughed and continued to wash my hair and hum to myself.

"Billie, if you don't give me the deets right now, I am going to tell all the girls that you went berry picking with Steve this afternoon and had me cover for you." She tapped her foot in impatience.

"Alright, alright." I sighed. "Everything you assume happened, happened. We had sex. It was amazing. The best sex I have ever had, hands down. And I don't know if orcs come by oral naturally as a skill or if Steve is just a fast learner, but I have never come that quickly."

Joey just opened and closed her mouth, eyes wide.

"But we're still keeping it a secret," I said pointedly. "So keep your big mouth shut."

I was still sad that for anything to be permanent, either Steve or I would have to say goodbye to our home. Granted, Fýrifírar hadn't been my home for long, but I couldn't imagine my life without all the girls I was abducted with or the tribe that had welcomed me in. But the idea of being without Steve also pained me.

"It's just complicated. If we decide to be serious, then one of us has to move," I explained.

"You can't seriously be considering leaving. You've—we've put in months rebuilding the bar," she said, shocked.

"I know. I know. But I can't ask him to stay just for me."

"Didn't he come here because he hated his own stupid tribe?" Joey asked.

"You know it isn't that simple. He isn't in a rush to go back, but I don't know if he ever considered staying here permanently."

"Well, what if you are fated?" Joey asked, flopping onto a bench by the showers and scowling at me.

"We don't even know if we can be. Between us, there's only a quarter of an orc. Maybe that isn't enough for us to be mates?"

Joey thrummed her lips over her fingers, thinking. "So you're just going to 'see where it goes.' What does that even mean?"

I sighed. This whole conversation was making me sad. Joey wasn't asking anything I hadn't considered when Steve and I started things, but it was too soon to talk about forever. Steve and I had slept together once, and we'd been on two dates. The only way forward was to wait and see. Joey looked at me sadly as if she could see it all swirling around in my head. She knew from day one how badly I wanted forever.

"Well. I think he'll ask to stay," she said firmly.

I returned my attention to my hair. "I am going to try to take it a day at a time."

I wanted forever with someone, but it was too soon to decide with Steve. I had been on two dates. Two dates that were amazing and ended in mind-blowing sex. But was that enough to establish a long-term commitment?

154

CHAPTER TWENTY

STEVE

I tried to slip back into my room unnoticed, but Reykr was there, lying on his bed, arms folded behind his head, waiting for me.

"So, how was the meeting with Agnarr?" he asked, brows raised.

It took me a second to remember what he was talking about. Right. Billie had lied to everyone and told them I was meeting with Agnarr about the progress on the bar. How had my conversation with Agnarr gone? My imaginary conversation with Agnarr.

"Uh, it was good," I said, noncommittally.

Reykr's brows rose even higher. "Good? Did he ask for any details? Like when we expect to be finished?"

"Er, no. He, um, was just happy that we were making progress. I… I told him about lacquering," I finished lamely.

Reykr grabbed his pillow from behind his head and threw it directly at me, hitting me in the chest.

"Hey," I said, catching the pillow, "what was that for?"

"That was because you are a terrible liar," he said.

"What do you mean? I was with Agnarr!" I tried to sound indignant.

"Really?" He grinned. "You reek of sex because you were with Agnarr?"

I immediately flushed a deep green. *I didn't realize others could smell sex on me. I thought Billie just smelled of me this morning. Does that mean...*

"So, where do you think I was?" I asked.

"I am going to guess, based on the way Billie smelled this morning, that it was *you* who Billie took her to the berry patch and that no actual berries were picked."

I looked at him, flummoxed. Did I try to keep up the lie, or confess? He had such a knowing look on his face, and Reykr was my oldest friend. There was no way I could keep seeing Billie for the rest of the season without him noticing.

I sighed. "Yes, I was with Billie. Joey covered for us."

"Well?" he asked, eyebrows at risk of disappearing into his hairline.

"Well?" I played dumb.

"Did you fuck her?" Reykr asked.

"You don't need to put it like *that*." I dragged a hand over my face. Fucking is not how I would describe what happened between the two of us. It was more than *fucking*.

"But you did?" Reykr prompted.

"Yes. Okay? Yes. And you aren't getting any details from me, so don't ask."

Reykr hooted for me and punched a fist in the air. "Finally!"

I did not feel as if it was possible for me to flush a deeper shade of green. However, I couldn't stop the small smile from creeping across my face.

Reykr gave me a big stupid grin, "Do you want my advice?"

"I don't know, do I?"

"If you don't want everyone to know about this, you need to go take a very thorough shower," he said smugly.

I groaned. "Could *everyone* smell us?"

"Orkin can smell sex. Can't you smell it?" Reykr looked confused.

"I can smell Billie, and I can smell when she's...er... interested in me, but don't know that I can smell when other orkin or people smell of sex," I tried to explain what I was smelling because there was clearly a difference between smelling Billie and smelling of sex.

"You can smell when Billie is turned on?" He arched a single brow at me.

"Yes? I mean, she smells more strongly of Billie." I tried to explain, but I felt I was failing.

"Interesting," was all Reykr said. "So what is this going to be? Are you taking each other as mates? I am guessing you haven't discovered you are Elskas?"

"No, we talked about that. We don't know if we are even capable of being Elskas," I didn't really want to have this whole conversation with Reykr, but now that he knew, I couldn't see a way of getting out of it.

"So, are you chosen mates?" He followed up.

"We're... dating." I cringed as I said this because I knew Reykr would have no idea what I was talking about.

"And what is *dating*?" he asked, incredulous.

"We are going to continue to spend time together and get to know each other and then decide at the end of the season if we are ready to make a permanent commitment," I explained.

I knew the next question Reykr would ask before he opened his mouth.

"So if you decide to be chosen mates, one of you will have to move to the other's tribe?" he asked.

"Yes. But I have already decided. If she'll have me, I am staying. I already feel more at home here than I ever did at Snaerfírar. And it isn't just because of Billie. This tribe feels so much more welcoming and interested in each other's well-being. Their sense of community is stronger. And, I like it here more." I wasn't able to look Reykr in the eye at the end.

"Well, I can't say that I am surprised," he said. "But I think you should continue to think about it and see what happens with Billie before you decide. I won't tell anyone. You know I barely like talking to Tyr, and Berit anyway,"

I let out a sigh of relief as I gathered my belongings and headed to the shower. "Thank you for listening and for keeping this to yourself," I said to Reykr as I left.

"I won't tell a soul. But you'll have to get better at lying. And showering," he replied with a mocking expression.

I just rolled my eyes as I headed out the door.

The next morning, I had breakfast with everyone to avoid further suspicion. Billie was also at our usual table, but she sat at the far end with Joey and Osif and seemed to be deep in conversation about mead. I ate quietly, again grateful for the breakfast options outside of gautr that Snaerfírar had. Today was flaky pastries with some cream and jam in the middle. I devoured them with vigor, considering my time spent with Billie had led to some skipped meals in the last few days. It wasn't very long before everyone at our table stood, and we headed toward the bar together. I hung back a bit, pretending to tidy up the plates, hoping that Billie would notice and stay. I looked up from the stack of plates I was creating and was grateful to find it was only the two of us left.

"Hey," I said, trying to sound casual.

"Hey, yourself." She grinned.

"Want to walk with me to the bar?" I asked.

"Obviously."

I couldn't help but smile. Was this what it was going to be like being with Billie? Me just constantly grinning like an idiot? We left the longhouse, walking close to each other but not too close.

"So, how was the rest of your night?" I asked, wishing I could have spent it with her.

"Oh, you know, the usual shower, interrogation by Joey, etcetera."

"Ah, it sounds like we had very similar nights. Reykr had many questions. He knows, by the way."

I wasn't sure how she'd respond to Reykr being in the know, but I didn't want to lie to her about it.

"How much does Reykr know?" she asked, brow raised.

I coughed uncomfortably. "I didn't give him *those* kinds of details. He knows we're dating. And I explained what dating is."

"Well, I am glad we each have someone who knows now. Though, that isn't going to make working side by side any easier." She gave me a heated look.

"We will have to ensure we stay apart during the workday and get plenty of time together outside of it." I looked around quickly to see if we were near anyone. It was only the two of us on the path, so I caught Billie by surprise and pulled her into a rough embrace before consuming her with a hungry kiss. She parted her lips for me immediately, allowing me to plunder her mouth while I stroked my hands up and down her back. She tangled her fingers in my hair, matching my enthusiasm and deepening the kiss.

All too soon, she pulled back.

"We need to…" She paused. "Sorry, losing my train of thought here. We need to get going, or this will continue." She waved her hand back and forth between us.

Regretfully, I agreed, nodding. When we reached the bar, all the others were well underway with their work, and it was only Joey who shot us a knowing look. Billie and I parted ways, deciding to work in completely different spaces, which was probably for the best.

I spent the entire morning focused on work because I couldn't let my mind stray to Billie and risk doing something stupid and obvious. However, several times, she walked by me when I was tempted to stroke a palm down her arm or pull her in close so that I could inhale the scent of her hair.

When Osif called for a lunch break, I was tremendously grateful. It was taking a lot of mental energy to focus on lacquering a wall instead of laying naked with Billie, perhaps pulling one of her nipples into my mouth and dragging my teeth across it while I watched her face contort with pleasure.

I was putting away the tools when Billie told Joey, "Go on without me. I want to check the attic before lunch. I don't know how long it will take to do those walls as well."

I pretended to keep working at putting away the supplies as the bar emptied, leaving just the two of us.

"Did you want me to join you in inspecting the attic?" I asked Billie.

"I wish you would," she said, looking me up and down before turning and running up the rickety stairs.

I reached the landing to find Billie already unlacing her tunic.

"Let me help you with that. We need to be quick." I quickly loosened her laces and pulled her tunic over her head, revealing her magnificent chest, nipples already hardened. I plucked at each of them with my forefingers and thumbs, earning me a delicious whimper from Billie. I pulled her closer and latched down on one nipple, between sucking on it and dragging my teeth along the puckered tip, just as I had imagined earlier. I slid my hands up Billie's bare back, pulling her closer to me. Billie slid her hand between us and dragged the heel of her palm up and down my cock.

"I want this," she said, stroking me. "Right now."

She began unlacing my pants as I continued to explore her breasts with my hands and my mouth. I groaned as I felt her small soft hand dip into my waistband and wrap around my cock. She tugged up and down slowly, causing bolts of pleasure to shoot out through my body. I looked around. There was no furniture, and I didn't want to take her on the rough wood floor. I saw the back window was open, with no glass in it and got an idea.

"Billie," I breathed in between peppering kisses up from her chest to her neck, "could we do this… could I take you from behind while you hang onto the window?" I panted and nodded to the back window so she understood what I meant.

Billie followed my eyes and smirked. "That seems like an excellent idea."

We were a tangle of arms and legs and lips as we headed toward the window, unwilling to stop touching. She had my pants nearly undone, and I was still attempting to suckle on her nipple while we made our way across the room. I moved my hands to undo her pants while I kissed down the valley of her breasts. She finally got my pants all the way down, and it was a tight squeeze, but she freed my cock. Grabbing me firmly, she stroked me up and down, causing me to moan into her chest. I couldn't get enough of her.

But just when I went to turn my attention back to her deliciously sensitive nipples, she dropped to her knees in front of me. Without any warning, she wrapped her lips around my cock and took me as deep as she could. I felt the head hit the back of her throat as she hollowed her cheeks, sucking me while pumping my knot with her hand. It was too much.

I let out a strangled cry, "Billie!"

She didn't even slow her pace. She just kept sucking me down like she was starving and my cock was the best thing she'd ever tasted. I twined my fingers into her hair as I rocked my hips forward each time she swallowed me up. I briefly wondered how my cock going this far down her throat could possibly be enjoyable, but the thought disappeared from my mind as she popped me out of her mouth and started dragging the tip of her tongue under the sensitive underside of my shaft all while using one hand to tug on my balls gently. Pleasure was exploding everywhere throughout my body. I felt tingling in the base of my spine, and my balls tightened

"Billie, if you don't stop soon, I am going to come all over your face," I moaned.

"That sounds pretty hot," she said between licks. "Is that where you'd like to come?" She looked up at me through her lashes while she dragged the flat of her tongue across the head of my cock.

"While that sounds… incredible…" I seemed to be having difficulty forming words. "… that is definitely something to keep in mind for the future. I would very much like to come inside you."

Billie rose from her knees and turned her back to me, facing the window. I slid my thumbs into either side of her pants and pulled them down to her thighs, revealing her beautiful ass. I kneaded her cheeks and admired the way her flesh rippled under my fingers. I closed the gap between us so my cock was wedged between her ass cheeks.

"Bend over, put your hands on the windowsill, and spread your thighs," I said. Having been with Billie once before, I knew she liked it when I took control. I knew exactly what I wanted.

Billie did as she was told, and I was rewarded with a magnificent view of her shining pink cunt. I dragged my cock up and down her slit, over and over, wetting myself with her juices and coating her with my precum. With each pass over her sensitive clit Billie whimpered.

"Steve, stop teasing me and fuck me now."

I notched the tip of my cock at her entrance and began to press in slowly. With her pants still around her thighs, she couldn't spread her legs very wide, making everything tighter. I grabbed onto her hips and continued the delicious torture of sliding all the way into her warm cunt. I felt every part of her exquisite channel as I drove further in. After a few more seconds, our thighs met, and my knot brushed up against the lips of her pussy. I didn't move for a moment; I just enjoyed the feeling of being buried to the hilt in Billie's wet heat. I bent over her so my chest was flush with her back, and I could wrap my arms around her and tweak her nipples. Billie gasped at the sensation, and her channel clamped down on me. She tried to arch her back to swallow more of me up, but I was as deep as I could go without knotting her, and she was still too tight for that.

"Steve, if you don't start fucking my brains out right now, I am going to lose it," she said through gritted teeth.

I sincerely hoped that "fucking her brains out" was a human saying because while I wanted to fuck Billie with every fiber of my being, I did want her brains to stay intact. I slid out of her slowly, almost to the tip, before setting a steady, deep pace. There was nothing, nothing like the feeling of delving into Billie's warm cunt over and over again. I tried to keep an even rhythm, but every thrust had me wanting to go faster and harder. I groaned into Billie's neck and dug my fingers even deeper into the flesh of her hips as I pistoned in and out of her. Billie reached up and grabbed my neck from behind, pulling me flush against her.

She turned and licked up the column of my neck, then whispered one word into my ear, "Harder."

CHAPTER TWENTY-ONE

BILLIE

ell, being fucked within an inch of my life while bent over outside the second-story window of my bar was not on my to-do list for the day, but I mentally checked it off with a flourish. I gasped as Steve ratcheted up his thrusts, holding onto my hips with bruising pressure. I arched my back into him, wanting more. The textured girth of his cock sliding in and out of me was causing stars to burst in my vision. I was close.

"My clit, use your fingers on my clit," I breathed.

Steve let go of my hip and somewhat clumsily tried to wrap his arm around my waist. I took my hand and guided him down to my folds, showing him how to find my clit from this position. It took a second, but once we were there, he circled my clit the way he knew I liked at the same rhythm he pounded into me from behind. The sensation coming from both positions had me crying out with pleasure, unable to keep quiet.

"Is this—is this good?" Steve wrapped himself around me, kissing my neck.

"Are you kidding? This is fucking incredible."

Steve widened his stance just slightly and pushed in just a bit deeper, breaching me with his knot. My entire body lit up at the added friction. I was on the edge of tipping over into oblivion. Steve ramped up his thrusts into mindless rutting while adding pressure to the tight circles he drew around my clit. I pushed my ass back into him at the same pace, wanting to devour his entire cock with every thrust, feeling his knot pop in and out. My body started to lock up as Steve gave a feral groan.

"Come with me." I wrapped my arm around his neck again so his face was flush with mine, both of us panting and sticky with sweat.

Steve's cock grew impossibly thicker as I clamped down on him, flying over the edge. I opened my mouth in a silent scream as I came, vision blurring. Steve pumped into me once, twice more, and I felt him unload spurt after spurt of cum, locking us together as his knot grew larger. I leaned back against his sweaty chest, panting as I came down. He nuzzled into my neck, inhaling my scent and brushing tender kisses across my sticky skin. He wrapped his arms around my waist, holding me as we both settled.

"That was—" he started, voice husky.

"It sure was," I cut him off.

"Is this how sex always is? This…er…" Steve fumbled over his words, but I knew what he was trying to ask.

"No. Sex has not always been like this. Sometimes, it's outright boring if you have a partner who doesn't care about what you enjoy."

"But seeing you come undone is half enjoyment." Steve sounded baffled.

"Well, then you are head and shoulders above half the guys I've slept with." I laughed.

"And that's good?"

I looked over my shoulder into Steve's concerned eyes. "Yes, very good," I said, kissing him. "We need to get cleaned up before people return from lunch, though."

"I think just a minute more," he said. "What do we have to clean up with?"

"Uhhh…"

"I'll run and get one of the clean rags we're using for the lacquering," Steve volunteered.

"And you're just going to leave me here with your cum dripping out of me?" I asked.

"Well, unless you have a better idea?" Like I might pull baby wipes out of a magical unknown pocket.

"Yeah, let's start having sex in my bedroom. Where I have a sink. And a toilet." I said, rolling my eyes.

"Okay, I'll slide out and run to get rags—just hold your knees together?" he said helplessly.

"Yeah, I'll try that. I am sure it will keep the gallon of cum you just unloaded inside me in place." I snorted.

Steve slipped out with an audible squelch, and I pressed my knees and thighs together to try to prevent cum from completely filling my pants, which were still only half down.

Steve hiked his pants up and ran downstairs for rags. I couldn't help but laugh while he was gone. Our appetites for each other were getting us into trickier and trickier scenarios. But I couldn't help it. Every time I saw him, my body reacted with *must fuck now.* It was barely a minute later when Steve returned, rags in hand. We both cleaned up the best we could, though I was definitely still sticky. *So much cum. Why so much cum?* I got the most of it off and out of me and redressed myself.

"And what should we do with all this?" I waved my hand at the small pile of rags we created.

"Leave them up here for now. I will come back after dinner and dispose of them. We aren't working on the attic tonight anyway."

Well, it was the best plan we had for the narrow window of time we had. I straightened my clothes and redid my bun. Assessing Steve, he needed to pull his fingers through his hair and adjust his tunic. Then we'd both look mostly presentable and not as if we'd just fucked out a window. I worried a bit about the smell, but nothing could be done about it. We were out of time. Maybe the other orkin would think I was perpetually horny, and I was kind of fine with that. I went downstairs first, telling Steve to wait a minute in case anyone had arrived. Finding the main bar empty, I called Steve down to join me.

"Quick, where were we at lunch?" I asked him.

He gave me a look that plainly said, *how the fuck should I know?* Great. Another lie for me to cover up. Our noisy group approached, and my brain spun into overdrive. Why would Steve and I skip lunch? Ugh, why couldn't I think of anything? I took a few steps away from Steve, so it didn't look like we'd been doing…what we'd been doing.

Joey and Reykr were the first to walk in, followed by Berit and Tyr. Joey and Reykr gave us both knowing looks but said nothing. Berit and Tyr seemed unaffected and returned to the walls they'd been working on. I joined them to stay far away from Steve. We were almost done with all the internal walls, and it was getting close to time to move in furniture.

As we worked, Tyr asked, "Have you considered doing a cleansing ritual before we open the bar?"

"A cleansing ritual?" I cocked a brow.

"There is a certain herb you burn around a new building

to ensure prosperity and a good future. We do it at our tribe whenever we build a new home," Berit explained.

I wasn't sure if I believed in any of that—I was not a spiritual person at all—but if it was important to them, I'd give it a go.

"Sure, when do you want to do it?" I asked.

"Well, it is supposed to be done at the full moon, which happens to be tonight," Tyr interjected. "That is why we thought about it; we discussed it at lunch."

"Okay, do you want to meet back here after the last meal?" I asked. This all seemed a bit weird, but who was I to judge their traditions? I didn't want to offend their tribe or Steve by association. If they burned herbs to cleanse a new building... cool.

"Sure, we will bring everyone from Snaerfírar," Berit said, finishing the last of the log he was working on.

Dinner was a loud and boisterous affair. Everyone was excited because we were getting so close to finishing the bar. Steve kept sneaking what he thought were surreptitious glances at me. We hadn't planned a "date" for tonight, but he didn't know I intended to take him back to my room after the Snaerfírar smoke ritual. I needed him, and I needed him badly. Once we finished dinner, we parted ways. I winked at Steve before leaving, knowing I would see him shortly. I was off for another shower before we met Steve and the rest of his tribe for the cleansing ritual. With the way Steve and I kept at it, I would have to start showering twice daily. This would not be good for my curls. I really needed to talk to the healer again about some conditioner situation.

Showered and ready, I practically skipped to Joey's room and barged in without knocking. We'd gotten so close that I was completely unfazed to find her half-dressed, nude from the waist up.

"Well, aren't we in a hurry," she teased as she pulled a tunic over her head and laced up her boots.

"Do you believe in this smoke-cleansing situation?" I asked, tapping my foot impatiently.

"I dunno. My grandparents used to burn incense at religious ceremonies, but I was too young to remember. I am like you; I don't really believe it, but what's the harm?" She finished with her shoes and stood.

We linked arms and headed to the bar.

"So, how are things with Steve?" She waggled her brows at me.

"Well. We fucked during lunch, and it was mind-blowing," I said, biting my lip. "I don't know if it is the fancy cock, the raw-dogging, or the fact that I am super into him, but I have *never* had sex like this before."

"Girl, if you keep up at this pace, you will have to let people know. They aren't going to believe your secret berry-picking expeditions forever. You're still drinking the birth control tea, right?"

"Ha. Definitely. It still makes me a little nervous that it is just a *tea*. I would rather have a pill or something like Piper's arm implant, but Emla ensured us the tea worked, so I'm counting on it. And drinking it every morning like a religion," I assured her.

I didn't want to think about babies with Steve yet. I wanted to think about pinning him down and teaching him every single sex position I could imagine.

When we arrived at the bar, we found only Tyr and Berit carrying two torches with dried herbs tied to them.

"Where are Reykr and Steve?" I asked immediately.

Tyr and Berit gave each other an odd look that made me feel a bit uneasy.

"We needed one more torch, so they ran back to Emla to get more herbs," Tyr said.

He sounded confident, and that seemed logical, so I decided not to question it further. Tyr handed us one of the torches and a fire starter. I cocked a brow at him.

"You start ahead of us because it is your space. We follow behind. It will create a dense, sweet-smelling smoke. Start with the attic, and we will follow and start on the main floor. Take the smoke into each corner of the room." He pushed the small of my back toward the door.

Joey and I looked at each other uncertainly but stepped inside. Joey took the fire starter and struck the flint, creating a spark. It lit the dried herbs immediately. Joey tucked the fire starter away, and we headed upstairs together, holding the torch. As the herbs continued to burn, a thick smoke emanated from the torch. It smelled sickly sweet, like rotten fruit. We took the torch from corner to corner in the attic until the whole room was filled with hazy smoke.

As we breathed in the smell, I started to feel a bit light-headed. I hadn't thought to ask if the smoke was safe for humans. Starting to get nervous, I looked at Joey just in time to see her eyes roll back in her head and her whole body start to sag, only being held up by the arm linked with mine.

"Joey?" I cried, dropping the torch to catch her as she fell to the floor. It went out almost immediately.

I was on my knees, holding her crumpled body. I checked to see if she was still breathing and was going to cry out for help when my vision narrowed to pinpoints, then went out entirely.

CHAPTER TWENTY-TWO

BILLIE

I was dreaming that Steve was carrying me back to my room. His strong arms held me up as we walked, and I nestled into his chest. Only his chest didn't smell like him at all. It smelled of some other man's musk. I tried to cry out in my dream but couldn't make any noise. I couldn't lift my arms or legs. Was this what sleep paralysis felt like, or was this part of the dream? My brain was too foggy to answer this question, and I drifted back into darkness. I was at the mercy of whoever was carrying me.

It felt as if no time had passed when I groggily opened my eyes. My whole body felt stiff and sore. I couldn't see anything around me. I blinked again, trying to get my eyes to adjust to the low light.

I was on my side on an earthen floor with Joey knocked out next to me. I moved slightly, trying to look around. We were in a cave, and a small fire was lit at the entrance, with Tyr and Berit sitting there. *What in the actual fuck?*

I shifted quietly and nudged Joey's shoulder. Tyr and Berit weren't looking at us but out looking out the cave opening, whispering. I shook Joey harder, and she finally opened her eyes. She blinked rapidly and assessed the situation much quicker than I had.

"I knew those bastards were up to something," she whispered, squinting at Tyr and Berit.

"Well then, why the fuck didn't you say anything to me?" I whispered back.

"I didn't want you to think I disliked your man's friends. But whatever. They hadn't thought through their kidnapping plan very carefully. You'll notice that neither of us is tied up?" She nodded to my wrists, which weren't bound.

I hadn't thought of that. Neither of us was restrained in any way. Did they expect us to wake up and go along with their half-cocked plan, whatever it was? I was in Joey's hands. She would be in charge of whatever we did in this situation. She had military training. She squinted at the two orcs.

"I surprise one, no problem. The question is whether or not we can get the second one down once he realizes what's going on. Do you have anything we could tie him with?" she asked.

As if I had methods of restraining giant orcs on my person. "Uh, no, do you?"

Tyr shifted and looked back at us. We instantly went motionless, eyes closed, and stayed that way until we heard Tyr and Berit pick up their conversation again.

I opened my eyes to find Joey unlacing her boots very quietly. *Why are we taking our shoes off at a time like this?* Had Joey completely lost her mind?

She pulled up her laces and showed them to me. *Oh, okay, restraints, got it. Check.*

I quietly held my knees to my chest, keeping my eyes on Tyr and Berit while I pulled the laces out of my boots.

I had never even punched a person before. There was no way I could restrain a nearly seven-foot orc. But Joey had already silently rolled into a crouched cat-like position. She jerked her head toward Tyr and then tapped her chest. Okay, she was on Tyr, and I was on Berit. She stalked up behind them with graceful, silent movements, and I followed behind, trying to tell myself we could pull this off. As she got up to Tyr and Berit, she stood, swung around, and did a full roundhouse kick to Tyr's chest, knocking him to the ground, then tying his wrists and ankles before he was even aware of what had happened.

I gaped at her, shoelaces in hand. Berit was also entirely surprised and hadn't jumped into action yet. Joey didn't pause. She descended on Berit, hands outstretched to detain him. Berit hesitated momentarily before going to his side, where he must have had a weapon. I finally got over my shock and jumped into action. As Joey went after his arms, I went for his hair. In a frantic tussle, we were shockingly able to get Berit to the ground. Joey was tying his arms behind his back with shoelaces, and I still had a firm grip on his hair.

"What can I do?" I asked.

"Gimme your laces. I want to make sure his hands are firmly bound." Joey didn't even look up from the knots she was tying. I handed her my laces, and she added them to the bindings already around Berit's wrists. Berit seemed to be in shock.

"But you're so… tiny." He looked from my face to Joey's.

"Yeah, in all those times we worked at the bar together, you never asked me what I did *before* I was abducted. *I was a soldier*. That right there was just basic training. You two are fucking idiots." She kicked him in the shin to add insult to injury.

I wasn't sure if Joey was mad about having to take out giant orcs or being underestimated. Probably both.

"Well, what are you going to do with us?" Berit asked, unable to contain his fear.

"I don't know. It depends on what you planned on doing with us!" I did not want to be the recipient of Joey's look at Berit and Tyr as they sat utterly bound.

"It was all Tyr's idea—"

"Well, isn't that fortunate for you." Joey rolled her eyes.

"A few days ago, we started noticing that one of you… Billie, in particular… started to smell of arousal while working at the bar. Tyr, because he is the tallest and best-looking male from Snaerfírar decided it must be because of him. He wanted to show Billie they could be Elska mates, but couldn't get her alone. So, he decided it would be best to take her away from the rest of the tribe. When you showed up with her, I decided to take my chances with you…" he trailed off as if saying his plan out loud was the first time he realized how stupid it was.

"So you decided, based on me smelling like arousal alone, that kidnapping and forcing a matebond with someone from a rival tribe was the best course of action?" I asked, voice dripping with venom.

"Well, it doesn't sound like a good idea when you put it that way," he admitted lamely.

"Did you ever stop to think that maybe our tribe wouldn't be pleased if you abducted us?" Joey asked, speaking slowly as if she were explaining something to a toddler.

Berit brightened up. "Yeah! I did! I mentioned that! But Tyr said if one of us were to come back with a matebond, then all would be forgiven."

"Oh my god. You two are so fucking stupid I cannot even." I put my face in my hands to stop myself from popping off.

Now that we were out of danger, I was more annoyed

than anything to be put in this situation. Berit and Tyr were completely immobilized due to Joey's handiwork.

"Berit," I crossed my arms, feeling thoroughly irritated at the whole situation. "Did you ever stop to think that perhaps I smelled of arousal or sex or whatever you weirdos can smell because I was fucking an orc that *wasn't* Tyr? Obviously, if I were pining after Tyr, I would have taken some steps to remedy that. I never even considered him. I was and am deeply involved with someone else." I kept my voice saccharine, wanting him to realize exactly how stupid they'd been with all of the assumptions they'd made.

"Uh… who?" He seemed shocked.

"I've been fucking Steve, you moron." I threw my hands in the air in exasperation.

"Steve?" Berit gave me a look of disbelief. "But he's so small compared to the rest of us. And he spends so much time *thinking,* whatever that means."

"You know, a male that is actually capable of *thinking* does have benefits, you absolute twat waffle." I was actively stopping myself from punching Berit in the face, though he definitely deserved it.

I heard Joey giggle, knowing Berit would have no idea what I was saying. I couldn't help but give her a grin. Now that it was clear we were never in danger, this situation was absolutely laughable. My only concern was how far we were from the tribe and if these two idiots could lead us back. Joey and I would be fine, but the problems this could cause for the tribe and tribal relations would be astronomical.

STEVE

Billie was gone. Even though we didn't have plans for the evening, I grew worried both she and Joey disappeared after last meal. We hadn't expressed intent to each other, but I assumed we'd spend the evening together. I must have been getting a second helping when she and Joey headed out.

I went to Billie's room after dinner and knocked on her door. No answer. Knowing that most of the Fýrifírar didn't have locks on their doors, I gently pushed it open, hoping Billie wouldn't be annoyed with my invasion of her privacy.

But she wasn't there. Her bed was made, and her cloak was hung next to the door. Wherever she was headed, she hadn't planned on being gone long.

I left Billie's room and went directly to the bar, the only place I could think she would be. I jogged there, starting to fear what may have happened to her, and was surprised to find Rekyr already at the bar.

"Billie is missing," I told him, and looked around to see if she was standing outside somewhere.

"So are Tyr, Berit, and Joey," Reykr said flatly.

I headed inside the bar to find it reeked of the sweet smell of svefanil, the herb our healer used to knock someone out when they needed to reset a bone. There was even a burnt-out torch with the herbs tied to it upstairs in the attic.

Reykr and I were both astonished.

"Do you think they are with Tyr and Berit somewhere?" I surveyed the rest of the bar for any other signs of abduction.

"I don't see any other reasonable explanation. What a disaster. Joey and Billie wouldn't have left without telling Piper. Tyr and Berit had to play a role. If we don't fix this, Fýrifírar will be furious that a rival tribe stole away two of their females. Do you think you can track Billie's scent?"

I inhaled deeply, trying to catch a whiff of Billie underneath the overpowering stench of the svefanil. It took a second, but I caught it—her spicy, floral musk was there. I glanced at Reykr and nodded.

"Do you think you can follow it?"

"I have only ever used my hunting skills to track animals, but I am going to do my fucking damnedest."

I was a member of the guard. I was never considered the strongest or the best because I was only a half-orc, but I had always excelled in tracking. It was the one area in which I outshone others. I had a keen eye for picking up details that others missed.

I followed Billie's faint scent out of the bar and into the woods with Reykr on my heels. We reached a path into the forest that split, and it was harder to catch Billie's scent while surrounded by the smell of the furutré. I knelt down and examined each fork. Only one had fresh footprints, with the trees on either side having disturbed and snapped branches.

"They had to go this way, because this trail is fresh," I told Reykr, pointing out what I saw.

Luckily, the moon was full, and orkin eyes were keen even in the dark. I could see the lazy trail left behind by Tyr and Berit. I couldn't help but wonder what they had planned with Billie and Joey. The idea of one of them carrying Billie while she was unconscious and sampling all of her soft curves made my blood boil. If they had taken Billie and Joey intending to try to take them as mates, I was going to kill both of them with my bare hands.

It wasn't long before I started to smell smoke, the telltale sign of a fire burning nearby. I followed the smoke to a small cave opening just off the path and was slack-jawed at the scene I found.

CHAPTER TWENTY-THREE

STEVE

yr, Berit, Billie, and Joey were at the mouth of a small cave, with a fire lit in front of them. Tyr and Berit had their wrists tied in several intricate knots, with their heads hanging down. It appeared as if Joey was berating him. This was not the scene I expected to find. Reykr and I gave up the ruse of trying to sneak up on them and just walked out into the open.

Joey stopped mid-sentence and turned to me and Reykr.

"Well, fancy seeing you two here," she said sarcastically. "I am guessing these two buffoons left a trail about a mile wide for you to follow?"

"Pretty much." I shrugged before I was almost bowled over by Billie, who came rushing to me with her boots flapping around her ankles. She jumped into my arms and wrapped her legs around my waist before kissing me soundly on the mouth.

"My hero," she teased.

"It seemed like you had the situation pretty well taken care of." I smiled down at her—of course, she and Joey handled the situation, my fearless Billie.

"That was only because of Joey. I have no idea how to restrain the person—or orc. But in case you weren't aware, don't get on Joey's bad side."

"Noted." I pulled her in for another kiss. Reykr cleared his throat behind me, and I looked over Billie's shoulder at him.

"While this display of affection is sickeningly sweet, we must plan what to do now." He nodded at my two tribemates. "Should we kill them?"

"What?!" Billie gasped. "No!"

"Why not? They drugged you and kidnapped you." I spat scornfully.

"Yeah, but they were way too stupid to pull it off. Look at how easily you found us. We were gone maybe a couple of hours. I think the only one with lasting damage may be Tyr."

Billie called to Joey, "Hey, is that kick to the chest going to cause long-term trauma?"

"Nah, he's fine. Aren't you, buddy?" she spoke to him like a toddler.

Tyr nodded glumly.

Reykr looked appalled. "So you are saying they should receive a lesser punishment because they were too stupid to kidnap you effectively?"

"I mean. They didn't really do any harm." Billie shrugged.

She might be conversing with Reykr and Joey, but as she wrapped her legs more tightly around my waist, I could tell she only had one thing on her mind.

"Maybe we shouldn't tell Agnarr and Piper about this." Reykr scratched his chin thoughtfully. "Since there appears to be no significant harm done, I would hate for them to feel obligated to kill these two idiots."

"I think we should leave it up to the women. Ladies, what do you think their punishment should be?" I asked.

Billie and Joey looked at each other thoughtfully.

"No talking to any of the females, especially not the humans," Joey proposed.

"And they must go home once we're done with the bar," Billie added. "But they need to stay finish out their fair share."

"Why no talking to females?" Reykr asked.

"They kidnapped us because they could smell arousal on Billie. Tyr thought he could take her as his mate. He didn't know she was getting railed on the daily by Steve," Joey responded coolly.

I almost dropped Billie in outrage. "What?" I spluttered.

"He could *smell* Billie, so he assumed she was interested in him. Your friend has a pretty big ego." As Tyr continued to shift, Joey casually pressed a booted foot down on his chest to prevent him from moving.

I let go of Billie, letting her quietly slip down my body as I clenched and unclenched my fists. It didn't matter that Billie was okay. Tyr had tried to claim ownership of her, and she was *mine*. A rage as I had never felt before boiled up in me. I would strangle him with my bare hands. As I started to head toward Tyr, Billie stopped me, pressing her palm against my chest. I could have easily brushed her aside, but I glanced down to see she was serious.

"Listen. I know you're pissed that Tyr just assumed I would be interested in him and not you. And that he kidnapped me. But you don't need to beat him up for me. I am not interested in Tyr at all. He's paid the price by being taken out by one swift kick of an embarrassingly small female." She waved her hand at Joey, still putting all her weight on Tyr's chest.

"But he took you without even *asking* you," I ground out.

"Yeah, and that was really fucking stupid. Now, not only does he not have me, but he won't have anyone. That seems like enough, right?" She was attempting to placate me.

I grumbled noncommittally.

"I don't need you getting your hands dirty for an orc that a barely five-foot-tall human has already detained. Why don't we let Reykr and Joey handle them, and you and I can go home?" She cocked a brow at me.

"I'm listening," I said.

"This will be the last night we have before the entire tribe knows about us, considering the abduction, rescue, etc. So why don't we spend it with just the two of us?" She raised her brow further.

I didn't need further explanation. I scooped her up, wrapped her legs around my waist and her arms around my neck, and started walking back to the village.

"Oh sure, leave us to deal with these two. We don't mind at all!" Reykr called sarcastically.

Billie just waved over my shoulder before nuzzling into me. She began kissing down my neck as I carried her.

"That was really hot, you know," she murmured as she kissed across my collarbone.

"What was really hot?" I huffed, somewhere between annoyed at Tyr and turned on by her kisses.

"You coming to my rescue," she said. "Wanting to fight Tyr. I've never had someone who wanted to fight for me."

I squeezed her ass and buried my head in her hair, taking in her smell. "I would have happily fought Tyr for you. He may be bigger than I am, but I am better trained. And he is kind of dumb."

"Kind of?! He kidnapped two women and didn't even bother to tie them up. Did he think we'd wake up and be happy to be in a cave with our kidnappers?" She locked eyes with me incredulously.

I laughed. "Probably. Like I said, he's not very bright."

"Well, I'm glad you found me before we had to march them back to the village and decide what to do with them," she said, kissing me as we headed back to the village.

I felt myself growing hard with each one of her kisses, "Billie, we are still a ways away from the village. Can you pause the kisses until we get to your room? It's hard enough to keep my cock under control while carrying you like this."

"Sorry," she responded in a mock, serious tone, "I shall reserve my acts of appreciation until we are in my room."

"Thank you." With that, she nuzzled into my chest as we returned.

Billie sighed happily in my arms as I carried her back to her room. It had been quite an interesting night and would end far better than I anticipated. Billie traced a finger along the neck of my tunic and inhaled the scent of my neck.

"Billie! You are killing me!"

"What?" she said innocently. "I'm not doing anything!"

"You think I can't feel your tiny hands exploring me, or you breathing in my scent? We are minutes away from your room, and then I plan to fuck you until you see the stars. Can we agree on that plan?" Billie gave me a wicked look that told me everything I needed.

My erection was almost painful at this point and tried to put it out of my mind, but Billie ground her hips into me.

"Do you want to have sex right here on the forest floor, or do you want to have sex in your nice comfortable bed?" I asked, voice low.

"Fine, fine. I will behave. I promise."

Within no time, we'd reached the edge of the village. Because it was so late, the moon was already high in the sky and it seemed as if all the tribe had gone to bed. I walked as quickly as I could to Billie's room, keeping an eye out for anyone. Luckily, we didn't cross paths with anyone, and as we reached Billie's door, I opened it with one hand without putting her down. I shut the door behind us and quickly laid Billie on her bed.

I was on top of her before she had a moment even to react. I kissed each of her cheeks, then took my time kissing down her neck, gently biting down on one of her tiny, perfect earlobes. Billie squirmed under me, wrapping her legs around my waist again so she could grind her hips into mine. My cock was already awake and straining against my pants as the smell of Billie's arousal grew stronger. I continued kissing down her neck but slipped a hand under her tunic to find her breasts. I was met with the strap she used to keep them in place.

"Can we do something about this?" I asked as I continued to kiss her.

"Mmm, you'll have to stop kissing me for just a second, but I promise it will be worth it," she teased.

I leaned back, straddling her as she lay flushed and perfect on her bed. She pulled her tunic over her head, tossing it on the floor, the chest band following close behind. Then, her glorious tits were on full display. I kneaded at the flesh on the underside of her breasts before drawing my thumbs across each of her dusky, puckered nipples. She arched into my touch as I swooped down to take one of her nipples into my mouth. I flicked my tongue back and forth over the stiff peak before sucking it deeply into my mouth, all while pinching the other nipple between my thumb and forefinger.

"Oh fuck, Steve, that feels good." Billie tangled her hands in my hair and pulled me even closer to her chest as I continued to devour her breast.

She reached down to the hem of my tunic, pulling it up, "I want your skin against mine."

I pulled my tunic over my head with one hand, tossing it

on the floor with hers. It was a frantic scramble of arms and hands and lips, as we tried to touch, kiss, and lick each other everywhere. I was insatiable when it came to Billie. The idea that she had been in danger nearly split me in two, and I didn't realize I had grown to need her so badly in the short time we'd spent together. I wrapped my arms around her, pressing her to me as tightly as I could while I worried and nibbled at her lips. She opened her mouth, and our tongues tangled together as she held me even tighter. Her need seemed to match mine in every way.

Billie licked and sucked on my tongue before pulling my lower lip between her teeth and biting down, causing a zip of pleasure to shoot straight to my groin. I ground my hips against hers, my erection feeling painfully trapped in my pants. As if on cue, Billie's hands strayed to the laces of my pants, pulling at them, never removing her mouth from mine. She struggled and then whined into my mouth as she fought to remove my clothes.

I pulled my lips from hers, panting. "Let me help," I quickly unlaced and yanked my pants down, watching her follow suit with her own. Finally, we were both naked, with our clothes piled in a heap on the floor next to her bed.

"You were right," I said. "A bed is much better than a blanket in a berry patch." I returned to my position on top of her, caging her in with my arms. She giggled beneath me.

"It will make cleanup much easier, considering the amount of cum orkin produce," she said, wrapping her legs around me and pulling me into her again.

And then I had a thought, she had licked and sucked me, but I hadn't done the same for her. If she tasted as good as she smelled, it would be divine. Instead of grinding my cock into her, I kissed from her lips down to her collarbone, then to her breasts. I paused to flick my tongue over each nipple until she shuddered under me. I continued my trail of kisses down her soft stomach and across her hip bone before pushing her knees apart to make room for my shoulders. I looked up to Billie to see some hesitancy in her eyes.

"May I?" I teased.

"Only if it is something you really want to do," she said hesitantly.

Having already licked her cunt thoroughly once before, I filed the response away for future reference. At some point a man had made her feel like this was a chore. I leaned down and examined her lower lips. They were swollen and puffy with want, leaking her desire. I licked up and down each lip, savoring the musky taste that could only be described as Billie. I used my fingers to spread her lower lips, revealing her clit. I tested it gently by using the tip of my tongue to circle it, as I had in the berry patch, not touching it directly. Billie writhed underneath me, moaning and spreading her legs wider. I was onto something. I continued to circle her clit with the tip of my tongue when I heard a ragged moan escape her lips.

"More," was all she said as she gripped my hair, holding me to her cunt.

I increased the pressure I used with my tongue while slipping two fingers into her tight channel. She was already warm and soaking for me. I pumped my fingers in and out as I continued to tease her clit with my tongue.

"Oh fuck, oh fuck," she cried, clamping her thighs around my head.

I felt her joints lock up as she barrelled toward her climax. I continued circling her clit with my tongue and pumping my fingers in and out of her rhythmically as she locked down around me. Suddenly, a flood of her juices came across my face, and she went limp, legs and arms splayed wide.

"Goddamn, Steve, that was amazing," she gasped. "I need you to fuck me now. Right now."

I was very happy to oblige. I kissed my way back up her body, pausing on her nipples and her neck before kissing her deeply.

"Damn, I never thought tasting myself on someone else would be so hot." She kissed me more fervently, devouring my mouth with her own. I kissed her back, savoring the flavor of her still on my tongue. My cock was wedged between the two of us and desperate to find its home in her warm cunt.

"Are you—are you ready for me?" I asked.

Billie nodded her head vigorously. I pressed against her wet folds, breathing through my nose so I could take it slow. I pushed my cock into her welcoming body slowly, feeling the grip of her around my cock.

"More," she breathed.

I continued to press into her, slowly, very aware of our size difference. Billie spread her legs even wider, nodding at me, showing me she wanted to continue.

I pressed into her further until my knot finally met resistance, and Billie nodded.

"Is this okay?" I asked.

"More than okay," she responded, wrapping her legs around my waist.

I started to thrust shallowly, not wanting to overwhelm Billie with my size or my knot. Billie locked her legs around my waist and murmured, "More."

I ratcheted up my pace and thrust deeper, but not knotting her. She wasn't ready. She'd need to come at least once more. Her cunt was like a vice around me, sucking me in with every thrust.

Billie hung on, digging her fingers into my shoulders and wrapping her legs more tightly around my waist. If this is what she wanted, I would give it to her. I rammed my knot into her again and again as she cried her pleasure. I knew she was on the medicinal tea, but the thought of her, ripe with our young, swollen breasts and stomach, flashed across my mind, and my thrusts took on animalistic pistoning, my knot squelching in and out of her obscenely. I felt her clamp down around me, ready for another climax.

I pounded into her soft body while drawing one of her nipples into my mouth. Billie moaned underneath me, grabbing at my hair as I devoured her.

I continued to flick my tongue back and forth across her peaked nipple, but I wanted to do more. I wondered if I could stroke her clit while delving in and out of her. I leaned back as I continued to thrust and just admired her perfect form as I slid in and out of her, causing her breasts to bounce up and down. She had her hands dug into my waist, and her mouth formed a perfect 'o' as I continued. From this position, I could fit my hands between us. I spread her lower lips and circled her clit with the pad of my thumb, all while keeping the same steady rhythm.

"Holy fuck Steve, that's so good," she cried. "Keep going. Just like that."

My balls began to tighten and tingle at the base of my spine, telling me I was close, but I wanted another orgasm out of Billie before I finished. I kept my pace steady and added slightly more pressure to the circles that I was tracing around her clit.

"Jesus Christ," she screamed as she clamped down on me.

My cock swelled as she strangled in her tight cunt. I unleashed torrent after torrent of cum into her, locking myself in place inside her. I leaned forward onto my forearms and peppered her face with kisses, surprised to find tears in her eyes.

"Are you okay? Was it too much? Is the knot hurting you?" I asked quickly, concerned.

She gave me a small smile and then wrapped her arms and legs around me, pulling me impossibly close to her—our sweaty bodies pressed together everywhere.

"I cried because it was so good," she whispered before pulling me in for another salty kiss.

CHAPTER TWENTY-FOUR

BILLIE

Feeling utterly sated and boneless, I relished the comfortable weight of Steve on top of me. He leaned up on his forearms to see me, and he had a stupid giant grin on his face that I couldn't help but return. It was going extraordinarily well for an evening that started with a kidnapping.

Steve stroked down my face gently, running a fingertip along the curve of my jaw. He looked so fucking happy to just to be with me that I couldn't help but start to cry again.

"Hey, hey," he said gently. "What are you thinking?"

"I've always been told I have such a big heart and willingly gave it to too many people only to find it discarded. It is really new for me to be with someone who wants to be with me as much as I want to be with them." She sniffled. "I can't believe you found me and Joey after those idiots took us."

"Well, not only am I one of the best trackers in our tribe,

but they are also truly idiots and left a trail an orkling could follow." Steve pulled me into him again, this time turning us so we could side by side.

"I kinda like being stuck to you this way. It makes post-sex cuddling a requirement."

"Is it not normal for humans to lay together for a while after sex?" He raised his brows at me.

"Not if it's a casual thing. And even if it is more serious, the dude usually goes straight to cleanup or falls asleep immediately."

Steve shook his head in disgust."I can't imagine wanting to do anything but lay here and admire you as you come down from your peak." He stroked down the side of my hip, pausing to grab a handful of my ass.

I giggled. It was so *fun* to experience all of these firsts with Steve. It felt like everything was brand new, with no preconceived notions of what we should or shouldn't do. We lay there, absentmindedly stroking each other, when a flit of concern flashed across Steve's face.

"What is it?" I trailed my fingers down his arm, barely brushing the hairs.

"When you finished the second time when I was inside you, you screamed someone else's name—was that a former partner?"

I cocked a brow at him, bewildered. I hadn't screamed anyone's name. I truly had no names to scream. I scrunched up my face, trying to remember what I'd said then, and came up with a blank.

"What name did I say? I was too lost in you—now I don't remember."

"Someone named Jesus?" He assessed me with a furrowed brow.

I clapped a hand over my mouth to cover the belly laugh

that escaped from me. My whole body shook as I laughed, and Steve groaned. Oh, tightening my stomach muscle must have tightened all of my muscles, causing me to clamp down on his still-hard cock. I couldn't help it. This made me laugh even harder.

Steve went from looking confused to affronted. "If this is a joke, I would very much like to be let in on it!"

I gasped for breath as I tried to stop laughing and reached out to Steve, pulling him in for a kiss. He returned but still looked as if he didn't quite believe me.

"Jesus Christ is definitely not a past partner." I tried to keep my laughter at bay as Steve looked at me suspiciously. "He's a god to some people on Earth—and in the religion I was raised in. So it's kind of like saying, oh gods? Or, oh fuck? Jesus fucking Christ happens to be one of my swears."

Steve looked mollified.

"I don't have any exes' names that are worth screaming. This is the best sex I've ever had." I blurted it out without thinking and instantly blushed a deep red.

I hadn't planned on admitting *that* this early in our relationship. That seemed like a much further down-the-road conversation. Yet, given Steve had nothing to compare to, it wasn't quite the same.

"Well, I know it isn't the same coming from me," he said, "but this is also the best sex I've ever had."

"Oh yeah? I'm better than your hand?" I kissed the bridge of his nose and each of his cheeks as he blushed.

"Definitely better than my hand." He tangled his fingers in my hair at the nape of my neck and kissed me again.

I knew we hadn't agreed on forever. We were in a holding pattern until we decided it was serious, but just for a moment, I let myself think of what life might be like with Steve. We could move in above the bar and run it together. We'd have long nights with drunk orkin, but we'd sleep in late and then wake up and fuck until it was time for the bar to open again. That sounded like a life I could get behind. But I wasn't ready to make that leap yet, and I still wasn't sure I was worth Steve leaving his entire tribe for. I let that thought sink in like a stone and wondered if I was worth that to Steve.

He must have noticed the faraway look in my eyes because he reached out and smoothed the creases across my brow.

"What are you thinking?" he murmured.

I raised my hand to the ceiling, tracing out thatch patterns far beyond my reach. "I'm just thinking about you. Me. What comes next?"

"Well, for now, I am very grateful that tonight's plans involve a towel and a proper way to clean up the mess I've made of you." He pulled out with an audible squelch as his knot had softened, leaving me in a veritable lake of cum. This was definitely going to be an extra blanket situation in the future.

As Steve walked toward my washroom, I admired the toned muscles of his ass and thighs before turning my gaze to his muscled back and shoulders. I gasped as I noticed a long, thin tattoo trailing from the base of his spine almost to his neck. It looked like little ocean waves crawling up his spine. There is no way that had always been there. I would have noticed.

"Steve!" I clambered out of the bed, getting cum literally everywhere. We definitely needed a long-term cum solution. This was insane. He looked back at me, surprised.

He turned back to me, surprised. "I said I would get you a towel." His brows arched in concern as the puddle of cum grew around my feet.

"No, no! Look at your back!" I pulled him into my small washroom. My mirror wasn't large, but it was big enough for me to see myself from my chest up. I pulled Steve in front of the mirror and flipped him around.

"Um, what exactly are you expecting me to see from this position?" Brows raised at me like I'd lost my mind.

"Look over your shoulder, you space cadet!" I commanded.

"Space cadet?"

"Just look over your damn shoulder," I huffed.

Steve craned his neck to see his back in my mirror, and his eyes got big. It was definitely a new tattoo. I wasn't just an idiot. Well, maybe I was an idiot, but I wasn't mistaken about what I saw.

Steve looked back at me and spun me around, exposing my back to him. From his sharp breath, I didn't need to ask. I knew what he saw. His warm finger traced down my spine.

"Elskas," was all he said.

He spun me back around and pulled me into a crushing embrace, cum spatter and all. My head was spinning. I was starting to think about the possibility of forever with Steve and now here it was. *Forever.* Forever.

I felt like I needed air. We never expected this. We had very little orkin blood between the two of us, and we'd be excluded from the whole Elska bond. Apparently, we were wrong.

"Billie, you look a little pale. Why don't you let me get some warm washrags and a towel for the bed, and we can lay down and discuss what this means for us?" Steve stroked a finger across my cheek before planting a delicate kiss on my lips.

I headed back to the bed, my feet and legs sticky, while I heard Steve running the taps. My head was spinning and my legs were shaking. All I had ever wanted was a forever. And now there was a naked *forever* in my bathroom getting towels to clean me up. It was a lot.

I hadn't even gotten to the bed, given my state, before Steve was behind me. He laid a large towel over the center of the bed before directing me to lie down, starfish style. Starting at my toes, he used a warm cloth to meticulously clean each of my feet. I giggled.

"Sorry, it tickles." I blushed.

"Don't be sorry," he said before moving slowly up my calves, cleaning every part of me.

As the cloth he was using started to get cold, he went to get a new towel. He came back to me with a new warm towel and resumed cleaning my thighs, gently massaging me as he went. It was hard not to sigh into the warm feeling of after-care, something I was not used to. As he finished my thighs, he dragged the towel across my hips before dipping between my legs and gently, oh so gently, cleaning my very overstimulated mound and lower lips. He did this all with a level of extreme concentration on his face.

Once he finished, he returned to the restroom, and I could hear the tap running. He must be cleaning up himself. I wasn't the only one covered in cum. I flipped to my side and pulled my blankets up to my chin, waiting for him to return. While the weather was changing, the fire hadn't been lit, and now that our frantic fucking was over, I was getting chilly.

Steve returned, still in all his naked glory. He was muscular without a ridiculously defined six-pack that you only saw on the cover of *Sports Illustrated*. His shoulders were bulky, and I was reminded of how he easily lifted me. I quirked up my lip, thinking of what that could mean for future options. His smattering of black silky hair across his chest and happy trail made me practically salivate. Though we'd been together multiple times, this was the first time I'd really gotten to see him afterwards. His penis, now soft, was still impressive, and I found myself longing to take it into my mouth to wake it up.

Get it together, Billie. We have a pretty serious conversation to have. You cannot be led by your desire to suck his cock! I shook myself to get my head back into a place to talk about mates and everything it meant.

But Steve had noticed me staring. "Do you like what you see?" he asked, giving me a shy smile.

"Yes. Yes—very much so."

"Well, unfortunately, you have covered up your delicious body and all your soft curves." He fake-pouted.

"Well, there's nothing stopping you from joining me." I lifted the blankets.

He quickly closed the distance between us and crawled into bed with me, pulling me to him with his muscled arms. I melted into him. He was so warm. He trailed his hand down my spine before grabbing a handful of my ass and pulling me in for a kiss. It started as a brief brush of our lips, but it wasn't long before our tongues were tangling together, and I could feel his cock hardening against my stomach. We were insatiable for each other. He was a drug I was happy to be addicted to. But I pulled myself back, disentangling myself.

I propped myself up on my elbow. "We have to discuss this whole Elska thing. I don't think either of us expected it."

Steve, incapable of keeping his hands off of me, traced along my collarbone to the tip of one of my pebbled nipples as he thought about my words.

"Sir. Hands to yourself as we talk about this. It is serious business." I gave him a mock angry face.

"Okay, okay, how about here? Can I put my hand here?" He placed it on the curve of my hip.

"That is acceptable," I replied seriously but followed with a giggle. "So this whole mate thing is forever?"

"Yes. Forever. Once your mate dies, most mates find it hard to go on—as you heard when I explained about my dad.

He lived for quite a bit longer, but he was a shell," Steve looked sad, tracing his fingers along the marks on my back.

"What usually happens?" I asked.

"Mates live out their lives together, and when one finally succumbs to old age, the other follows quickly. There are mates that have lived successfully without each other. I believe Astrid would be an example of this, but I wouldn't be surprised if a part of her aches daily for her mate."

I hadn't thought about how long Astrid had lived without her mate. She seemed so strong and in control. Perhaps it was the weight of being jarlin that had kept her going. Or, before her mate died, they produced three orklings to which she was very close. I thought about being tethered to Steve for life. Maybe I was still cock drunk, but that didn't sound bad at all.

"Do you want to be tied to me for the rest of your life?" I asked, skeptical.

"I've wanted forever since our first conversation," Steve said plainly before pulling me in for a kiss.

I kissed him back, unable to help myself, but pulled away quickly.

"Hey, hey, hands and lips where they belong," I chided. "What makes you so certain about me?"

I'd never had someone want more than a casual hookup. Someone wanting forever was exciting but scary.

"You are so full of joy and possibility," Steve said. "You look to the future and see nothing but opportunity ahead. You have a huge heart and give your all to those lucky enough to call your friends. And you have spent a lot of time figuring out what you want from your life—I feel like I want that. I don't want someone to drift along with me. I want someone with a goal, a desire, and a life they want to create. And I wanted to create that life with you. I think that is what I have been missing."

That sent me reeling. Steve wasn't just saying yes to the Elska bond. He was saying yes to *me*. He saw me in a way I didn't think anyone had ever seen.

I couldn't help the tears starting to well up in my eyes. To have someone see me, for all of me, and want me—it was more than I was prepared for on the same night as a kidnapping.

CHAPTER TWENTY-FIVE

STEVE

Elska mates. I had never dreamed of such a thing for me. I thought being a half-orc might preclude me from the option—especially if it was with a human. Yet, here she was, lying next to me, naked, and chewing on her lower lip.

"Hey, what are you thinking?" I asked.

She took a while to respond as if wanting to phrase what she was going to say very carefully.

"We don't have fated mates on Earth. We have partners, and we have marriage, which is the most permanent way of committing to someone, but even then, people separate all the time. The idea of being bonded for life to someone is exciting but also scary."

I couldn't hide the hurt in my eyes. I was elated and wanted to run out and tell the whole tribe I'd found my mate —naked and all. And Billie was only… considering.

"I can't say that I feel the same hesitancy. I've known all along, bond or not," I said, trying to keep myself from choking up.

"Steve." She stroked my arm. "I also worry that since you've never really been with someone, maybe you're just infatuated because I am your first," she said very quickly as if it would hurt less. It didn't.

I knew I was inexperienced, but that didn't change the fact that I had never met anyone like Billie. I had never felt drawn to anyone the way I was drawn to her. If she'd let me, I would follow her around, feeding her snacks and petting her hair. I could tell she wasn't happy by her furrowed brow and pursed lips. Everything felt very precarious.

"Steve, it isn't that I don't want you as an Elska mate," Billie clarified. "That isn't it at all. I am just inexperienced in my own way. I have never had someone want me seriously. Fuck, I've never had someone want me longer than a month. So to have a gorgeous, funny, caring orc in front of me, offering forever, is a lot to take in."

"So the idea that someone might want you forever is brand new?" I asked.

She nodded, tears starting to well in her eyes. I knew she'd said no touching while we had this conversation, but I couldn't help it. I wrapped my arms around her and pulled her into an embrace. This was either a really good choice or a really bad choice because Billie started crying in earnest. She had her arms pulled in front of her chest, so I was basically bear-hugging her as she cried into my shoulder. I stroked her hair and let her cry. She didn't pull away from me, so I hoped I was providing at least some level of comfort. She cried for a long time, and I just held her and wondered where the conversation would go from here.

Eventually, her cries turned into soft hiccups, and she

pulled away from me. Her face was a blotchy mix of different shades of red and tear-streaked, but she still looked beautiful to me.

"I'm so sorry. Here you are, offering me everything I always wanted, and I can't just say yes."

My heart fell as she continued.

"It isn't you. It is a permanency I have never been offered. And I can't agree to a lifetime with someone, no matter how amazing they are, without at least thinking about what it will mean for me. You realize this means I would expect you to move here, right?"

"Yes. I already told Reykr I was staying if you'd have me."

Billie looked shocked. "You really are so sure about this? About us?"

"I was sure before the mate marks appeared. Now I am convinced." I shrugged.

Billie rolled that over in her head. "And what happens if you reject an Elska bond?" she asked.

The mere idea of this made me sick to my stomach and my chest feel tight, but I wasn't going to bind Billie to me without giving her a choice. "The marks fade over time, but you never get another Elska. This is your one chance. You could take another chosen mate, though," I said it, even though it killed me.

Billie shook her head. "No, no, that's not what I want at all. There is no one else from Fýrifírar that I am remotely interested in. And it isn't as if I am going to go after Tyr or Berit. Aside from the fact that they kidnapped me, they seem to lack basic common sense."

"And Reykr?" I had to ask, though it was like a dagger to my heart, wondering if my mate might be interested in my best friend.

At this, Billie laughed. "Steve, you mean the world to me,

but sometimes you don't pick up on subtle cues. Have you not noticed Joey and Reykr?"

I thought back. I couldn't think of anything that stood out to me about Joey and Reykr. They worked in the same space together often, but they never seemed to be deep in conversation.

"How can you tell?" I asked.

"They haven't figured it out yet, but they don't like to be apart. As soon as one of them musters up the courage to say something, I have a feeling they will fall hard and fast." She raised her brows and cocked her head to the side suggestively.

"Why didn't you tell me!?" I asked in mock outrage.

"It's pretty obvious, my dude." She rolled her eyes.

"We are getting away from our actual conversation, but we will return to this Reykr and Joey talk. Let me get this straight. You want me. You don't want anyone else. But the idea of forever is overwhelming to you?"

She nodded. My brain whirred. How long would it take someone who had no concept of *forever* to decide? Days? Months? I didn't know if I could hold on that long, waiting for a decision. It would wreck me.

"Well, what do you want to do then?" I asked, trying to give her the freedom to make a decision, even though I knew she was already feeling intense pressure.

She searched my eyes as if somehow I would give her the answer. I stroked down her arm but said nothing as she thought.

"Could I have two days?" Billie asked hesitantly.

I breathed a sigh of relief. I could do two days.

"A two days sounds—very, very fair," I responded.

"One condition, though."

My fragile relief started to crumble.

"I need two days where I don't see *you*. I won't be able to decide if you are standing there, being all wonderful and tending to my every need."

I gave her a fierce frown.

"You can't go *two days* without seeing me?" she asked.

"Maybe I just don't want to," I said loftily.

She laughed, thankfully. "Just two days. And that day doesn't have to start until tomorrow."

I barely had time to look at her in surprise before she swung a leg over my hip and pulled me in for a bruising kiss. Based on my memories of this night alone, I could go for two days.

BILLIE

The next morning, Steve snuck out early. We decided to tell those who needed to know about the Elska marks. I had a feeling that this was Reykr for him. For me, it was Piper and Joey. I didn't head to breakfast. I went straight to Joey's door and opened it without knocking. To my great surprise, I found Joey and Reykr fast asleep, tangled together in Joey's bed. Reykr's entire thigh was hanging out of the covers, exposing a great deal of his ass. I almost whooped with joy, but I didn't think either would appreciate it.

Well, fuck, I needed Joey. How was I going to extricate her from Reykr? Both of them started to shift and wake at the light coming in from the open door. Reykr opened his eyes first and scrambled to cover himself, waking up Joey in the process.

"What the fuck, Billie?!" she whisper-shouted at me.

"Oh *I'm* sorry," I said sarcastically. "How was I to know that I might find Reykr in your bed when you've said literally nothing to me about him?" I crossed my arms in front of my chest and stuck out my tongue.

"I wasn't sure it was—I didn't know—" She stumbled over her words.

"I think what she is trying to say is that my returned interest took her by surprise," Reykr said in a growly voice, clearly displeased to be found in such a compromising position.

"Okay, well, I won't say anything, and we have more pressing matters at hand. Reykr, Steve is going to need you immediately."

Reykr looked alarmed. "Is he okay?"

Without saying a word, I turned around and pulled up the back of my tunic, exposing the Elska marks running down my spine. I heard both Reykr and Joey gasp. Joey ran to me, completely nude, and traced a finger down my spine, causing me to shiver.

"Hey, watch it, that tickles!"

"Does this mean what I think it means?" she breathed, still staring at my back.

"Yes, Steve has matching marks," I replied.

Reykr let out a low whistle of surprise.

"So why isn't Steve with you right now?" Joey asked, brow raised. "Isn't this supposed to lead to spontaneous, insatiable fucking?" Joey asked, brow raised.

I turned around so I could face Joey. "I told him I needed some time. I didn't expect this. We didn't think we had enough orc between the two of us to warrant an Elska bond.

And for fuck's sake, put some clothes on. I can't have a serious conversation with you while you're standing there naked."

"Well, I'm sorry, you barged into my room before the sun was even warm," she said petulantly.

I turned to Reykr. "He's going to need you. He's headed back to your rooms now."

Reykr nodded. "How much time did you ask for?"

"Two days."

Giving me another nod, Reykr stood, wrapping his waist with a blanket, and headed to the washroom. By this time, Joey had pulled on a tunic and pants and was assessing me, face scrunched up in disapproval.

"You told him you needed two days?" she asked, shocked.

"How long do you think a normal person needs to decide whether to commit to an irreversible soul bond?" I snapped.

"Jeez, alright, alright," she said, grabbing her boots.

I was irritated that I had to explain it to her and Reykr instead of having this conversation with Joey alone. I was also hurt that I didn't know how fast things were going between them. Reykr came out of the washroom, dressed in his clothes from yesterday. He nodded to Joey and me before slipping out the door and closing it behind him.

As soon as I was sure that he was out of earshot, I hissed, "And when were you going to tell me about that? Hmm? You know all the details about me and Steve."

"Well, up until last night, I thought it was a one-way street!" Joey spit back. "He was so quiet. I had no idea that he was interested. We were both high on adrenaline after we deposited Tyr and Berit in their rooms, with strict instructions not to leave until we came for them in the morning. We shut the door, and without a word, he scooped me up and took me back to my room. I don't think we even said a word to each other. I have no idea what is going on. And you robbed me of my chance to have that conversation by bounding in here with an Elska mark down your spine."

Oof, I had made a mess of this. "I'm sorry. I'm sorry. I didn't even stop to think you might have someone in your room. I should have waited."

"If I had walked into your room 20 minutes ago, would I have found a similar scene?" she asked smugly.

"Mmm, yep." I blushed. "Maybe we need to start keeping a sock on the door?" I joked.

"I'd rather not let all the women know about my situation with Reykr, especially since I don't even know my situation with Reykr." She threw her hands in the air.

"Okay, okay, that's fair. I won't tell a soul about Reykr. Will you keep the Elska thing on the DL for now?" I asked.

I really didn't need all of the other women knowing about it. And I felt my stomach churn at the idea of people finding out before I'd made up my mind.

"So you found out you are soul mates and told him you needed time to *decide*? What kind of bitch ass move is that? You know you want him," She glared at me, pressing her palms onto the small table in her room.

"I do want him. But we've been *dating* or whatever for like two weeks. Doesn't that feel a bit soon to make a forever commitment? And you know my past! I've never had someone interested in forever with me. What if he gets bored of me? Or irritated that I snack in bed? Or that I take over an hour to do my stupid hair?"

"Billie, are you blind?!" she yelled. "He looks at you like you hung the moon. I have never seen a man—orc—more in love."

"That doesn't mean it will last forever," I crossed my arms, ready to dig in my heels. I wasn't ready to believe a weird tattoo on my back would mean someone wanted to be with *me* until they died.

"Actually, that is exactly what the Elska bond means. Come on." She grabbed my arm.

"Where are we going?" I asked.

"We're going to see the only person who can make you understand," she said, dragging me to the door. "We are going to see Piper."

STEVE

I was pacing our room when Reykr finally walked in.

"Where the hell have you been?" I demanded.

"I could ask you the same thing." He looked me up and down, as I was obviously in my clothes from the day before.

That's when I noticed he was also in his prior day's clothes.

"Oh, were we spending the night with a certain petite spitfire?" I asked.

"Well, since your *Elska mate* already knows about it, I don't see any reason to keep it from you," he said, his tone oozing with harsh judgment, intensifying the tension in the room.

"Hey. That just happened. You and Joey are the first two to find out. I am genuinely as surprised as you are," I said, my voice filled with unexpected shock.

"Ha," he barked out a laugh. "You think I am surprised? I saw this coming a mile away."

"What the fuck? How?" I asked.

"Um, you are clearly obsessed with her. But if that wasn't enough, you told me you can smell it when she is turned on. All male orkin can smell when a female is ripe, but when it is your mate it is enough to drive you insane," he said knowingly. "You've been particularly insane in the last few weeks."

"And you didn't think to tell me?" I cried.

"I knew you'd figure it out eventually. It seems as if the kidnapping was enough to push you over the edge."

"What do you mean?" I asked with a huff.

"Well, sometimes mate marks just appear spontaneously, but they often appear when one mate senses the other is in danger," he explained. "I wouldn't be surprised if they showed up late last night."

"They did. Billie saw them when we were…" I trailed off.

"When you were fucking her?" He smirked.

"Must you be so crass?" I spit out.

"Would you call what you did last night 'tender lovemaking'?" he asked, giving me a withering stare.

He did have a point there. I dragged my fingers through my hair, my head still spinning. Mate. I had a mate.

If she'd have me.

"Well, what do I do now? Just sit around while she makes up her mind?" I asked plaintively

"Did you agree on anything?" He asked.

"She said she'd stay in the kitchen with Joey and Runa, working on mead and cocktail recipes so I can work on the bar and we can have some space from each other," I said, trying to keep the melancholy out of my voice. I didn't want to think about spending two days working without Billie, especially because I'd have to work with Tyr and Berit, whom I still wanted to strangle. I sighed.

"Think about it this way," Reykr said. "Work yourself to the bone to keep your mind off of it and so she'll be proud of how much you've accomplished when she returns."

While that didn't sound nearly as appealing as working alongside Billie, it was a solid plan.

"Okay, let's shower and head to the bar," I said.

"Shower, breakfast, then bar," Reykr corrected.

Realizing I hadn't eaten since the night before, I agreed.

Reykr and I arrived at the bar to find Tyr and Berit already there, looking terrified but working away. Osif and his crew were there as well. Good. We'd need every pair of hands to complete this in time for the equinox. Billie would have her bar in time for the celebration if I had to work myself to bone. I would prove to her that I was here to stay.

Osif ambled up to me. "Where's Billie?"

"My *mate* is spending time with Emla to learn how to make more drinks and finalize the menu," I growled. "We are going to finish the bar in her absence."

Osif raised his brows in surprise but didn't say anything.

"Alright, all," I called in a booming voice to get everyone's attention. "Billie is taking some time to focus on the menu and the drinks. We will finish the bar and make it absolutely perfect in time for the equinox."

I was met with a lot of muttering and even some eye-rolling from Osif's orkin when I heard another low voice growl behind me. "Do you all want to eat, drink, and be merry on the equinox, or do you still want to be working away while the rest of the tribe celebrates in the longhouse instead of the beautiful new bar we've restored?" Reykr crossed his arms in front of his hulking frame and gave them all a look that would have immediately brought me back to work.

There was some grumbling, but all the orkin returned to

their tasks. We were almost ready for the soft furnishings and the serving ware, but not quite. After ensuring everyone was working hard, I took it upon myself to sand and seal all the tables. Reykr joined me and we worked in silence for a long time before he finally said something.

"Do you want to talk about it?" he asked, not looking up from sanding.

I continued sanding. Did I want to talk about it?

I sighed. "She doesn't understand Elska mates. She's worried about us getting tired of each other. She said you don't go from 'dating' to being mates this quickly. I explained that it was normal here, but she said she still needed time. So I am giving it to her." I didn't stop working. It was easier to talk about without having to make eye contact.

"And how do you feel about that?" Still sanding.

"I want to give her time. I don't want her to feel like she has to choose me. I am finishing this bar whether or not she does. But it has to be her choice. I don't want anything with her if she doesn't want it with me," I said sadly, my gut twisting at the idea of finding my Elska mate only to have her snatched away. It felt almost cruel.

But I knew Billie. She wanted me, but she didn't understand. And she was scarred by all the pathetic human men in her past who didn't treat her like the treasure she was. I doubled my efforts on sanding, ensuring that the wood of every table was soft as silk under my fingers before sealing them. The day seemed to slip away. I paused to shove down a meat pie that Joey insisted I eat before I returned to work around midday. The sun was setting as I looked out at the lawn, admiring all the sanded and sealed tables.

Osif approached me. "Steve, I must let my orkin break for the last meal. They've worked hard all day. Some have families to return to."

I waved my hand at the workers. "That's fine." I raised my voice so it would reach everyone could hear me. "Thank you all for your hard work today. I know if we keep at it we can finish tomorrow!"

Instead of cheers, I got grumbles, but all the orkin agreed they'd be back early the next day. Soon, it was just me, Joey, and Reykr. They both assessed me in silence.

Joey was the first to speak. "You're going to stay working, aren't you?"

"Yep. Bram delivered all the glassware, cutlery, and such today. I am going to clean it and put it all away."

Joey sighed. "Then I'll stay, too. I'll wash, you dry?" She gave me a tired smile.

I almost hugged the tiny woman, but knowing her, she might kick me for even trying. "Thank you. I really appreciate it."

Reykr gave me a mock salute and headed out while Joey and I walked into the bar.

"I'm kind of surprised he didn't stay," I said as we entered the bar's kitchen.

Joey rolled her eyes. "He's going to get you food, you moron. I know you've forgotten you need food, but he hasn't."

I felt a blush creeping up my neck, embarrassed that I thought my best friend had left me in my time of need. "Right, right. That makes sense," I muttered. "Let's get to work."

We washed and washed and washed. By the time Reykr returned, we had finished all the glasses. I'd dried them and lined them perfectly along the shelves behind the bar so Billie could easily access them. Reykr forced me to sit on the floor of the bar and eat. I devoured everything without tasting it and stood to keep working.

"No," Reykr and Joey said in unison.

I opened my mouth to fight, but Reykr cut me off. "You're no use to her dead. I will ensure we finish tomorrow, but you are dead on your feet. Bed." He steered me toward our room.

He nodded at Joey as we headed out, and she gave him a small smile. I briefly felt bad for interrupting whatever plans they probably had with each other for the evening, but I was so tired the thought drifted out of my brain almost immediately. Reykr watched me hawkeyed as I changed out of my dirty clothes and climbed into bed. It felt heavenly. Reykr was still watching me as I sunk into a deep sleep, void of dreams.

BILLIE

It was still early when we arrived at Piper and Agnarr's house, nestled among the trees at the edge of the village. I knocked and waited. And waited. Joey and I shifted uncomfortably in the silence.

"It's too early for them to be at breakfast," Joey said. "Knock louder. Maybe they are still upstairs getting dressed."

I knocked again, this time with much more force. Another few minutes passed and then the door opened. We were greeted by a shirtless Agnarr, pants barely laced.

"Uhh, sorry if we woke you," I said awkwardly, "It's kind of an emergency."

"You didn't wake us," he said. "We were just…busy."

Jesus Christ, is everyone having sex today?

He led us into the dining room. "What kind of emergency is it? Was someone injured at the bar? It is early for you to be working." Agnarr looked concerned.

"Um, not that kind of emergency," I said.

I turned my back to him and pulled up my tunic.

"Well, well, well, what do we have here?" he asked, sounding incredibly pleased. "Who is the lucky orc?"

I dropped my tunic and turned back to him, blushing. "It's Steve."

"Ohhh, even better! We can use this to build relationships with the Snaerfírar. He's such a beloved member of his tribe. When I was there, they treated him with deference and respect. His parents were in high standing in the tribe. His taking a human mate will open up trade and diplomatic opportunities." Agnarr rubbed his hands together enthusiastically.

"Excuse me," I said tartly, "but I haven't said yes. If you recall, humans don't have fated mates. Finding out that someone you've been sleeping with for only a handful of days is now your *forever* is a lot to take in."

Agnarr's face flashed with concern before he said, "I understand. You'll need to talk to Piper, and I should probably talk to Steve. What did you tell him?"

"I told him I needed a couple of days to think about it and that I would stay in the kitchen while he worked on the bar."

"Does anyone else know?" Agnarr asked.

"Just Reykr," I said. Agnarr arched a brow. "They are best friends, and I can't expect him to handle this on his own. While I might be overwhelmed with the idea of forever, I can empathize with the anxiety he must be feeling at me wanting time to decide."

I wasn't a bitch. Well, only when I wanted to be. I decided to leave out how Reykr found out. Reykr and Joey were even more tenuous than Steve and me. Though I did have to admit to myself, my best friend dating my mate's best friend did sound pretty great.

"I will go to Steve and Reykr. I can also help them with the bar today. Piper should be down any moment, and you three can discuss how you want to proceed. Does that work?" he asked.

I felt relief flood through me. He wasn't mad. He wasn't expecting me to say yes or no. He was giving me all the tools I needed to make an informed decision. I felt better already. I sat down at one of the chairs at the dining table, ready to wait for Piper. Agnarr stared at us awkwardly for a moment.

"I'm just going to go finish getting dressed. I am sure Piper will be here any minute," he said very quickly as he headed back up the stairs.

Joey and I burst out laughing as soon as Agnarr had left the room. We'd definitely interrupted Piper and Agnarr's morning sex. Not too long after Piper arrived. She didn't look embarrassed at all. She was fully dressed, and her hair was freshly braided.

"I knew you'd expect me to take awhile, you know, what with all the cum." She waved her hand vaguely toward Agnarr.

I snorted, and Joey let out a laugh that could only be described as hysterical.

"So Agnarr tells me there is some sort of female emergency going on?" she asked, looking suspicious. "I'm not sure I believe it's an emergency if you two are involved, knowing the shenanigans you get up to in the kitchen and the bar. Wasn't it just a few weeks ago you were throwing furniture out a second-story window?"

"Oh, it's very much an emergency." Joey's eyes widened as she nodded and nudged me to start explaining.

I said nothing but stood and pulled up the back of my tunic. Immediately, I felt Piper's finger tracing the markings down my spine.

"Wow, yours are so different than mine. Is it Steve?" she asked.

I whipped around, "How did you know it was Steve?"

"Um, you used Agnarr as a cover-up to go have sex in the berry bushes. You thought that wouldn't get back to him? Also, we both know everything that happens around here." Piper crossed her arms matter-of-factly.

I opened my mouth to say something, then closed it. I wasn't sure what else there was to say.

"So what is the emergency?" she asked.

"Well, I haven't said yes," I said.

"Ohh, I see," she responded sympathetically. "Scared of forever?"

I wrung my hands. Piper was spot on.

"We just don't have anything like this on Earth," I said anxiously. "What if we get tired of each other? Or want to separate?" I worried about this, too.

"My parents are divorced, and I knew so many people in unhappy marriages. I thought I always wanted forever, but now here it was, a hulking, sensitive, kind orc, standing right in front of me—I was scared. But I don't know if it is Nifl-heim, or the orkin, or just a magic we don't understand, but the Elska bond felt very real. I have never connected with someone the way I connect with Agnarr. It is almost as if I know what he feels before he tells me. I don't even like being apart from him." Piper exhaled, then asked, "How's the sex?"

"Wh-what?" I spluttered.

"Oh, come on now, we both know you're no prude. How's the sex?" she asked again.

I didn't need to think twice. "The best I've ever had. Head and shoulders above any human dude."

"And you didn't find it odd that Steve, who was purportedly a virgin when he showed up here, was giving you mind-blowing sex?" she sassed.

"Jesus, you really do everything that goes on around here," I said, shocked.

"It's part of my job." She shrugged.

I thought about what Piper said. It *was* odd that the sex was so fantastic with someone who had no experience. I just thought he was a quick learner—with an amazing cock.

"So," Piper continued, "the sex is amazing, the bond is real, whether or not we understand it, and I am guessing Steve is all in? Is he happy to move here?"

"Yes, he's all in. And he said he feels more at home here than he ever felt at Snaerfírar."

Piper looked thoughtful before brushing a whisp of hair from her face. "Well, then, what are you waiting for?"

"I don't know. I just can't say yes to this without having some time to untangle it in my brain. You didn't say yes right away," I accused.

"You're right. I didn't. Take some time. But try not to kill poor Steve."

I stood without even thinking about it and started to head to the door. Joey went to follow me.

"Hang on there, Joey. You and I need to chat about a particular older orkin with a tough exterior?" Piper gave her a knowing look.

Joey's jaw dropped, but she stopped walking. I grinned to myself before waving to both of them. "See ya later."

I left Piper and Agnarr's house and headed toward the kitchen, my head feeling heavy. I rubbed my temples. This was a lot to think about this early in the morning. If I were back on Earth, I would still be asleep. I was groggy and overwhelmed. What was I going to do about Steve? He wanted forever, but I knew how "forever" could turn out for the people with the best intentions—even for couples who seemed made for each other. Divorce. Unhappiness.

I was surprised to find myself already at the kitchen doors. I pushed them open and was greeted by the normal morning crew with enthusiastic hellos. I plastered on a smile and asked if Runa was in her office. Receiving several affirmations, I headed to her door. It was open and she was looking over a giant stack of disorganized papers.

"Hi." I tried to sound chipper.

"I'm surprised to see you here, Billie. Shouldn't you be working on the bar?" she asked without looking up. "Summer equinox is only two days away."

I sighed. I would have to tell her. "I need to spend some time away from the bar. I don't think it will be ready for the equinox, and the tribe will have to live with it. We'll celebrate it a few days late."

Emla raised her brows at me. "You think the tribe will be okay with that?"

"Well, they'll have to be. I have some thinking to do about what I want before I finish," I said plainly. I didn't have any more to offer.

"So you've come here to think?" Emla looked even more skeptical.

"Not just think. I thought maybe I could practice some cocktails while I mulled things over. I would love to offer more than just mead when the bar opens."

"And you want me to help teach you how to make cocktails?" She crossed her arms in front of her chest and squinted at me as if she could figure out why I was really here if she stared hard enough.

"Only if you have time." My words tumbled out, anxious

that she'd tell me I would be better off spending time in the bar.

"Of course, I have the time." Emla rubbed her eyes with her thumb and index finger, "But eventually, you'll have to tell me why you're really here."

Buoyed by her agreement, I was able to say, "Maybe."

Emla stood and ushered me over to a far corner of the kitchen, grabbing a bowl of fruit I didn't recognize on the way.

She placed the fruit, a knife, and a cutting board on the counter before me. "Cut these into quarters. All of them. Then maybe you'll be ready to talk, and we can start making cocktails."

She walked away before I even had a chance to object. Grumbling, I grabbed one of the fruits and started quartering it. It looked like a cross between a lime and a grapefruit. I tentatively licked one of the quarters. Sour but not bad. More lime than grapefruit. I started thinking about the cocktails I could make from home with this lime-type fruit.

I mulled it over, but after about the tenth piece of fruit, my mind wandered back to Steve. I circled around the same question over and over. Was I ready for forever? I didn't have an answer. I pulled myself one way, then the other, thinking about happy couples and unhappy couples I knew. People I knew that were divorced and people that were happily married for twenty plus years. How could I ensure that we fell in line with the latter? I was nowhere close to an answer when Emla showed up to teach me some cocktails.

She brought several different jugs with her. Some seemed to be liquor, the others juices and mixers. I had fun trying different options with her but stayed tight-lipped about Steve. Eventually, the time for the last meal approached. Emla wordlessly produced a tray of food and shooed me on my way. She could sense I was in no mood to socialize. I headed back to my cabin and ate my dinner in silence.

I didn't have the brainpower to think about anything anymore. I finished my meal and lay back on my bed. It wasn't long before I felt tears welling in my eyes. Silent tears turned into hiccuping sobs. I wanted a clear-cut answer of what to do, but there didn't seem to be one. I drifted off as I cried, exhausted from a day spent overthinking.

CHAPTER TWENTY-SEVEN

BILLIE

My head was heavy with exhaustion—I hadn't slept well. I lay awake until the sky started to lighten with the sun's rays. I spent my second day in the kitchen, much like the first, thinking about Steve from every angle and not coming up with a solution. I shook my head and grabbed a second cup of tea that didn't remotely resemble coffee but did seem to have caffeine—or the alien equivalent of it. I was chopping different fruits and macerating others in preparation for my second cocktail lesson.

Yesterday, I successfully created two cocktails that Runa assured me orkin would like but were distinctively me. If I got another two down pat today, I would have a solid menu for when we opened—if we opened. I hadn't let my mind wander to the progress on the bar, and I wasn't about to start now. Runa would be here any moment, expecting me to have prepared all the ingredients for our cocktail lesson.

I went back to cutting fruit. Unfortunately, I was halving

the same berries Steve and I had picked together, incredibly unsuccessfully. I wondered what he was doing. Was he working on the bar like he said? Or was he just as distraught as I was? I felt like my heart was in my throat as I thought about the pain I was putting him through, and either the knife slipped, or I wasn't paying attention, but I slit right through the tip of my index finger, where I'd been holding the berry.

I looked at my finger briefly as if it wasn't my own. Blood was rapidly starting to flow, but I didn't feel any pain. It all felt surreal. Without much thought, I raised my hand over my head, dropping the bloody knife on the cutting board. I walked to Runa's office in a daze, barely aware of the blood starting to trickle down my arm. I stood in Runa's doorway and quietly waited for her attention. I didn't want to interrupt. By the time she looked up from her paperwork, I had blood dripping into my armpit.

Runa jumped up with more speed than I thought she was capable of and rushed to me. "What the hell happened, girl?" She pulled my finger down and quickly wrapped it in one of the cloth napkins stacked by her office.

Oh, that made sense. Wrap it and then raise it above your head. I forgot about that part.

"Go fetch Emla and tell her to meet us in Billie's room," she snapped at a kitchen worker walking by. "Tell her to bring supplies for stitching."

The orc looked startled but took off immediately. Runa applied pressure to my finger with the cloth napkin and steered me out of the kitchen toward my room.

I felt tears welling up in my eyes. "But what about the cocktails and the bar?"

"Honey, I think it is time for you to admit that you are in no place to open a bar while you are still deciding your future." Runa wrapped one arm around my waist, keeping the hand on my finger and marched me to my bedroom at an alarming pace.

When we arrived, Emla stood at my door. She wordlessly opened it and ushered us both inside. Runa sat me in my armchair while Emla pulled up a footstool and placed her bag of supplies on the floor. She quickly laid everything out on my bedside table. I recognized everything you would need to stitch someone up, with the exception of a vial of amber-colored liquid. She pulled the stopper out with her teeth and poured about a shot's worth into the glass I kept at my bedside.

She handed it to me, and I took it with my uninjured hand. "Drink it down quick. It tastes awful."

I examined it skeptically. "What is it?"

"It will help with the pain. Do you want to feel me stitch up your finger?" she asked gruffly.

I swallowed it down immediately, feeling it burn my throat. "Emla, have you ever tried this on humans?" I sputtered.

"You are the first human to be silly enough to require stitches." She didn't even look up from my hand she was now unwrapping. "Oh, this isn't terrible. I say three to four stitches at most."

As she cleaned my finger, I realized I couldn't feel it at all. There was a part of my mind that found that terrifying, but it seemed to be smothered by whatever drug she'd given me. I watched, detached, as she sewed three neat stitches into my finger before covering it with salve and a bandage. She collected all of her supplies and placed them back in her bag.

She assessed me, now slumped in the chair, barely able to keep my eyes open. "It makes orkin a bit groggy. It looks like you may need to lie down for a while." She turned and left with a detachment that only came from years of working in medicine.

Runa helped me remove my shoes and tucked me into bed. As I drifted into a dreamless sleep, my last thought was how worried Steve would be.

I opened my eyes to find myself in the predawn quiet, much like I had the day before. It took me a minute to figure out why I'd slept in my clothes. As I strung together the previous day's events, I jumped out of bed. I told Steve I would meet him at the bar before anyone else arrived. I brushed my teeth but left my mane wild. I looked like an anxious lion, but I didn't care. I didn't want Steve to think I didn't care about our meeting today. That was the last thing I wanted. My stomach churned at the idea of him not knowing what he meant to me. As the bar came into my vision, I saw an orc— my orc— standing on a ladder, carefully hanging colorful pendants across the front of the bar.

From the outside, my bar was a vision. Everything was done. Someone had even added beautiful window boxes with flowers spilling out of them. Above the double doors hung an engraved sign, which had to have been made by Osif, that said *Billie's Bar* in a beautiful scrawl. I wondered if Joey helped him with the spelling. I took in the entire scene, my beautiful bar with Steve, in the early morning light, adding the final touches. I watched Steve continue to hang the pendants and realized I was holding my breath. I wanted him off the ladder.

I didn't want to startle him, so I called quietly, "Steve?"

He swung around on the ladder too quickly for my liking but didn't fall. "Oh, it's you!" He broke into a smile that nearly took up his entire face. Fuck, he was so… swoonworthy. He quickly descended the ladder and then turned to me, still smiling. But his smile faltered as I stood there, twisting my fingers in front of me. Right. I already had his answer, and he was waiting for mine.

While I fucked around in the kitchen, Steve must have worked day and night to get my bar going. All of it. For me. Even down to the little pendants he was hanging before the day was warm. I wondered what he'd done with the inside. He wasn't just telling me he was here to stay, he was showing me. He finished our bar and our home. I was wavering back and forth about the future and he was showing me he was here, ready for right now.

Something inside me snapped. I sprinted to him, throwing myself into his open arms and wrapping my legs around his waist and my arms around his neck. I buried my face in his shoulder.

"Steve," I whispered, "I've been so focused on the future I forgot to consider right now. I don't want a life without you in it, whatever future may come." My voice was choked with emotion as tears started to fill my eyes.

Steve attempted to run his fingers through my hair, instead getting them tangled in my wild curls. I leaned back, tears sliding down my cheeks, to be able to look Steve in the eye.

I expected concern or frustration, but he was still smiling. "Billie," he said, his deep voice gentle, "I know the idea of forever scares you, but we have the rest of our lives to figure it out. You are all that I want."

I nodded, still crying, and pulled myself in for a sloppy, wet kiss. We clung to each other for a moment. I kissed from his lips down his neck, savoring his scent. I was home.

STEVE

I loosened my grip on Billie, allowing her to slide down me and plant her feet on the ground. "Are you sure?" I was sure, but I wanted to check in one more time.

Billie nodded vigorously, shaking her beautiful wild curls as she did. "Very, very sure."

I took her hand and pulled her toward the double doors of her bar—or maybe now it was our bar? "Do you want to see inside?" I asked, unable to keep the excitement out of my voice.

"You finished the inside, too?" she squeaked as I pulled her along.

"Of course, I finished the inside, too! What would be the point of working on this for all hours of the night if the inside wasn't ready?" I yanked the doors open and ushered Billie inside.

The inside of the bar was pristine. The brand-new windows let in an abundance of sunshine, and all of the wooden surfaces gleamed in the early morning light. Piper had handled all of the soft furnishings, ensuring that each window had curtains and a padded bench in front of it. I'd arranged all the glassware and alcohol behind the bar. Joey and Osif had written the menu above it—one in English and one in Orkin—since our mysterious ability to understand each other didn't seem to extend to the written word. After taking it all in, I wanted Billie's response. This would be our last time alone here for a while.

She stood there, still clinging to my hand, smiling, with tears streaming down her face. "Steve, how did you finish it all?" she asked in wonder, still gazing around the bar.

"Hard work. And help from the tribe. We owe a huge thanks to Osif, Joey, Piper, and Reykr. And Berit and Tyr, actually. But I think they were mostly trying to make up for kidnapping you." I grinned ruefully. "But it was worth it. Worth it for my mate. Worth it for you."

Billie's already watering eyes got even wider. "Mate, my mate," she whispered.

"Upstairs is all done too, if you want to—" I cleared my voice meaningfully—"*see* it before everyone arrives?"

Billie wordlessly raced to the stairs, pulling her tunic off as she went. I didn't hesitate to follow, quickly removing my own tunic. I marveled at the curve of her ass as I chased her up the stairs. This was our life.

CHAPTER TWENTY-EIGHT

BILLIE

It was only after Steve roughly took me up against the wall that I got to take a look around our new home. I cleaned up in our washroom and noticed a new colorful mat in front of the sink. When I exited, I actually looked around the living space. It was only one room, but it was spacious. A giant four-poster bed was in one corner, piled with soft blankets and pillows. It was so large I was a bit stunned, but then I remembered—orc mate. Very large orc mate.

The kitchen area had a round table with four chairs and a new sofa and coffee table in front of the fireplace. Everything I could think of was here. And what stunned me even more was that it was all to my taste. This must have been Piper and Joey. I was still taking it all in when Steve arrived at the top of the stairs. I had been wondering where he went while I was cleaning up.

He handed me my tunic, smiling. "I figured you would want to put this on before the rest of the team showed up."

"Thank you." I pulled it over my head, careful of the giant bun I'd tied my hair up in.

"Are you ready?" Steve asked, noticing all the emotions I was feeling: nervousness, excitement, overwhelm, and giddy.

"I guess we're about to find out." I grabbed his hands and kissed each of his knuckles. "Thank you. Thank you for all of this. For the bar. For waiting. For understanding why I needed time." Tears started again. "Thank you so much."

"Anything for you. And everything." Steve pulled me into a hug. "This is just the beginning of surprises."

"What else could you possibly have planned?" I gasped.

"You'll find out soon enough." He smirked at me with his brows raised.

"Gah, how am I supposed to focus on our big day when I know you have more surprises in store?" I scrunched up my face in a mock pout.

"I am sure you'll manage," was all he said as he headed downstairs.

The rest of the day passed in a blur. Joey, Reykr, Piper, and even Agnarr showed up before anyone else. The rest of the building crew arrived about an hour later, including Tyr and Berit. By midday, everything was prepped and ready for the entire tribe to celebrate the equinox at the refurbished bar. I stood behind the bar top, chewing my lip, waiting for everyone to arrive. Reykr, Steve, Joey, and I were going to bartend. Piper was in the back with a kitchen crew that had shown up—a gift from Runa.

I guess Agnarr was being jarl by standing ready at the doors. "Are you ready?"

I looked at my team, all smiles. "Yep, we're ready!"

Agnarr flung open the double doors and walked out into

the lawn. "Come one, come all to celebrate the equinox!" he yelled in a booming voice.

I had expected orkin and humans to trickle in, but it was as if they had been waiting. The bar was packed to the gills instantly. I went into autopilot. Mead, cocktail, cocktail, more mead. I was soon sticky with drink and grinning like an idiot. All of the girls hugged me and tried to buy me a drink. I refused, knowing I'd be working until the last patron left, but I cheered them on as they all took a shot of orkin liquor that tasted kind of like the gross cinnamon whiskey all the kids drank back home.

The mood in the bar was electric, with orkin and humans alike buying each other drinks and celebrating. It was almost midnight, and the mood had reached a fever pitch where everyone was drunk but not too drunk. I was pouring Agnarr another mead when Steve snuck up behind me and grabbed me around the waist. I shrieked.

"It's time to go," he whispered in my ear.

"Go? Go where?" I turned around to look at him brows raised in disbelief.

"My next surprise." He grinned at me mischievously.

"We can't leave the bar on opening night!" I insisted, practically stamping my foot.

Steve looked down the bar at Reykr and caught his eye. Reykr nodded and before I knew what was happening, Steve lifted me off the ground and carried me over his shoulder like a rag doll. He walked out from behind the bar top through the crowd, which was now all cheering madly. Clearly, they knew something I didn't.

"Thank you for tonight," Steve boomed. "We will be back in three days. Joey and Reykr will hold down the fort while we are gone. Try not to burn the place down." Steve saluted Rekyr, then turned to open the double doors and walked us out into the night.

Steve walked in silence for a moment, ignoring all of the questions I peppered him with. *Where are we going? Who is going to take care of the bar?* All fell on deaf ears.

When he finally put me down, I was surprised to find myself on the saddle of a hestr.

"Where could we possibly be going in the middle of the night?" I demanded.

Steve pulled my cloak from a saddle bag and wrapped it around me, buttoning it under my chin, before swinging himself up behind me. "Um, I believe I asked a question," I said. Actually, I asked several."

Steve finally broke his silence. "Agnarr explained the ceremonial pools to me. And the mating frenzy. He assured me the bar would operate smoothly while we were gone, with Reykr and Joey at the head."

I opened my mouth to fight him and realized I had no fight in me. Three days alone with Steve? Three days to explore each other, commit to each other, and solidify our relationship? It was probably the most thoughtful thing a partner had ever done for me—outside of building me a bar.

"Okay." I leaned into his warm body.

"Okay?" His voice came from behind me, tinged with surprise.

"I trust you. It seems like you thought of everything, let's go to the pools."

Now, over the shock of it all, I was delighted. It felt like the orkin version of a honeymoon. I never expected a honeymoon. Steve was going to kill me with his thoughtfulness.

We quickly left the village and followed the well-worn path amongst the giant furutré, lined with glowing mushrooms. Everything was beautiful and magical in the low light. This quiet journey on my *honeymoon* was more than I ever expected. I had a mate. A husband? That was a bridge to cross. Piper had a wedding, but that was more of a show of unity for the tribe. I wasn't sure if it was something I needed.

We traveled in silence, with me leaning my weight against Steve, wrapped in his scent and warmth. Not wanting to be caught in the forest at night, I tried tamping down my desire for him and focused on the journey. I shifted my weight so I wasn't pressing so heavily against Steve's cock, telling myself I would get plenty of it later. However, as the night wore on, I could feel Steve's impatience—and his cock—growing.

"How far are we?" I asked, rubbing my ass up and down the length of his cock.

"If we gallop? Less than an hour," he said, grinding against me.

"She's been going at a steady pace. I think she could gallop for a bit. We could reward her with some apples after," I said.

Steve didn't need any convincing. He pressed his knees into the hestr, urging her forward. She moved from a steady trot to a gallop, seemingly unbothered. Steve kissed up and down my neck, messaging my breasts, his cock fully hard against my ass. Our hestr hurdled toward it as if knowing we needed to meet our destination. She came to an abrupt halt outside the caves, and Steve was thoughtful enough to lay down an enormous amount of grain for her before scooping me up.

"Billie, I can't wait any longer," he whispered in my ear. "My cock is going to erupt at the mere thought of you."

I dragged him into the caves, pleased to find there were beds *and* a hot spring. There were springs of various depths and sizes in the center of the caverns. The walls were lined with rooms carved out for a bed, a washroom, and one that looked like just supplies. I only had one thing on my mind: making Steve come.

We headed to the bedroom, and I disrobed immediately,

Steve following suit. His dark green cock was more swollen than I had ever seen it and was leaking copiously at the tip.

"On the bed," I breathed.

He clambered up wordlessly, spreading himself out before me. I'd seen his cock before, but for the love of God, it was magnificent. Textured and knotted and *almost* too big. I knelt before him and took his entire cockhead into my mouth, sucking it ravenously. He tasted salty and sweet, and I wanted more. I hollowed my cheeks, sucking him in as deeply as I could.

"Billie." He pulled me gently up by my hair. "I need to eat too." His eyes were dark pools of unmasked hunger.

Oh. *Oh.* "Do you want to—" I paused.

Surely, Steve wouldn't even know what sixty-nine meant. I had only ever done it a few times. Being a curvy girl, I always felt self-conscious about sitting on someone's face. Honestly, I didn't believe girls who said they weren't. It felt so... exposed. I was lost in my own train of thought about face-sitting when Steve took matters into his own hands. He dug his hands into my hips and lifted me over him, settling one knee on either side of his head, which spread me wide upon on top of him. I pitched forward in shock as his tongue snaked out and plunged deep into my core before licking up and down each fold methodically. So this is what it was going to be like having a partner? Someone who cared about me as much as I cared about them?

I shuddered under his touch, already inching toward combustion when I gathered my senses and realized if I leaned forward just a bit, I could pull the head of his cock into my mouth while working the rest of it with my fist. I lapped at the slit at the head of Steve's cock, while stroking him up and down enthusiastically. All the while, I felt warmth spreading out from my core as Steve switched to sucking on my clit and delving two fingers in and out of me.

I had to pause licking his cock because I was panting so hard and trying my damnedest not to grind against his face. I felt my whole body locking up as he rhythmically pumped in and out of me with his thick fingers and laved at my clit with his wonderous tongue.

"Steve," I panted.

"Just let go, stop worrying," he said, barely stopping what he was doing to respond.

I let myself collapse on him, and he pulled my thighs even tighter around his face. With his mouth on my clit and his fingers inside me had me feeling like my whole body was sped up and quickly running toward the edge.

"Steve, fuck, oh fuck. Oh, it's too much. I can't—" I gasped, starting to feel like I might burst.

Steve may as well have been deaf because he continued with the same rhythm and pace, unrelenting. My vision started to grow hazy, and then I felt my whole body lock up as I combusted. I felt myself gush all over his face. Steve removed his fingers and continued to lap at me gently, cleaning me and, from the sounds he was making, savoring the taste of me. I felt entirely boneless as I came down, panting heavily. I'd never come that hard in my life.

As my vision returned, I realized Steve's hard and dripping cock was still inches from my face. I had just entirely failed at sixty-nining. I started to pull myself up on shaky arms and legs.

"Steve, I'm so sorry I didn't even get you to finish," I said, suddenly embarrassed.

I clambered over him and sat next to him where he lay in bed with a giant grin on his face, his lips and chin still shining with my juices.

"Are you kidding me?" he laughed. "I just saw you come completely undone from my fingers and mouth alone. I'd do it again now if I thought you could take it."

He reached out and stroked down my side. I contemplated our options. Then, a lightbulb went off in my head.

"I think I am a little too overstimulated to do *that* again, but I do have something else we could try," I said, giving him a mischievous grin.

"Oh?" he said, looking intrigued.

"Go get some of those oils lining the edge of the pool," and I directed, "and I'll be ready for you when you get back."

CHAPTER TWENTY-NINE

STEVE

I left Billie thoroughly sated on the bed, and headed to the hot springs. She was right. Numerous bottles of oils and soaps lined the edge of the pool. I grabbed the oil, wondering what she had in store for us. I returned to find a scene nothing short of perfection. Billie was spread out on the bed, knees bent, with each of her hands massaging her nipples. Wordlessly, she reached out a hand, taking the bottle into her hands.

"Climb over me," she directed.

I swung my leg over her hips, ready to mount her, rutting into her until I filled her with my seed, but it seemed she had something slightly different in mind.

"Scoot up higher," she said, opening the bottle of oil.

I shifted upward so my legs were on either side of her torso, my cock shamelessly leaking all over her amazing breasts. Billie poured some oil onto her hand and then stroked me up and down until I was glistening. Then, to my surprise, she wiped the remainder of the oil onto her breasts and tossed the bottle aside. She looked up at me, eyes hooded with lust, and took my cock into her hand. She positioned it into the valley between her breasts, then used both hands to press her breasts together, with my cock trapped between them. It was all finally starting to click together.

"Billie, you want me to... fuck your breasts?" I asked uncertainly.

"That's exactly what I want you to do, Steve," she said, pressing them more firmly together. "Look at these babies. It would be a waste not to," she said, pressing them more firmly together.

I couldn't ignore how amazing it felt to have my cock slide up and down between her oiled skin. I tentatively thrust into her the same I would her cunt. It felt different, but I had zero complaints. I slid in and out again, this time going a bit further, with my knot brushing along the undersides of her breasts. It wasn't long before I was thrusting up and down with vigor, my knot blissfully reaching further and further with each thrust.

Billie watched me with a pleased grin on her face while she fondled her nipples. Then, it was time for another surprise. This time, as I thrust forward, Billie dipped her chin down and licked my leaking tip before I pulled back. I gasped. Billie looked very pleased with herself.

"Is this something that humans do with each other?" I asked.

"Is it something you want to do with me?" she asked.

I nodded vigorously.

"Then it doesn't matter what humans do. It's just you and me from now on, babe."

Thinking of it being just the two of us forever was heady and overwhelming. I wanted all of Billie. I thrust again, and this time she took the entire head of my cock into her mouth and sucked down on it before releasing me. She repeated this again and again as I slid up and down her until I couldn't take it anymore. I felt my balls tighten and tingle at the base of my spine as I hurtled toward completion. As my cock started to thicken even more, Billie pulled the tip of it into her mouth, swirling her tongue around it and the underside of the head. I couldn't even warn Billie as I unleashed rope after rope of thick cum into her mouth, but she drank it down, continuing to suck me until she could take no more, releasing me to finish coming across her chest.

I leaned back to see Billie, my Billie, my Elska mate, covered in my shimmering cum, smiling up at me. I couldn't help but smile back. I didn't know what I had done to deserve this happiness, but I would take it and hang onto it with all I had. I peppered kisses down the side of Billie's face, nipping on the lobe of her ear.

BILLIE

Steve scooped me up and carried me to the hot springs from the bed. I could really get used to being carried around by my giant orc mate. He made me feel positively dainty. He walked into the springs carefully, finding his footing as he went. As we neared the pool's center, we were in water up to his chest, and I was almost completely submerged in his arms. He gently sent me down. It took me a minute to find my feet, realizing if I wanted to keep my head above water, I would have to stand on my tiptoes.

The spring was delightfully warm, with a light cloud of steam shrouding the air around it in an almost magical mist. I trod water over to the pool's edge, sampling the different bottles and potions neatly lined up next to a stack of fluffy towels. I picked up a light pink one and popped it open. It smelled almost like jasmine. Wondering what it would do, I poured some of it into the water. I gasped as the water immediately started to bubble up—spreading quickly.

"Steve!" I called.

By the time he looked at me, I was completely surrounded by bubbles. This was like a bubble bath on crack. The bubbles just kept growing. I started giggling, and Steve let out a booming laugh as he waded over toward me.

"Did you dump the whole bottle in?" He continued to laugh.

"No!" I said indignantly. "Just a few drops!"

"Well, it smells amazing, but I can't say that I am a fan," he said, brow cocked.

"What do you have against bubble baths?" I laughed, scooping up bobbles with both hands and blowing them toward him.

"It's not that I dislike the bubbles. It is that they block my view of your beautiful body."

Well, now I was going to melt into a puddle of goo. I looked down to see my body was, indeed, completely blocked from Steve's view.

"You have a lifetime of seeing all of me to look forward to," I assured him as I swam over.

I took some more bubbles into my hands and started soaping up and down Steve's arms, enjoying the feeling of his corded muscles. I stroked my hands up, rubbing the soap across his collarbone and down his powerful pectoral muscles, and I felt goosebumps rising on his skin as I touched him. Then I worked my way down his stomach, working the soap in circles, admiring his green skin.

Steve cleared his throat as I shifted to massaging soap down his stomach. "Um, can I clean you while you clean me?"

"I would love that," I said, not taking my eyes off his chest.

Steve scooped up some of the magical bubbles and started massaging the soap into my shoulders. As his fingers pressed into my muscles, I moaned. He wasn't just washing me. He was massaging me. He kneaded my shoulders gently, utterly distracting me from cleaning his stomach. I let my arms fall to my sides as he worked each shoulder gently. Steve took a step closer so he could massage up my neck, and I felt his erection prod into my stomach. Steve said nothing, still attending to my sore muscles.

"Your ringlets frame your face beautifully in the damp air," he whispered into my ear as he slid his hands down from my neck to my tits.

I blushed. Growing up, I hated my curly hair, straightening it within an inch of its life during my emo phase of the early 2010s, but I had grown to love it as an adult. It was wild and untamed, and I liked that it reflected that part of me. The idea that Steve liked it made warmth pool in my belly.

"Thank you," I responded, trying to get back to washing Steve's stomach.

But now he was plucking at my nipples, gently pinching them, his erection growing much more insistent. I wrapped my arms around his neck, and Steve hoisted me up even higher, so he could take a nipple into his mouth, licking and sucking it. I wrapped my legs around his waist, feeling his cock pressed between us. We were not going to finish this bath. Steve drew on one of my nipples while working the other between his thumb and forefinger. It wasn't long before I was panting. I wanted him. I had never wanted someone this often and this badly. I reached in between us and pumped his cock up and down, marveling at his girth and texture. This cock was *mine,* and I had so many plans for it.

I shifted myself up higher in the water so I could stroke Steve's cockhead up and down my slit. "Can we—how do you want to?" I asked, my mind muddled with need.

"There's a built-in seat around the edge of the pool," Steve said, pausing the gentle tugs he'd been giving my nipple with his teeth.

He headed to the edge of the pool while I kissed up and down his neck. Steve reached the bench and settled with my knees on either side of his hips. I reached down and stroked his cock up and down again, slipping a thumb over his tip. I pulled him toward me, rubbing his cock in circles around my clit, but it wasn't enough.

"Are you ready to go again?" I whispered into his ear while dragging my fingers along the underside of his cockhead.

"I think that's fairly obvious," he gasped as I wrapped my hand firmly around his knot, squeezing it.

I notched him at my core and slowly began to slide down. I knew that water could mess with natural lubricant, so I didn't want to ram myself down on him immediately. I slowly slid down his length, feeling him breach each layer of me as I settled myself deeper. When I felt myself hit his knot, I let out a gasp. I was stuffed so full I could feel every ridge and pattern of his cock. I breathed in through my nose, readying myself to take all of him. I pulled him in for a kiss, hoping to loosen myself up by touching him in other ways. I tugged on his lower lip with my teeth, causing him to open up for me. Our tongues tangled together, learning each other, all while he was buried deep inside me. I wrapped my legs around his waist, allowing me to sink down even deeper. I felt his knot press against my core and couldn't hold out any longer.

I slid off him almost completely before slamming my hips down into his, taking all but the knot, which pressed against my lower lips. I gasped at the way he filled me. This wasn't the vague fullness I was used to. I could feel every ridge, vein, and texture of Steve's cock. The fact that this was the sex I had just signed onto for life was at the forefront of my mind. Steve gripped my hips, taking control. He slid me up and down off his marvelous cock, my tits bouncing in front of him.

"Billie," he gasped, "I need more."

He wanted to go deeper. Thinking quickly, I grabbed one of the towels, laid it next to the pool, and then got on my hands and knees.

"Here," I said, "take me here."

Steve scrambled out of the water and joined me on the towel, where I was ready, on my hands and knees. He took no time finding my weeping slit and dragging his cock up and down it.

"Stop toying with me and fuck me like you mean it," I ground out, ready to have Steve fill me completely.

He stopped teasing my clit and lined his cock up at my entrance. He pressed in slowly, causing me to gasp at each inch he pressed further in. I spread my legs wider, leaning on my forearms to give him better access. His warm hands massaged my ass cheeks, pulling me wider to accommodate him.

"Fuck, Steve, you feel so good," I gasped as he continued to bury himself in me.

He continued to massage my ass cheeks as he slid in even deeper.

"You feel—incredible," he said, breathing through his nose.

I could tell it was taking all of his willpower not to ram into me completely. He inched in further and further until I felt his knot graze the lips of my pussy. He wrapped himself around me, pressing his chest to my back.

"Is this okay?" he asked.

"Mmm… Your cock is amazing," I moaned.

Steve grasped each of my hips with his enormous hands and started to thrust in and out of me at a slow, steady pace. I felt pleasure spider out from my core until I could barely hold myself up, having to drop down from my forearms and lay on the towel as he pushed in and out of me methodically. Every thrust felt as if it unleashed something deeper within me, and it wasn't long before I was panting Steve's name.

"Steve! Fuck. Harder! Fuck me harder!" I screamed as he pumped steadily in and out of me.

I felt his thick fingers dig deeper into my hips as he ratcheted up the pace, thrusting in and out of me with all he had. Having come multiple times over, it wasn't long before I was able to take his knot. Spreading my lower lips wide, he slid in with a pop and out as he continued to thrust. I was on sensory overload and didn't know how to respond. I was panting at the onslaught of sensation. I felt myself building toward a climax, but it was too soon. I wasn't ready to be done. I wanted to savor this with Steve. I let my head rest on the towel as he continued to pump in and out of me, loving every moment. I relaxed into Steve, enjoying the drag of his cock against my channel. He felt exquisite, and it took all my willpower not to barrel toward my climax immediately. As Steve stroked in and out of me, he arched over me, grasping one of my breasts in his hand. It was almost too much to bear; I was panting so much that I needed water.

"Water, I need water," I gasped.

Steve slid out of me and brought a cup out of nowhere so I could gulp down some hydration. I tossed the cup aside as he crouched over me again, dipping into me seamlessly. He continued his steady stroking in and out, increasing his pace as he approached his finish. My entire body felt as if it was a live wire that he stroked back and forth with each thrust. I locked down on him, swept up in the crescendo of pleasure. I came and came screaming his name. How did every time feel better than the last? I felt like a wrung-out sponge, completely lifeless.

Finally, I felt Steve take one final plunge, taking me as deep as he could, pushing his knot deep into me. He exploded ribbon after ribbon of cum inside of me as I fell face-first into the towel. I treasured that he was the only one to ever come inside me as I felt my insides gush with his hot cum. He guided me down to our sides so we could lay locked together. Steve wrapped his much larger frame around me as he continued to pulse inside me. My heart was beating so rapidly, and my breath was coming so fast it would take me a minute to come down from the high. I was going to need to be better about hydration if this is what sex was going to be like.

After some time, lying in comfortable silence, a thought cropped up in my mind. "Are you... does Snaerfírar do the ceremonial braiding?"

"Já, a mated male, always has his hair in plaits," he said from behind me.

"Well, then, it's time." I shifted and found Steve's knot softened enough for me to slide off it.

Copious amounts of cum dribbled out of me, but I didn't care. We could bathe in the magical bubbles later.

Steve sat up as I knelt behind him and delicately combed through his damp hair.

"Do you have any preferences?" I asked.

"I want everyone to know I am yours. Beyond that, I don't care," he said.

For our first time around, I settled for a simple French braid; I could get more creative as time went on. I plaited his hair easily, having grown up with sisters. As I finished, I looked at him and admired his profile.

"A mated male," I said, "No one will doubt it."

STEVE

Once Billie finished braiding my hair, I pulled her into my lap. I kissed every inch of her face, stopping with the tip of her nose. She said nothing but gave a happy sigh and snuggled into me further. I wrapped my arm around her waist and pulled her as close to me as our bodies would allow. Having her braid my hair felt like a surreal finish to our evening. However, there was one tiny doubt in the back of my mind.

"Was that—was that okay?" I knew all signs pointed toward her enjoying herself, but I was still new at this. I wanted to make sure I checked in with her.

I felt, more than heard, her chuckle as she wrapped her arms around me.

"That was the best sex I've ever had. I have never once had to stop a partner midway to get me a glass of water because I was panting so hard." I could hear the smile in her voice.

"So you aren't sad about being shackled to an inexperienced half-orc like me?" I said, voicing my lingering concern.

"Not at all. I am excited to experience everything new with you—maybe we'll find some new favorites I haven't tried," she said, grinding her hips into mine.

"Hey, enough of that, we need sleep," I admonished her gently—not really minding at all.

She sighed."I suppose you are right. And I would rather sleep in the bed than on a stone floor."

Bill rolled out of my lap and found clothes and towels in a chest on one of the chamber walls. I cleaned her gently with warm water before cleaning myself, tossing the cloths aside. I stood over her, smiling. I bent down and scooped her up, dragging her back to the bed. Before joining her, I pulled the covers up to her neck, ensuring she was comfortably wrapped in blankets. I climbed in behind her, wrapping myself around her, thinking there was nothing better than being curled around my Billie.

We made love two more times in the early morning, slowly, languidly, barely awake, savoring each other. It was almost midday when we woke again, both in need of another dip in the pools. And fresh blankets.

"Shall we bathe?" Billie asked.

"Probably for the best."

"Hey, hey, we need to clean up. We can't keep starting more."

"Fine," I reluctantly agreed, standing and heading toward the springs.

Billie followed me, curls in complete disarray from our activities. I loved it. We slipped into the hot pools and started cleaning ourselves, deliberately staying on opposite sides of the pool so we would actually get clean and not end up fucking on the edge of the spring again.

"So does today count as day one?" Billie asked, soaping up her hair.

"Yes, only day one" I said, eying her mischievously.

"So we get two more whole days?" She grinned.

We spent our entire time in the caverns, napping, fucking, talking, making our way through all the food Runa had carefully packed for us. It was all I had ever dreamt of, and I was sad to see it come to an end. Billie could tell.

"Hey, nothing has to change," she said, stroking my face. "We'll move into the bar, work late into the evenings and fuck in the early morning light."

"That sounds like a life I could fall in love with," I whispered

"Well, it is a life I look forward to." She pulled me in for a kiss.

It was late in the afternoon. We could fit in one more round before going to bed early to return to the tribe. I kissed Billie earnestly, making my meaning clear.

"Oh, are we going to go again?" she asked, voice sultry.

"Only if you are up for it," I responded.

I could fuck Billie day in and out, but I knew she was much smaller, more delicate than I was.

"I can definitely do one more round before heading home," she said, swinging a leg over me.

Billie was perched atop me, wild curls framing her flushed, smiling face. My heart nearly burst at the sight of her, my lusty woman, ready for more. She was a marvel. My forever, my *mate*. A life with Billie was a life I was ready for.

LEXICON

Old Norse is a parent language to many of the Northern Germanic Languages. It is a "dead language" and there is controversy between scholars and historians about the pronunciation and use of many words.

The language used by the orkin is a combination of Old Norse, present day Icelandic, and some proto-Germanic terms. It is not meant to reflect any specific language, history, or people.

While some Old Norse mythology has inspired some aspects of the universe *Abandoned on Niflheim* takes place on, there is little correlation between what I have depicted and any original texts, myths, histories or oral traditions of Old Norse and present day Northern Germanic cultures.

Planets

Niflheim /niv-uh l-heym/ – planet where Piper and other females have been left.

Midgard /mid'gard/ – orkin term for earth.

Tribes

Fýrifírar /fyːri-fiːrar/ – orkin living in the forest of Niflheim.
Vátrfírar /vaːtr-fiːrar/ – orkin living on the coast of Niflheim.
Snaerfírar /stnaiːr-fiːrar/ – orkin living in the snowy region in the highest settlements of the Fjall Mountains.

People and Sayings
Já /yaː/ – yes.
Jarl /yärl/ – chief or earl (masculine).
Jarlin /yärl-in/ – chief or earl (feminine).
Kveoja /kʰvɛðja/ – language spoken on Niflheim.
Elska mate /ˈɛlska/ – fated mate.

Flora and Fauna
Hestr /hest-err/ – beasts for riding and carrying goods, similar to horses. They have 8 legs, short curly hair, and a snout more similar to a cow.
Baldrian /bald-ree-an/ – soothing herb, similar to valerian.
Furutré /ˈfuɹa-treː/ – tree found in Niflheim, similar to pine.
Örn /œrtn/ – a large bird, similar to an eagle, local to the Snaerfírar.
Fjall Mountains /fjatl/ – mountain range down the spine of the continent.
Björn /pjœtn/ – bear.
Skogkatt /skuːgkAt/ – large, long-haired fairy cats who live in the mountains and climb rocks.
Valhnot /vahl-nut/ – tree nut local to Fýrifírar, medium brown in color.
Grautr /græʉt-er/ – grain like porridge served for first meal, usually sweetened with fruit and syrup.
Niflfýri - forest of mist that separates the Fýrifírar from the Snaerfírar.

Time

Dagr /ˈdɑgr̩/ – day.
Vika /ˈvika/ – week.
Mánuthur /ˈmauːnʏðʏr/ – month.
Ár /auːr/ – year.
Áratugur /auːr aˈtʰʏːɣʏr/ – decade.

EPILOGUE

I chose not to include the epilogue in this book mainly because I was on the fence about Billie and Steve's future. It is now fully written and available for anyone who signs up for my newsletter. It is spicy and sweet and takes place one year later.

If you sign up for my newsletter you will be sent the epilogue one week after release date.

Steve's Barmaid Epilogue

ACKNOWLEDGMENTS

I am sitting here, having finished the last of the edits for *Steve* and I am literally crying in gratitude. This book wouldn't exist without my author family. We tend to keep our identities private, bu every single one of you helped me on my journey with this book. I cannot wait to meet you.

I owe an enormous amount of gratitude to my cover artist, Rowan Woodcock. He sells my books. I get to meet him next year and am already working on being chill and cool. (I will fail).

To my little sister, without whom I wouldn't be the person I am today. You bring me joy and inspiration everyday.

And finally, Kiki. I love you with all of my heart.

Xoxo,
Jen

ABOUT THE AUTHOR

Jen has been reading for as long as she can remember. She used to get in trouble for reading *Little House on the Prairie* under her desk in elementary school. Jen's day job is advocating for adolescent mental health, something she doesn't see giving up any time soon.

Jen is married to a very polite Englishman she brought back as a souvenir from her college study abroad trip. She has identical twin mutants who make her question her sanity daily. She enjoys reading about alien peens, napping, and watching soothing cooking shows.

She is a goth kid at heart and truly wishes she could wear platform combat boots and black nail polish on all occasions.

www.authorjeniferwood.com